T0147100

A Waffle Lot of Murder

The All-Day Breakfast Café Series by Lena Gregory

A Waffle Lot of Murder

An All-Day Breakfast Café Mystery

Lena Gregory

LYRICAL UNDERGROUND
Kensington Publishing Corp.
www.kensingtonbooks.com

LYRICAL UNDERGROUND BOOKS are published by

Kensington Publishing Corp.
119 West 40th Street
New York, NY 10018

All Kensington titles, imprints, and distributed lines are available at special quantity discounts for bulk purchases for sales promotion, premiums, fund-raising, educational, or institutional use.

Special book excerpts or customized printings can also be created to fit specific needs. For details, write or phone the office of the Kensington Sales Manager: Kensington Publishing Corp., 119 West 40th Street, New York, NY 10018. Attn. Sales Department. Phone: 1-800-221-2647.

Lyrical Underground and Lyrical Underground logo Reg. US Pat. & TM Off.

First Electronic Edition: October 2020
ISBN-13: 978-1-5161-1045-2 (ebook)
ISBN-10: 1-5161-1045-5 (ebook)

First Print Edition: October 2020
ISBN-13: 978-1-5161-1048-3
ISBN-10: 1-5161-1048-X

Printed in the United States of America

Greg, thank you for believing in me!

Acknowledgments

This book would not have been possible without the support and encouragement of my husband, Greg. We've built a wonderful life together, and I can't wait to see where our journey will lead next. I'd like to say a big thank you to my children, Elaina, Nicky, and Logan, and to my son-in-law, Steve, for their understanding and help while I spent long nights at the computer. My husband and children are truly the loves of my life.

I also have to thank my best friend, Renee, for all her support, long conversations and reading many rough drafts. I still wouldn't know how to use Word without her help. I'd like to thank my sister, Debby, and my Dad, Tony, who are probably my biggest fans and have read every word I've ever written. To my agent, Dawn Dowdle, thank you for believing in me and for being there in the middle of the night every time I have a question. Words cannot express my gratitude to my editor, Elizabeth May, for giving me this opportunity and for her wonderful advice and assistance in polishing this manuscript.

Chapter One

"That letter is not gonna open itself, ya know." Savannah snatched the envelope Gia had been turning over and over for the better part of five minutes, slid the tip of one rhinestone-studded maroon nail beneath the flap, and slit it open.

"Yeah, well…" Gia climbed back onto her step ladder and returned to the cornucopia she was arranging on a shelf behind the All-Day Breakfast Café's counter in honor of fall's impending arrival. At least, everyone assured her fall was coming. Hard to tell without the leaves changing color and the crisp clean air that would have heralded the change of season in New York. Whatever devastating news awaited her inside the envelope could wait until she was done decorating. "Remember what happened last time I received a letter from the town council?"

"That's a little dramatic, don't ya think?" Savannah waved her off and started reading. "How long has this been sitting here? It's dated over a week ago."

Gia spread some hay around the shelf beneath the arrangement. "I don't know. A few days, I guess. I picked up the mail on Friday but didn't get to go through it all until this morning."

"Mmm-hmm…" Savannah shot her a knowing look and lifted a brow. "AKA, you saw the town council return address, tossed the letter aside, and ignored it for the weekend."

And there's the down side of having a best friend who knew you too well. "It's possible it went something like that."

Earl and Cole, who were both sitting at the counter drinking coffee, and good enough friends to get away with it, laughed.

Earl, the elderly gentleman who'd been her first customer when she'd opened the café, pointed to her work in progress. "You have an empty space there."

Gia straightened, then leaned back, careful not to tumble off the step ladder. Sure enough, he was right. She shifted a couple of gourds to fill in the hole. "Better?"

He wiped his mouth with a napkin and set it aside, then pushed his empty plate away, sat back and studied her creation. "Yup."

"Makes me realize fall's comin'." Cole, who worked the grill a few days a week to help her out and to alleviate his own post-retirement boredom, stood and took his and Earl's empty breakfast plates, then rounded the counter to put them in the bin Gia kept there. "I gotta get started prepping to open."

"Sit a few more minutes. Have another cup of coffee if you want. I already cut up all the vegetables last night." Though they'd had a huge Sunday morning breakfast crowd, the evening had slowed enough for her to get started preparing what they'd need for Monday morning.

Savannah held the letter out to Gia. When she didn't take it right away, Savannah shook it. "Look."

Gia made no move to take the letter. Her last experience with the town council had left a bitter taste in her mouth, but if Savannah's enthusiasm was any indication, this letter might not threaten such dire consequences. "I guess they're not trying to shut me down again."

"Nope. On the contrary, this is awesome. Who knows? Maybe they want to make nice after your last encounter." She grinned and thrust the letter toward Gia again. "Now take this, and see for yourself."

Gia set the small pumpkin and gourd she was holding aside, climbed down from the step ladder, and took the letter from Savannah.

"See?" she squeaked.

"Savannah, I haven't even started reading it yet."

"Well, I'll save you the trouble. You've been invited to participate in the annual Haunted Town Festival." She squealed and clasped her hands together.

After quickly scanning the letter, Gia tossed it onto the counter. "It says I've been cordially invited and I can have a table and a house. What does that mean, exactly?"

Savannah grabbed a can of Diet Pepsi from the small refrigerator beneath the counter, despite the perfectly good soda fountain sitting right above it, and popped the top—how she managed it with those long nails, Gia had no clue. "The Haunted Town Festival is huge, probably the biggest event of the year around here."

"All the proceeds go to the animal shelter, so people come from all over to support it." Cole refilled his and Earl's coffee cups.

"Thanks," Earl said and took a sip. "He's right. All of my kids come with their kids, been doing it every year since they were little, and none of them have ever missed a festival."

Cole lifted the coffee pot toward Gia.

"No, thanks." She'd already had three cups—any more and she'd be too jittery to work. "What do they mean by a table and a house?"

"Okay." Excitement brightened Savannah's already brilliant blue eyes. "So, the Festival is held on the old farmlands just outside of town. There are a large number of abandoned outbuildings out there, and most of them are used for themed houses. Like haunted houses and the like. You get to set up your house with whatever theme you want, and then, on the night of the Festival, you have a bunch of people work your house and scare the people coming through."

"Those houses are hard to get. The same groups get them every year." Earl frowned. "I wonder whose house opened up?"

"I heard Tim and Cathy retired and moved up to Pennsylvania to be by their youngest who just had her third baby in less than five years," Cole said.

"Certainly sounds like she could use the help," Earl agreed. "But what did they do with their plumbing business?"

"Their oldest son took it over, but he must have decided not to do the house this year. Who knows?" Cole shrugged. "Maybe it was too much, with taking over the business and all, or maybe he just didn't want to do it without the rest of the family."

"Either way, I guess you lucked out that a house is available." Savannah tapped a nail against the letter. "There's a number right there. You'd better call right away. That house will go fast, if it hasn't already. I sure hope they held it for you, being they sent an invitation and all."

"I don't know." It sounded involved, and if it was too much for someone who'd been doing it for years, how was she supposed to pull it off? Of course she didn't know why the last person had backed out. "What about the table? What's that?"

"The table is great advertising, the chance to get word out and offer a variety of samples from your menu. We can put out a few different dishes, easy to eat things you can pick up and eat on the go; homemade muffins, scones…" Cole snapped his fingers. "Oh, you know what would be perfect? Some of those pumpkin spice waffles you were playing around with last week."

"And don't forget the cold brew coffee." Savannah grabbed an order pad and pen and started jotting notes. "Maybe we could even do a smaller version of your breakfast pies, like make them in little mini pie tins people could carry with them or sit at one of the picnic tables and eat."

The table sounded like a great idea, get word out about her business, let people taste some of her menu items. "Maybe I could just do the table and not the house."

"Nah," Cole said. "The table is work and great advertising, but the house is the fun part."

"Then it's settled." Savannah scooped the letter off the counter and held it out to Gia.

Gia held up her hands. "Wait, guys—"

"And don't forget home fries. They'll be sure to bring in customers." Earl winked at Gia.

"Thank you, Earl, but I—"

"You know what?" Savannah fished her cell phone out of her oversized mustard-yellow bag, checked the number on the letter, and dialed. "I'll just call them myself."

"Wait. I didn't even—"

She held up a finger and turned away. "Hello? Yes, hi. I'm calling for Gia Morelli at the All-Day Breakfast Café...Yes...Sure, I can hold..."

"Savannah, wait—"

She turned back toward Gia and covered the mouthpiece. "You're the one who's always talking about missing fall in New York, missing the old traditions you had, driving out on Long Island... Yes, I'm still here."

Earl picked up where she left off. "Hitting up the farm stands, pumpkin picking..."

"Roasted sweet corn, apple cider," Cole added.

She shot them a dirty look. "You two aren't helping matters."

They just laughed at her. Traitors.

Savannah sighed. "I'm on hold again."

"All right, so maybe I have been missing New York, and perhaps I've mentioned it once or twice."

Savannah pinned her with a you've-got-to-be-kidding-me glare. "Ya think?"

Gia scowled, though she couldn't really argue. As much as she loved Boggy Creek, straying from the familiar was proving difficult at times, especially with the arrival of her favorite season.

"Well, you'll never stop missing your old traditions if you don't start making new ones," Savannah said.

"I guess you're right."

"Of course I am." She smirked. "I wouldn't have said it if I wasn't."

"I think the table is a great idea, but maybe we could skip—"

Savannah held up a finger and returned to her call. "Yes. Yes, we haven't decided on one yet, but I'll get back to you later on and let you know…"

"Looks like you're doing the Festival." Earl laughed out loud with no regard whatsoever for the look of horror that had to be plastered on her face if the sinking feeling in her gut was any indication.

"But I—"

"Ah, let her have her fun." Cole grinned at Earl. "Now for the good part."

"Oh, what's the good part?" At the moment, nothing sounded good, or fun. It all seemed like an overwhelming amount of work and less time she could spend with Thor, her Bernese Mountain Dog. Hard to believe he had just turned a year old and she'd had him for almost that long. At the same time, it seemed he had been a part of her life forever and she couldn't imagine being without him.

Earl nodded toward her, his eyes filled with understanding. "First off, I know that look. It's the same one my daughter-in-law gets every time she's invited to something that doesn't include her little girl. So let me ease your mind. Thor can be with you while you set up and work on the house, and he can be there before and after the haunting hours. Guests are allowed to bring their pets, but Zoe gets a bunch of high school students together and sets up an old stable as a doggie day care center for the workers."

Zoe had been watching Thor since Gia brought him home, and she was amazing. "I guess that would be all right."

"It's for his own safety. During the peak hours, you are 'haunting' your house, so it's dark and creepy, and you can't really keep an eye on him."

"Speaking of pets, have you ever considered some kind of pet breakfast food?" Cole turned the pad Savannah had been using around and jotted something down. "We could make something up and offer it at the Festival to get an idea if people and their pets like them."

Hmm…that was a good idea. A homemade breakfast treat for dogs. She could set up a stand by the door of the café for them. "I like that idea. Maybe something with peanut butter. Thor loves peanut butter."

"And bacon," Earl added with a grin. "Who doesn't love bacon?"

Gia was beginning to warm to the whole event. At least, the table part of it. The house she wasn't so sure about. She'd never even visited a haunted house, never mind trying to set one up and work it.

"Woo hoo!" Savannah pumped her fist in the air. "We got it!"

"The house?"

"Yup. Now we just have to come up with a theme."

"A theme?" Gia's stomach turned over. What had Savannah gotten her into?

"Yeah, you know, like vampires or werewolves or something."

"Nah." Cole shook his head. "How about something different? Something unusual."

"Clowns." Earl tapped the pad Cole was jotting ideas on. "Write that one down. Every single one of my kids is terrified of clowns. We could do a circus themed house."

"We?" Hmm...maybe, if they all pitched in and worked on it with her the whole thing wouldn't be so bad. She had to admit, it would be nice to spend time with her friends somewhere other than work.

"Of course. What? Did you really think we'd throw you to the wolves without backup?" Earl grinned. "Besides, you don't really think I'd miss this, do you? I bet some of my kids would love to participate too. And my grandson is old enough. It sure would be nice to spend some time doing something fun with him."

"Don't forget Willow and Skyla," Cole tossed out. "And maybe Trevor and some of the kids who work in his shop want to join us too."

"And my brothers." Savannah frowned. "Wait...Didn't the Ramseys do clowns last year?"

"Oh yeah, you might be right." Cole scratched clowns off the list. "How about zombies?"

Savannah waved off the idea. "Zombies are overrated. Besides, every haunted attraction has zombies."

"True." Cole tapped the pen against the pad, his brow furrowed in concentration.

Apparently, the Haunted Town Festival was a serious event in Boggy Creek. At least, it was to her friends.

Gia warmed to the idea. An event that involved the entire community sounded great. It would be good for business, and she was always looking for ways to immerse herself in the community. She'd grown to love Boggy Creek over the past year. She wanted to be a part of everything that made it so special. Still...she had no clue what she was doing. And Gia had never been very adventurous. She preferred the familiarity and safety of her comfort zone. In spite of that, the one impulsive decision she was forced into making—her move to Boggy Creek, Florida—turned out to be the best thing she'd ever done.

Savannah waved a hand in front of her, trying to recapture her attention. "Ghosts? Aliens? Horror movie monsters?"

They tossed around ideas for the next few minutes, until Cole glanced toward the clock hanging above the cut out between the kitchen and dining room and jumped off his stool. "Yikes! We got so carried away we forgot we had to open."

Gia headed for the front of the shop, where a couple already waited on the sidewalk for her to unlock the door.

Savannah fished her keys out, then slung her bag over her shoulder. "And I have to get to work. I have paperwork to do, and I have to get in touch with a seller to find out what time I can get my potential buyer into a house."

Gia unlocked the door and held it open for her two customers. "Good morning. Have a seat wherever you'd like, and I'll be right with you."

Savannah scooted behind the couple before Gia let the door go. "I'll pick you up about seven, and we can go see our house and decide where to set up the table. Barbara Woodhull, one of the event coordinators, is meeting us out there at seven thirty."

"Sure thing." There was no point in arguing. Apparently, her friends had decided she'd be participating, so Gia gave up. Besides, she might even enjoy it. She'd been missing fall, which had always been her favorite season. She had been a bit homesick and down lately, despite her love for Boggy Creek and its residents. Maybe a new annual tradition would help ease some of the nostalgia that had been hounding her. But she still couldn't help wondering what she'd gotten herself into.

Chapter Two

Still not convinced she was doing the right thing, Gia climbed out of Savannah's new Mustang convertible and ran her fingers through her tangled curls. Riding with the top down in the little blue sports car was amazing but left her long, dark hair looking like a rat's nest.

Savannah ran a hand over already perfect long blonde hair. She'd been smart enough to pull it back into a bun before they'd left. She smoothed her long cream-colored skirt.

Oh well. Live and learn. Gia scanned for critters as they crossed the deserted hard-packed dirt field that barely passed for a parking lot. "Are you sure it's okay to be bumbling around out here when it's getting dark?"

Savannah lifted a brow. "Gia, the event takes place after dark."

"Oh." She swallowed hard and forced a laugh. "Right."

"Besides, Cole opened this morning, so we couldn't come out here until you closed."

"True." But it didn't make her any more comfortable on the deserted farm after dark. When half the town was lingering around, it would probably seem less frightening. Of course, that was the idea of the event, to scare people. It seemed they'd found the perfect setting.

Streetlights surrounding the lot lit up as she followed Savannah toward an old outbuilding that had seen better days. Rust spotted the corrugated metal where jagged holes had rotted through the walls. One spotlight shone above the large, partially open garage style door—at one time, they must have kept tractors or other farm equipment in the building. Another spotlight lit the small, closed door next to it.

Savannah pushed the roll-up door, and it screeched as it opened. She stepped into the lighted interior and yelled, "Barbara?"

Gia followed her in.

An enormous black animal crouched beside a pile of wood.

Gia screamed and lurched back.

Savannah caught her and laughed, then pointed to the stuffed black wolf the size of a small car. Gia's horror was reflected in its black eyes. Its lips curled back, revealing brown stained fangs and a row of jagged teeth.

"Scary, huh?" Savannah didn't seem fazed by the creature that appeared to be pouncing toward them. She patted its muzzle. "You should see it when they turn it on. Debby from the animal shelter does a huge section in the woods. She's been offered a house every time one opens up, but she prefers the section of woods between the last two houses. Because she runs the event, she likes to let donors have the houses. Anyway, they hook this monstrosity up to an air compressor and set it in the trees. Then, every time the pressure builds up, the whole thing shoots forward into the path. You can hear the screams from all the way in town. Scares the life out of me every year, even though I know it's coming."

Gia walked around the wood base the animal stood on. If this was any indication of the attention paid to detail for this event, it must be amazing. "Where did they get something like this?"

"A theater company used it for a prop one year, then donated it to Debby for the Festival."

"Donated?"

"Debby can be very persuasive, and she's quite passionate about the Festival. It brings in a good portion of the funding she needs to run the shelter and provide food, blankets, veterinary care. Some of the animals she takes in spend their whole lives there, and they need care."

Gia's heart ached to think of Thor ending up in the shelter forever, not that the animals there weren't well cared for. Debby treated them all like her own—but nothing could be the same as going home to a family that loved you. Thor had brought so much to her life at a time when she'd desperately needed it.

Savannah shot her an I-told-you-so look. "You can go out to the shelter and pick out another one after the Festival."

"I never said—"

"You didn't have to; it's written all over your face."

"Yeah, well, Thor's been amazing. With just the two of us in the house, surrounded by all that property, there's no reason I can't bring home another one."

"Or two."

"Don't push it." But she couldn't deny she'd been thinking the same thing. Sometimes Savannah's intuition was scarier than the big black wolf staring her down. "And you stay out of my head. It's creepy."

Savannah laughed out loud, and a pang of love shot through Gia.

She'd never had another friend like Savannah, someone who knew her so well, accepted her for who she was, despite her faults, cared about her so much, and would do anything in the world for her without an instant of hesitation.

"Thanks, Savannah."

"For what?"

"Just for being you and for being such a good friend."

"Always." Savannah gave her a quick hug, then stepped back, looked around, and frowned. "I wonder where Barbara is. It's not like her to be late. From what I hear, she runs this event like a drill sergeant."

"Maybe she got held up at work." Gia started forward, strolling between piles of props, wood, paint cans.

"She doesn't work. As far as I know, anyway. Even though Debby is technically responsible for the event, Barbara Woodhull and Genevieve Hart put this whole thing together every year, coordinate everything down to the last detail. I can't imagine them doing that while holding down jobs."

"You don't know them well?"

"Not really. I've seen them around; Barbara seems a little stand-offish; she attends community events but stays to herself, if you know what I mean. You've probably seen her around town, early forties, always dressed to the nines. Come to think of it, I've never seen that woman have to stick on a ball cap or tie her hair up in a sloppy knot to make herself presentable." Savannah shrugged. "Anyway, Genny seems like a real sweetheart, very friendly. I've never participated in the Festival before, though I attend every year. Too bad you arrived too late to go last year. At least then you'd have an idea of what goes on."

Gia hadn't been in a position to enjoy a festival or anything else when she'd first arrived in Boggy Creek, but Savannah didn't need to be reminded of that. She'd stood by her side through it all.

Savannah picked up a rusted pickaxe, examined it, then tossed it aside and brushed the powdered rust off her hands. "Only local businesses sponsor and work the Festival, and the real estate office I work for doesn't participate."

Savannah called out again, then fell into step with Gia. "If you see anything that sparks an idea for a theme, let me know. People have dibs on some of this stuff, like the wolf that's only here because it's too big to store anywhere else. Mostly, this building houses things that have been donated throughout the year, so a lot of it is up for grabs."

"What's Debby's theme?"

"Werewolves. Everyone dresses like werewolves and stalks their victims… uh, I mean guests…" she grinned, "through the woods between houses. It keeps people from getting bored while they're waiting their turns."

"Some of this stuff is great." Gia held up a hardhat with an ax blade embedded in it, the handle sticking out. Then she pointed to a box filled with doll parts. "And some of it's just plain disturbing."

"No kidding." Savannah shivered. "And don't get any ideas; you're not using dolls, or pieces of dolls, or anything with creepy eyes that will be staring at me the whole time."

It was Gia's turn to laugh as she tossed the hardhat onto a small pile of wood scraps. "Hey, you're the one who was so gung-ho to do the scary stuff. I'd have been content hanging out at a table with food all night."

"Yeah, well…" They'd reached the closed back door of the building, and still no sign of Barbara Woodhull.

Gia turned back to the prop she'd just discarded, an idea taking hold. "Hey, do you think anyone's using the hardhat with the ax?"

"I don't know. Why?"

"Check it out." She picked up a shovel someone had propped next to the back door, one side of it covered in something red and sticky-looking that reminded her of congealed blood. "If we use the hard hat, this shovel, and the pickaxe you found when we came in, maybe we could do a haunted mine theme?"

"Hmmm…Maybe." Savannah tapped a nail against her lips. "We could make the house look like an abandoned mine. If we black out the windows, we can even create the illusion of being underground."

Claustrophobia threatened to suffocate Gia, and she tossed the shovel aside. "Maybe not."

Savannah frowned. "What? I thought that was a pretty good idea."

"We have to be able to work the house all night, and I don't want to feel like I'm trapped underground for hours on end."

"True." But Savannah's enthusiasm waned. "I can't imagine where Barbara could be. I'm sure this is where she said to meet her, and the door was partway open."

"Why don't you try calling her?"

"Good idea." She pulled her cell phone out and dialed.

Gia brushed splattered dirt off an old door someone had left propped against a pile of tires, the glass from its window missing, leaving a gaping hole they could cover with black fabric, then someone in a mask could poke their head through to startle unsuspecting guests. "What about some kind of a—"

"Wait." Savannah took the phone away from her ear and listened. "Do you hear that?"

Gia strained to hear. From outside, a muffled version of "Thriller" blared through the night. She couldn't help but smile. "Barbara's ringtone, I imagine."

"She must be out back. Come on." Savannah pulled the small door open and held it for Gia.

As soon as she sucked in the humid air, she choked.

Savannah paused. "You okay?"

She pressed a hand against her chest, willing away the tightness. "Yeah. I didn't realize how musty and moldy it smelled in there. Not to mention everything is covered in dirt and dust."

"For sure. Most of that stuff's probably been sitting around someone's storage shed or basement for years." Savannah started down the road, her sandals' three-inch heels sinking in sand that was much softer than that of the hard-packed dirt parking lot.

The ringtone stopped. The hum of insects filled the night, louder than Gia had ever heard. Or maybe that was just because she was trying to hear past it. "Try her again."

Savannah dialed but didn't press the phone to her ear. "Thriller" sounded again, and they followed the sound across the narrow dirt road that wound around past the back of the building and then between two fairly large, rotting wood sheds.

"This is the road the guests will follow. It winds between all the houses and through the woods. It ends by a big field down that way." Savannah pointed toward an open space.

With darkness mostly on them, Gia couldn't make out much more than a lack of trees or buildings in the distance. "How much land is out here?"

"I have no idea, but what's used for the Festival is only a small portion. If you head down that way," she gestured past the scattered row of buildings, "there's an abandoned orange grove and several abandoned farms that aren't part of the fairgrounds."

"Hey, look." Gia bent and peered under a bush a few feet into the wooded area bordering the road. Light flashed on and off to the sound of "Thriller."

Savannah turned on her phone's flashlight and handed it to Gia. "Here. Shine this into the bush so I don't stick my hand into a bunch of thorns or anything."

It was the *or anything* that worried Gia most. She shone the light beneath the bushes and held her breath while Savannah took a quick peek before reaching in and grabbing the cell phone, which had once again stopped ringing.

"Can I help you ladies?"

Savannah whirled toward the woman's voice, lost her balance, and fell over, sprawled half on the dirt road and half on the grass. Barbara's phone fell face up in the dirt.

"Oh goodness, I am so sorry." The woman wiped mud from her hands onto her already dirty jeans, careful to avoid the mud-covered knees, then reached out a hand to Savannah. "I certainly didn't mean to startle you."

"It's okay." Savannah took the woman's hand and climbed to her feet, then dusted herself off. The cream skirt was probably beyond saving, but at least she hadn't broken an ankle falling off her heels. "I'm Savannah Mills, and this is Gia Morelli. We had an appointment scheduled with Barbara Woodhull for seven thirty, but she didn't show up."

The woman looked at her watch and frowned, then used her wrist to wipe the sweat from her forehead. "Oh my. That's not like Barbara to be late."

"When I called her phone she didn't answer, but we followed the ringtone to the bush right there and were just picking up the phone." Savannah bent and retrieved the phone from the dirt and brushed off the blue, rhinestone-studded case.

"Hmm... That's weird." The woman squinted at the phone, through bloodshot, red-rimmed, swollen eyes. She sniffed and pulled a crumpled tissue out of her pocket.

"Are you okay?"

"Oh yes." The woman waved off the question and wiped her nose. "Allergies. I've been working on my house for the past couple of hours, and the dust and mold that's collected on everything all year is killing me."

A bulky man with a full head of long, thick gray hair and the lined face of someone who'd seen a lot of stress in his life shoved through the door Gia and Savannah had just exited. He wore a black T-shirt with Security emblazoned across the front. He took one look at the woman and frowned. "Genny? Is everything okay?"

"Yes, oh dear...maybe not. I don't know." She started to chew on her thumbnail, then scrunched up her face, looked at the dirt caked beneath her nails, and lowered her hand to her side. "I'm sorry to bother you, Jeb. These women had an appointment with Barbara, but she didn't show up, and they found her phone in the bush there."

"No bother at all, ma'am. That's what I'm here for." He nodded toward Genny, then turned his attention to Savannah. "What time were y'all supposed to meet up with Barbara?"

"Seven thirty."

"Huh…" He scratched his head. "Well, I haven't seen her around here tonight; have you, Genny?"

"Uh, no." Deep lines furrowed her brow. "Actually, I haven't seen her since last night, but she never lets that phone out of her sight. If she doesn't have pockets, she usually holds it in her hand."

The phone in Savannah's hand vibrated, then "Thriller" blared from the speaker.

All of their gazes shot to the phone. The initials KC popped up on the screen along with a background image of a man and a woman locked in a heated embrace, the woman facing the camera, her eyes closed, her long dark hair spilling over her shoulders.

Genny gasped.

Jeb took the phone from Savannah and studied the screen. "You said you found this out here?"

"Yes, right there beneath the bush." Savannah pointed. "We were trying to call her to see if she was running late, and we heard the phone ring, then saw it light up."

"All right." He handed the phone to Genny, and she stuffed it into the back pocket of her jeans.

So much for preserving evidence. Of course, they didn't even know if a crime had been committed, but still. You'd think he'd be a little careful just in case.

"I'll have a look around, but she probably lost her phone earlier, then went to retrace her steps hoping she could find it," Jeb said. "You ladies don't worry about a thing. I'm sure she'll turn up."

Despite Jeb's seeming lack of concern for Barbara's whereabouts, a sense of unease crept over Gia. His theory made perfect sense, and yet, despite Genny and Jeb being there, the acres and acres of property had the deserted feel of someplace long abandoned. And, if not for the floodlight positioned by the back door, it would now be fully dark.

Genny smoothed back strands of frizzy brown hair that had come loose from her ponytail with a shaky hand, leaving a smudge of dirt along her forehead. "Can I ask what you were meeting with Barbara about? Maybe I can help you."

Gia glanced at Savannah, not knowing if they should continue or not.

Savannah shrugged.

Gia held out a hand to Genny. "I'm Gia Morelli. I own the All-Day Breakfast Café, and I was invited to participate in the Haunted Town Festival."

Genny's worried gaze transformed instantly, excitement brightening her dull brown eyes. "Oh that's wonderful. Welcome, welcome. I'm sorry Barbara wasn't able to greet you. I'm sure something came up. But I'd be happy to show you around."

"Are you sure it's not too late?" The thought of trampling through the old farmland in the dark, when who knew what critters waited out there searching for prey, didn't appeal. A shiver tore through her. "We could come back tomorrow if that would be better."

Savannah rolled her eyes.

Gia ignored her. She couldn't help it if her experiences with wildlife were limited to stray cats in the alley behind the deli where she'd worked in New York City, an occasional rat on the subway, and pigeons that gathered in the park.

"Oh no, no. Don't be silly, dear. No need to come back. I know these grounds as well as, if not better than, Barbara. The circuit breaker is right inside. Just let me turn on the lights, and we'll get started." She hurried away, all thoughts of Barbara apparently forgotten.

Gia leaned closer to Savannah, afraid her voice might carry across the open field where Jeb had been swallowed up by the darkness, or into the cavernous metal storage building Genny had rushed into. "Are you sure it's safe out here at night?"

"Of course it is, Gia."

"Then why do they have a security guard on duty?" Hah. Gotcha there.

"Because people have started setting up their houses and stuff already. The lighting has been run, supplies are being stored in houses with no locks, and they worry about vandalism. Nothing more sinister than kids being kids, Gia. Sneaking into an old abandoned farm that has the added bonus of creepy props? Are you kidding me? What kid wouldn't be all over that?"

Me for one. She kept the thought to herself. She had a feeling Savannah's childhood had been drastically more adventurous than her own, especially since she'd grown up with a houseful of brothers.

Rows of lights Gia hadn't noticed lining both sides of the dirt road flickered on.

The brush beside them rustled, and something skittered into the darkness.

Savannah elbowed her in the ribs. "It was a lizard."

Gia laughed. "All right, all right. I'm trying here."

"Okay, ladies. Follow me." Genny started down the road. Her heavy-duty flashlight led the way, even with the lights lining the road. "Are you taking the empty house or just a table?"

"Both," Savannah blurted before Gia had a chance to change her mind.

"Wonderful." Shining the light into the center of the empty field, Genny gestured them forward. "The tables will be set up there, in the center of the 'town.'"

Thankfully, she continued down the dirt road without venturing out into the overgrown field. "That higher grass will be cut down before the event. The tables will be set up ahead of time. I believe the one that's available is at the front, right by the entrance."

"That will be a great spot, Gia." Savannah gripped her arm. "People waiting in line will have to go right past you. They'll have time to eat while they wait to enter the haunted section."

"Oh yes, it's definitely a great spot," Genny gushed. "The exit is on the other side of that last house there, so they'll pass pretty close to you on the way out too. Plus, there's picnic tables set up just to the side of you. It really is a prime location."

"Which house opened up?" Savannah asked.

Genny gestured with the flashlight, then stopped in front of a wood building the size of a small ranch and opened the door. "This one right here."

"Wow." Savannah walked around the side of the storage building, then looked down the road, and returned to them. "Right in the middle. That's great."

Gia stared at the pitch black interior. The scent of mold and something else, grease or oil, maybe, wafted out. Her eyes started to itch. She sneezed and rubbed her eyes. Boy, Genny wasn't kidding about allergies. If she was going to spend any kind of time in this building, it was going to have to be aired out. And doused with Lysol. Maybe bleach. And Febreze. And maybe she'd burn a few candles.

Genny reached a hand in and flipped a switch by the door. Bright, fluorescent overhead lights lit the interior. "Naturally, you can't leave these overheads on the night of the event. You'll have to use some kind of dimmer, decorative lighting. But this is great for set up. Not all the buildings have so much light. I had to hang drop lights in mine just to see my hand in front of my face."

Savannah followed Genny into the long, narrow building. The shape of the empty building reminded Gia of every summer camp she'd ever seen in a horror movie. "What about a dormitory?"

"I love it." Savannah whipped a pad and pen out of her purse. "We could set up a bunch of beds and stuff, make it haunted? Or maybe have monsters, like nightmares or something? We could call it Nightmare House."

"What a fabulous idea and different from anything else we have." Genny oohed and aahed as Savannah relayed her vision for the event. "I'll tell you what; I'll approve it right now. I love it."

"Can you do that? Really?" Savannah pressed her pad against the wall and frantically wrote ideas. "We don't have to wait for Barbara or Debby?"

"Not at all. You just move right ahead."

"Awesome, thank you." When Savannah's pen stopped working, she shook it, but it had given up. She stuffed everything back into her purse. "Thank you so much, Genny. We're really excited to be included."

Gia waited out front with Savannah while Genny locked up. "Thank you very much for showing us around. I can't wait."

Somewhere along the line, Savannah's excitement had become contagious. Unfortunately, the cost did have to be considered.

"Well, if you ladies are okay to see yourselves out, I'd like to get finished up in my own house so I can head home. It was nice meeting you both, and I'm looking forward to working the event with you."

Gia and Savannah said their good-byes, and Genny hurried off back the way she'd come.

Savannah fell into step beside Gia as they headed back down the dirt road toward the storage shed. "Isn't this exciting?"

"It is…"

"But?"

"I'm just worried about the cost."

Savannah waved off her concern. "Don't even worry about it. It won't end up costing that much. At least, the house won't. We'll try to use a lot of the junk we find lying around here, and we can ask around town for donations."

"Where are we going to get beds, Savannah? Even if we find cheap ones…"

Savannah laughed. "Don't be silly. They don't have to be real beds. We'll just get some old blankets and build platforms or something underneath to make them look like beds."

"I guess that would work. Then afterward, we can donate the blankets to the animal shelter."

"See." Savannah punched her arm. "Now you're getting the hang of it."

They walked through the storage shed and out to the parking lot.

From down the road, blue and red lights raced toward them, accompanied by the peal of sirens.

Chapter Three

Police Captain—thanks to a recent, permanent promotion—Hunter Quinn turned over an empty crate and straddled it across from where Gia and Savannah sat together on a stack of plywood toward the back of the storage shed. "So?"

"So what?" Gia had been sitting there with Savannah, rubbing her itchy eyes, for the better part of an hour, ever since several police cruisers had flown by them, only one of which had stopped. The officer insisted they remain where they were but refused to tell them anything about what was going on. Her patience had worn thin about fifteen minutes ago.

"You know, Gia, I'm beginning to think I was right about you. You are a magnet for trouble and a bad influence on my cousin." Hunt sighed and spared a glance for Savannah. Since he was one of the many male cousins she'd grown up with, and they were very close, and he was Gia's more or less boyfriend, Hunt was one of the few people who could get away with saying something like that without earning a tongue lashing from Savannah.

Some of Gia's annoyance abated. A little. She lifted a brow. "And am I a bad influence on you as well, *Captain* Quinn?"

That earned her a sad smile. He shook his head, weariness slumping his usually rigid posture. "What am I going to do with you?"

In that moment, all thoughts of giving him a hard time fled. "They found Barbara Woodhull, didn't they?"

He nodded. "Yeah."

A pang of guilt shot through her. Followed by a trickle of grief, even though she'd never met the woman. Barbara had been there, maybe beyond getting help when she'd needed it, only because she planned to meet Gia.

Hunt's expression hardened, and he pulled out his pad and pen. Even the slightest ounce of playfulness was gone. "I already spoke with Genevieve, and she explained what you two were doing out here, but would you mind walking me through what happened?"

"We came out here to meet with Barbara about doing the Haunted Town Festival."

Savannah tapped a steady rhythm against the boards with her nails. "The town council offered Gia a table and a house, so we were supposed to take a look at the house. I set up the appointment earlier this morning."

"Did you speak with Barbara then?"

Savannah nodded. "She said she didn't mind meeting us out here after the café closed."

"Did she say anything else? Anything that might indicate what she planned to do before her meeting? Did she plan to meet with anyone else that you know of?"

Tap, tap, tap; the staccato was going to drive Gia crazy if she didn't stop. Unable to take the sound—which was pounding in time with her headache—for another second, Gia reached out a hand and covered one of Savannah's.

"Oh sorry." A blush crept up her cheeks.

"No," Gia waved it off. "I'm sorry. I just…I have a headache. Probably from sitting in here for so long with all the dust and mold."

Hunt looked at her, not without sympathy, but it was clear he wasn't letting them leave yet either. "I'll get you both out of here as soon as I can, but I need answers first."

Of course he did. Gia's headache meant nothing when a woman lay… Wait. Why was he asking if Barbara had planned to meet with anyone? If the poor woman met a natural end, like a heart attack or an asthma attack or something, what would it matter?

Savannah scrunched her face in concentration. "I…um…no, I don't think she said anything other than she'd be happy to meet us out here and show us around."

"She was murdered?" The words blurted out before Gia could stop them.

Savannah gasped, and her gaze shot to Hunt. "Are you sure?"

He nodded slowly and lowered the pad and pen. "The security guard found her in the woods not far from the trail."

"Isn't there a chance it was an accident? Maybe she tripped and fell? Fainted? Hit her head?" Savannah shook her head, desperate for any truth other than what was so obvious in Hunt's hardened expression. "You have to be mistaken."

Turmoil darkened his deep brown eyes until they were almost as black as the night. "A security guard found her buried in a shallow, freshly dug grave beneath a line of azalea bushes, not far from the trail that leads through the property, and called it in. The cause of death appears to be blunt force trauma to the head, but the ME hasn't made the official ruling yet. I'm sorry, Savannah, but she didn't wind up there by accident."

"No. No, I don't imagine she did." Savannah started to tap her nails but then glanced at Gia and clasped her hands together in a white knuckled grip in her lap.

Though sympathy still remained in his eyes, Hunt returned to his questioning. "It's okay. Just take your time and think about it. Did she give you any indication at all of what she might have had planned for the day?"

"Um...I don't...I can't remember her mentioning anything about her plans for the day at all. I'm sorry. I was in a hurry, and I just wanted to get the appointment set up so I could get to work and before..." She shot Gia an apologetic look. "Well, before Gia could change her mind about doing the Festival. I was excited, ya know? You know how much I love going to the Festival every year, and this was the first time I was finally going to get to participate."

"I know." Hunt covered her hands with one of his own. "Are you okay?"

She nodded. "I'll be fine. It just came as a shock, you know? Not only that she passed away, but that she was murdered."

"I know. If you think of anything, though, anything at all, please call me. Something you might not even realize is important, can sometimes provide the clue we need to point us in the right direction."

"Do you know when she was killed?" Gia held her breath, hoping she wasn't dead because she'd been waiting for them.

He turned his gaze on Gia. "Probably late this afternoon sometime."

She let the breath out slowly. Not that it mattered, or made the situation any less tragic, but she hoped Barbara had been there for reasons of her own at the time.

"Is there anything you can tell me about what Barbara's plans were?"

"No. I'm sorry. I never spoke to her. Savannah made all the arrangements."

"Okay, how about after you arrived? Did you see anyone on the grounds, pass anyone leaving while you were pulling in? Anything at all?"

Gia thought back, even though she already knew the answer. "I remember thinking how deserted it was out here, not a soul around when we first got here. Then Genny showed up outside while we were looking for the phone."

"What phone?"

"Barbara's phone. When she wasn't here, Savannah tried to call her. She didn't answer, but we heard the "Thriller" ringtone, so we followed the sound and found her phone under the bush along the trail."

"Where's the phone now?"

"Genny has it. Jeb gave it to her, and she put it in her pocket."

He frowned and nodded but didn't write anything down. "Did you happen to notice which direction Genny came from?"

"I didn't. When I reached under the bush, Genny startled me. When I turned around, she was already standing there."

"I didn't notice either. I was watching Savannah, shining the light under the bush for her, then Genny was just there. Surely you can't think—"

"I don't think anything, just trying to figure out who was where. Did you see anyone else?"

"The security guard. What was his name?" Gia looked at Savannah.

"Jeb."

"He came out of this storage shed when we were standing on the trail. He said he was going to take a look around. Is he the one who called you?"

"Yes." He stood and tucked his pad and pen into his back pocket. "Did you two touch anything while you were here?"

Savannah's eyes went wide. Her voice shook. "I-I don't remember."

Gia put an arm around Savannah's shoulders. "It's okay. Let's just think about it. When we came in, the door was already open, right?"

Savannah sniffed and shook her head. "I can't remember."

"Which door did you come in?" Hunt asked gently.

"The front. The one like a garage door, not the smaller one," Gia offered.

"Oh right." Savannah nodded in agreement. "It was partway up, but I had to push it the rest of the way for us to get in."

The three of them walked toward the front door, Gia keeping her arm loosely draped across Savannah's shoulders. "I think Savannah touched that wolf after it nearly scared the life out of me."

"Yes, I think I did."

"Did you touch it too?" Hunt asked.

She shot him a *yeah right* look.

He shrugged in acknowledgement. "Okay, then what?"

They retraced their steps through the warehouse, the items that had seemed so innocent only an hour earlier, suddenly taking on a more sinister feel.

Gia pointed out the hardhat on top of the woodpile. "I picked that up, thought it might be fun to do a mine theme."

"Is that where it was when you found it?"

"No." She pointed to where she'd first picked it up.

"Wait." Savannah stiffened and pulled away from her. She turned in a circle. "Where's the shovel?"

"What shovel?" The sharpness in Hunt's gaze belied the casual tone of his voice.

"There was a shovel propped beside the back door. One side of it was covered in something red and sticky-looking, like fake blood or...some...thing." Gia's stomach heaved, threatening to expel the rushed dinner she'd shoveled down before heading out. "Hunt?"

"Did you pick it up?"

She nodded, unable to speak past the lump in her throat practically choking her.

"Where did you put it?"

"I don't know." She started to move closer to the back door, but Hunt held out a hand to stop her.

"I picked it up from where it was propped by the back door." But what had she done with it after that? Her head whirled. She couldn't think straight. Had she inadvertently picked up something important? Even worse, had she lost a potentially valuable piece of evidence?

"Gia," Hunt prodded.

Okay. She needed to pull herself together. She had been talking to Savannah. She'd dismissed the mine theme idea, but then what?

"You threw it aside." Savannah pointed to a spot on the partially rotted wood floor. "I had to step over it before I opened the back door to go out."

"So where is it now?" Gia asked, not wanting the idea the shovel might be the murder weapon to fully form, yet unable to stop it from jumping into her head. "You don't think...?"

"Are you sure that's where it was?" Hunt stared hard at Savannah, as if willing her to remember faster.

But Savannah took her time. She turned in a circle, frowned, looked at the spot where they'd originally found the shovel, then looked back at Hunt. "I'm positive."

"Me too." Though she couldn't be a hundred percent certain how it had landed, she was very sure she'd tossed it into the only circle clear of debris of one sort or another. "It was definitely somewhere right around there. I tossed it aside with my right hand, then went straight to the back door."

"All right. Thank you both. Gia, would you take—"

A gut-wrenching scream tore through the storage shed from somewhere close by, then cut off.

"Wait here." Hunt bolted for the door, yelling over his shoulder. "Don't move. And don't touch anything."

Chapter Four

Yeah, right. Like Gia didn't know better than to touch anything at a crime scene. In his defense, it's not like her curiosity hadn't gotten the better of her once or twice before.

Gia stood still for all of thirty seconds, then glanced at Savannah and hurried after Hunt.

Savannah kept pace at her side. "What do you think that was?"

"No idea," Gia huffed, "but it can't be good. Are there any animals that make a sound like that?"

"Not that I've ever heard."

A second scream shattered the silence.

Just before they reached the open garage style door, Gia hesitated. What if there really was something out there? Something dangerous, like an alligator, or a coyote, or a panther—though she'd never seen one, she'd heard they roamed the woods here—or a killer.

Savannah hurried past her through the door.

No way would she let Savannah face any kind of danger alone. She ran after her.

When Savannah stopped short, Gia plowed straight into her. "Hey—"

"Shhh…" Holding one hand out to stop Gia from moving forward, Savannah gestured for her to move to the side of the large metal building.

Gia slid into the shadows between the storage building and the trees beside it, praying she didn't run into any wildlife, but too caught up in the scene to back away.

A man dressed in dark slacks and a white or pale yellow button up shirt knelt in the middle of the parking lot, his head hanging low, his face cradled in his hands.

The man's sobs tore at Gia's heart, leaving her aching to go to him and help in some way. Fairly confident Hunt wouldn't appreciate the intrusion, Gia held her ground and struggled to see past Savannah's head. "Who is that?"

Savannah squinted as if to get a better view, then shook her head. "No idea."

Hunt crouched beside the man, one hand on his shoulder, leaning close, his words too low for Gia to make out.

The man certainly seemed grief stricken. He must have known the victim very well. "Barbara's husband, maybe?"

Savannah shook her head. "I don't think Barbara was married. A boyfriend, maybe? Or a brother?"

"Alfie!" Genny Hart rushed across the parking lot toward the man. "Oh, Alfie, can you even believe it?"

"Oh, Genny, nooo!" Alfie wailed and shot to his feet. He fell into Genny's arms and cried harder. "How could this have happened? I just talked to Barbara a few hours ago, and now she's gone."

Hunt stood and glanced at Detective Leo Dumont.

When Leo nodded, Hunt backed away, giving Leo room to step between Genny and Alfie. Leo gently disentangled the two, leaning close to speak quietly to Genny, then patted her arm and led her across the parking lot.

Gia started to step forward, hoping to get closer so she could hear what they were saying, but Savannah's iron grip on her arm stopped her.

Hunt saved her the trouble of trying to eavesdrop when he guided Alfie back toward the storage shed and led him inside.

"Great, now what?" Gia scooted out from between the bushes and the side of the building and brushed herself off, desperate to be rid of anything that might have dropped onto her while she was hiding. A shiver tore through her.

"Now, my dear..." Savannah picked a few pine needles out of her hair and brushed her hands off. "We go home, or at least back to your house since there's no way I'm sleeping until I know what's going on, and we wait to hear from Hunt or Leo."

Hunt often stopped by Gia's late at night, just to check in on her and sometimes to share a late dinner or watch a movie, and Savannah's fiancé, Leo, sometimes showed up with him. Since they knew she and Savannah were together, it was a good bet they'd be by if they could.

Gia stared at the open door Hunt and Alfie had disappeared through.

"Forget it, Gia." Savannah took her arm and started toward the parking lot. "He went into the storage shed for a reason, most likely privacy."

"That's true, but he also told us to wait there," Gia argued. "So, he probably thought we were still in there when he went in."

Savannah rolled her eyes. "Don't even try it. Hunt knows full well we didn't wait inside, no matter what he said."

"But we don't even know for sure if he was done questioning us."

"Oh please." But Savannah hesitated. She glanced back toward the spot where Leo had intercepted Genny, but they had already disappeared around the side of a building. Then she looked back at the storage shed and frowned.

Gia used her moment of indecision to head back inside.

Savannah sighed and mumbled something that sounded suspiciously like *pain in the neck* as she trudged through the doorway.

Gia didn't have to move far into the cavernous space to hear Alfie's sobs echoing throughout the building. She slid just far enough inside to see Hunt had returned to sitting on his crate toward the back of the building, and Alfie had taken a seat in the spot Gia and Savannah had vacated.

Though his gaze never left Alfie, Hunt stiffened, and she had no doubt he was fully aware of their return. Since he didn't say anything, it was probably okay with him if they stayed.

Alfie's gaze was fixed on his hands, which were clasped tightly in his lap. He was oblivious to Gia and Savannah's arrival. "I can't believe she's gone."

"You said you last spoke to her a few hours ago?" Hunt prodded.

"Yes, I'm sorry." He sniffed. "I'm having a hard time processing all of this."

"You and Barbara were close, I take it?"

"Oh yes." He groaned. "I don't know what I'm going to do without her. She was my best friend in life. We did everything together. No one understood me like she did. What am I going to do?"

A vice squeezed Gia's heart. What if that was her, and a detective was sitting across from her demanding answers about something that happened to Savannah? She started forward, intent on doing something, anything, to ease his suffering, knowing full well there was nothing she could do. There would be nothing anyone could do to ease her pain if something happened to Savannah.

Savannah gripped her hand and shook her head.

Gia squeezed back and lowered her gaze to the floor, tears threatening.

"The best thing you can do for her now is to answer my questions, try to help me find who did this to her," Hunt said.

Alfie sniffed and nodded, then straightened and lifted his chin. "You're right. I can do that. I have to do that. Barbara needs me now. And I'm always there when she needs me. There'll be plenty of time to fall apart afterward."

Hunt nodded. "What can you tell me about the last time you spoke? Was it on the phone?"

"No, no, I dropped her off here."

"What time?"

"I don't know. A few hours ago?" He frowned, his face twisted into a mask of concentration. "Maybe around two or three?"

"Why did you drop her off? Where was her car?"

"We were going to go out to eat after, spend some time planning our house for the Festival." He sucked in shaky breath and wiped his eyes. "It didn't make sense to take two cars, so I dropped her off here, and I told her I'd pick her up when I was done working."

How many times had Gia and Savannah done the same exact thing? They'd done it today, when Gia left her car at the café and they drove to the fairgrounds together. It seemed perfectly innocent and reasonable that Alfie would have done the same thing.

Hunt scribbled on his pad. "Where do you work?"

"I work from home. I'm a freelance information analyst."

Hunt wrote something down, then looked at Alfie and waited a beat.

"I analyze information for different companies, then write up reports for them."

Hunt nodded. "So, you were working from home after you dropped Barbara off?"

"Yes."

"Was anyone else there with you?"

"No, I was working alone."

Gia frowned, indignant on Alfie's behalf, even though the man didn't even seem to notice how the tone of Hunt's voice had hardened. Couldn't Hunt see how broken up he was? What was wrong with him? He couldn't possibly think this man had anything to do with Barbara's murder.

Savannah pinched her arm between two of those dagger-like nails.

"What?" Gia hissed, though she already knew full well what Savannah's problem was. They'd been down this road before. Only this time, Gia had to acquiesce. She didn't know Alfie from a hole in the wall. For all she knew, he might just be a really good actor, or so broken up over having killed his best friend, he couldn't get a grip on himself. Even though the law maintained his innocence until he was proven guilty, he would remain on the suspect list until he was proven innocent, which she had no doubt Hunt would set out to do.

"Did you see anyone else here when you dropped her off?" Hunt asked.

"Uh…yes, sir. Mike was walking across the field toward the outer buildings."

"Mike?"

"Mike Smith. I don't know much about him, but he works on the grounds here, maintains them all year, as far as I know."

"Okay." Hunt jotted something, presumably Mike Smith's name, on his pad. "What about anyone else? Was Genny here? Or Jeb, the security guard?"

He shook his head and inhaled deeply, his shoulders shaking, then his voice hardened. "No. I didn't see either of them, but Kayla Claybourne was standing right outside this storage building when I pulled into the parking lot. She turned and went inside when she saw me. I assume Genny must have been nearby, since she and Kayla go pretty much everywhere together. It's rare to see one without the other."

"But you didn't actually see Genny?"

"No, I didn't."

"Did Kayla acknowledge your arrival? Wave, call a greeting, anything?"

"No."

"Did you or Barbara acknowledge her?"

Alfie scoffed. "Definitely not."

"Why not?"

"Let's just say, Barbara and Kayla didn't get along. If you want my opinion, you should probably check into her."

"You think Kayla killed Barbara?" Hunt scribbled in his book.

Alfie's cheeks flared red. "Uh…well…no, no, not really. I just… I know they didn't like each other much."

"Do you know why?"

He chewed on a thumbnail and shook his head. "Barbara always said Kayla was just jealous of her friendship with Genny."

"Genny and Barbara were close?"

Sweat broke out on Gia's forehead and dripped down the side of her face. The thought of being on the receiving end of Hunt's rapid-fire questions brought a wave of anxiety. She brushed her hair back.

"Not as close as Barbara and I, but yes, they'd been friends since childhood." Alfie's posture slumped, and he rubbed his temples. "I'm sorry. I have a pounding headache. I'll be happy to help in any way I can. And I want desperately for you to find whoever did this to poor Barbara, but there's nothing else I can tell you. I really need to go home, take some ibuprofen, and lie down."

Hunt tucked his notebook in his pocket and offered Alfie a card. "Thank you for taking the time to answer my questions. If you think of anything at all, no matter how insignificant it might seem, please don't hesitate to call."

Alfie took the card and stuffed it into his shirt pocket. "Thank you, Detective."

Hunt just nodded, not bothering to correct him, then walked Alfie to the door. "Will you be able to get home okay, or would you like a ride?"

"I'll be okay, thank you." Alfie nodded to Gia and Savannah on his way out. His eyes were red and swollen from crying.

Gia resisted the urge to offer comfort.

The minute the door closed behind Alfie, Hunt turned on them.

"I thought—" Gia started.

But Hunt held up a hand to stop her. "Save it. I knew when I went out the door you two would be right behind me, just as surely as I knew you'd follow me back in."

Savannah grinned.

He punched her arm playfully. "But I do have to admit, it'll be nice to have a case you two have no reason to be involved in."

Though he phrased the statement lightheartedly enough, Gia couldn't help taking the words as a warning. Although, he was actually right. This case didn't involve them. She didn't even know any of the players. Thankfully.

Chapter Five

Gia climbed out of the passenger side of Savannah's car and shifted the seat forward for Thor. "Come on, boy."

He scrambled out and waited on the sidewalk for Gia to grab her bag and collect herself, which wasn't proving easy this morning.

By the time they'd finished up at the Festival grounds last night, it wasn't worth going all the way back to the café to pick up Gia's car. Zoe had dropped Thor off at the house for her, so Gia and Savannah went straight to Gia's, where Savannah had spent the night.

Unfortunately, neither Hunt nor Leo showed up or called, so she hadn't learned anything new about the investigation. She'd lain awake, staring at the ceiling most of the night, wondering what could have happened.

"You go ahead and take Thor to daycare, and I'll get started prepping." Savannah locked her car doors, then sorted through the keys on her ring for the key to the front door.

"Thanks, Savannah."

"No problem," she called. She waved over her shoulder as she hurried across the sidewalk and up the small pathway to the front door.

Gia took a deep breath of the muggy morning air. Dark clouds already filled the sky, and the forecaster had promised rain on and off all day. Though she'd grown accustomed to the afternoon showers that passed quickly, the overcast sky reminded her of New York. For once, the reminder brought no pang of homesickness. She'd never liked the long, cold, gray New York winters. The cold she could deal with, but she needed sunshine and blue skies.

With her bag slung over her shoulder, and a tight grip on Thor's leash, she walked toward the Doggie Day Care Center. She scratched Thor's head as they walked, and he looked up at her, his big brown eyes filled with love.

"Let's pick up the pace a little, honey. I want to make it there before it starts raining, okay, boy? I don't want you to get soaking wet and then have to spend the day in the air conditioning."

Thor dropped his tongue out and panted, then averted his gaze and trotted at her side. A moment later, he caught sight of a lizard that skittered across the sidewalk and up the side of the neighboring building and bolted after it. Apparently, he took her words to mean he should dilly-dally and chase lizards. She guided him back on path. "One of these days, you're going to catch one. And then what? Huh?"

"Gia, hold up." Trevor Barnes, the owner of Storm Scoopers, the ice cream parlor down Main Street from her café, waved from across the street and started toward her.

"Hey, Trevor, what's up? Isn't it kind of early for you to be in?" He didn't open until around noon, so there was usually no reason for him to be up and in the shop before the sun even rose.

"I just dropped Brandy off at day care so I can go out kayaking for a while before work." He petted Thor's head and offered Gia a lopsided grin. His slightly-too-long-in-the-front brown hair fell over his eyes. He shook it back. "Why don't you take a few hours off and come with me?"

"I'd love to, but I can't today. Willow's coming in late, so I have to work the dining room." Her only waitress took mostly online college courses, but she had to take a test that morning and wouldn't be in until lunchtime. "Besides, isn't it going to rain?"

"I won't melt." He smiled. "Now, when are you going to hire that second waitress you keep talking about so you can spend more time hanging out with me?"

"One of these days." She laughed, since they both knew it probably wasn't going to happen any time soon. Gia's luck with finding good employees had been less than ideal, and she was happy with the staff she currently had. Willow was a hard worker and got along great with the customers, and Cole had taken on more hours in front of the grill, freeing Gia up to work out front more often. Plus, Savannah and Earl pitched in now and then when Gia expected to be busy or someone needed time off. "Actually, Skyla offered to come in and help out a few days a week, but I haven't had a chance to talk to Willow alone and see how she'd feel about working with her mom."

Trevor waved it off. "Those two are closer than any two people I've ever known. I can't see it being a problem."

He was probably right, but she owed Willow the respect of asking. "Me neither, but I want to make sure."

"Well, let me know when you can get some time off. I miss kayaking with you." Trevor had introduced her to the peace and beauty of kayaking, and she loved it, but balancing the café, which, thankfully, was getting busier and busier, spending time with Thor, trying to get her house in order—she'd probably never finish unpacking all the boxes in the garage—and using what little time was left over to pursue some sort of relationship with Hunt, was proving more difficult than she'd anticipated. What she really needed was some downtime. And now she was going to toss in trying to do the Haunted Town Festival. What was she thinking?

"You know what? I'd love to go again as soon as I can get a few hours off. Maybe early next week."

"Just let me know, and I'll be there, but I won't hold my breath. Earl was in last night, and he said you're planning to do the Haunted Town Festival this year." Trevor laughed. "I wouldn't count on having any free time until it's over. From what I hear, it's a lot of work."

"Have you ever done it?"

"Nah. I'd love to, but I never felt like I had enough employees to do it right."

"Why don't you join me?" Gia had been worried about the same thing, but with both of them, they should be okay. "I'm going to be making pumpkin spice waffles, and I think they'd be great with your homemade vanilla ice cream."

Trevor's stomach growled and he pressed a hand against it. "Now see what you did? I'm starving, and that sounds delicious."

"If you give me a few minutes to drop Thor off, you're welcome to come in and have breakfast with Earl." Earl always came into the café before opening to have breakfast, every morning, without fail.

"I'd love to, but I'll have to take a raincheck. I'm meeting a couple of friends out by the lake..." He checked his watch then looked up at the growing clouds. "Wow. And I need to get going or I'm going to be late. I'd love to do the Festival with you, though, so keep me in mind. I'll stop in tomorrow before work and you can tell me what I have to do."

With that, he rushed off, tripped over his own feet, stumbled a few steps and almost went down in the middle of the road. After he recovered, he shot a grin over his shoulder, gave her a thumbs up, and kept going.

She shook her head. How he managed to be so graceful while kayaking and such a klutz walking was beyond her. The low rumble of distant thunder goaded her into resuming her trek toward the day care center.

Odd, Trevor hadn't mentioned Barbara's murder. Since he'd already heard Gia was doing the Festival, she assumed he'd heard about the murder as well. Then again, he'd heard about her doing the Festival from Earl last night.

Maybe he didn't bring it up because the rumor mill wasn't up and running yet this morning. With the shops opening along Main Street, including her café, that would soon change. Speaking of... if she didn't pick up the pace, she was going to miss breakfast with Earl. "Come on, Thor."

She opened the day care center door and ushered Thor inside just as the first fat drops of rain spattered the windows. A gust of wind almost yanked the door out of her hand.

"Hey there." Zoe rounded the counter and squatted down to pet the sides of Thor's face. "Looks like you got here just in time."

Rain battered the windows and door and ran down the sidewalk in a small river. "I don't know if I'll ever get used to the way torrential downpours just start out of nowhere."

"It wasn't out of nowhere." She stood and smiled at Gia. "The clouds have been building all night. It's been thundering on and off for the past ten minutes or so, and the wind picked up a few minutes ago. You just need to learn what signs to watch for."

"I guess. I'll have to pay more attention." But it still seemed the rain should start out as a drizzle then increase, rather than the clouds just opening up and dumping their contents all at once. She unclipped Thor's leash and handed it to Zoe, then petted him and hugged him. "You be a good boy, now, okay. I love you, baby, and I'll be back as soon as I'm done working."

"Don't worry, Thor's always a good boy. Isn't that right, big fella?" Zoe patted his side. "Come on, Thor. Brandy's already here waiting for you."

Thor cast one last longing look at Gia, barked once, and trotted after Zoe toward the back room.

Gia stood staring out the window as gallons of rain water shot from the drainpipe, down the sidewalk, and into the street. The thought of running back to the café in that mess didn't appeal.

After putting Thor in the play room with Brandy, Zoe returned to stand beside Gia. "I'm sorry I can't offer you a ride, I'm the only one here this early."

Wind-driven rain battered the windows.

"No worries. I'll give it a minute, and if it doesn't slow down, I'll make a run for it." Or she'd let Savannah and Cole get started while she went in the back and played with Thor. "Or maybe I'll just play hooky today."

Zoe laughed. "We both know that's not happening."

"True, but I can dream, can't I?" One of these days, she just might follow through. "Oh, while I'm here, I wanted to ask you about watching Thor during the Haunted Town Festival. Do I have to sign up ahead of time?"

"Nope, you don't have to sign up at all, and I'd love to have Thor. The high school kids get community service credit for volunteering for the

Festival, so there's never a shortage of helpers." Zoe frowned. "If they let the Festival go on as planned."

Uh oh. Seems Zoe had heard something more than Trevor. "Are they planning to cancel?"

"I don't know, but if I were you, I'd expect a huge crowd when this rain lightens up."

"Oh, why's that?" Not that she was ever opposed to a large crowd.

"Because rumor has it you were out there when Barbara was found."

Great, just what she needed. Everyone asking questions Hunt would have an episode if she answered. Maybe Savannah could hang around for a while and work the front while Gia helped Cole out in the kitchen. Not that she wanted to throw Savannah under the bus, but Savannah was more skilled at evading than Gia was. It was a skill she had to learn. Fast. "What are people saying?"

"Just that she was found buried on the fairgrounds and everything is roped off out there. She obviously didn't bury herself, so suspicions are running rampant."

Though she'd been a little surprised that Trevor hadn't known anything at all, she didn't expect that so much information would have leaked already. Hunt wouldn't be happy. It was easier to investigate if people weren't prejudiced by popular opinion. Easier for Hunt to investigate, that is, because Gia had no part in this case, and it didn't concern her. "How'd everyone find out so fast?"

"A few people showed up at the fairgrounds late last night to drop off supplies, and the police wouldn't let them in." She put a hand on Gia's shoulder. "Someone saw you and Savannah leaving."

Gia blew out a breath, thanked Zoe, and braced herself to run out into the rain. The upside of Florida storms; at least the rain was warm. It could have been worse.

A car pulled up in front of the door, and the driver tapped the horn in two short bursts. Earl cracked the passenger side door open a little and waved.

"You're the best, Earl," Gia whispered, as she shoved through the door and bolted for the car, every footfall splashing water all over her jeans. But it was still better than walking. She slid into the passenger seat and yanked the door shut as quickly as she could. "You're a lifesaver, Earl. Thank you."

"No problem. I saw you walking down here on my way in and had just parked when it started raining, so I figured you could use a ride."

A shiver tore through her.

Earl switched off the air conditioner. "Heard you had a busy night."

"Yeah." What else could she say? She wrapped her arms around herself, but the car warmed quickly with the air conditioner off.

Earl let it go. He made a U-turn in the middle of the mostly deserted street and parked in front of the café.

She wiped the fog off the passenger window so she could get a good view of the dining room. A few customers already sat at tables, all near the center of the room.

She glanced at the dashboard clock. She should still have another half hour to prepare. "Savannah opened already?"

"I don't know, I hadn't gone in yet, but it seems so. Probably didn't want anyone waiting out in the rain, and I saw Cole's car out back when I first got here, so no reason not to open, really."

"All right, then." She couldn't leave Savannah to do everything. "Thank you for the ride, Earl."

"Any time."

They jumped out of the car and ran for the front door. Earl was surprisingly agile for a man of his age—which Gia didn't know. From things he'd let slip, he had to be nearly—if not more than—eighty years old.

Gia held the door for him to precede her, then followed him in.

Savannah had already lain the waterproof mat in front of the door, and an umbrella stand with plastic bags sat on the corner. Though Gia had a number of umbrellas stashed away, none of them ever seemed to be conveniently located when she needed one.

As she let rain water drip off her head onto the mat, two pink ruffled umbrellas, sitting side by side in the stand, announced the Bailey twins' presence. Great, just what she needed, Boggy Creek's resident gossip artists. She swore the elderly women sometimes knew stuff before it even happened.

"Gia, dear, you're soaked." Estelle Bailey jumped up from her chair and glanced pointedly at her watch. "Well, I guess no one can blame you for being late after the night you had out at the Fairgrounds."

Late? Seriously? She didn't bother to point out that, technically, the café shouldn't even be open yet. She pushed her hair back off her face and tied it in a band she had on her wrist. "Good morning, ladies. How in the world did you two hear about that already?"

Estelle's face puckered.

"Oh for pity's sake, Estelle, let the poor girl get through the front door before you attack." Esmeralda picked up the cloth napkin from her place setting, then rounded the table and handed it to Gia.

Gia wiped her face, thankful for the moment's reprieve.

Estelle harrumphed but made no move to sit. "So, anyway, Beth from the salon told—"

No way could they have been to the salon between the time the body was found at eight or nine last night and not even seven in the morning, though it was hard to tell from the perfectly coiffed, blue up-do Estelle patted. Gia wouldn't be surprised if the woman had Beth from the salon on speed dial.

"—whose sister lives with Jack's cousin—"

A dull throb started at Gia's temples. It was too early for this.

"—told Patty, who's a paramedic, though she wasn't on call last night, that your boyfriend had the Fairgrounds taped off—"

Gia's eye twitched.

"—and was questioning that nice boy, what's-his-name, who was such good friends with Barbara."

Earl chuckled from his seat at the counter, then took off his hat as he wiped his mostly dry face with a napkin.

Savannah turned her back, though her shaking shoulders gave her away.

"Look, Estelle…" What could she really say? The woman had everything pegged as if she'd been there.

Estelle saved her the trouble of answering when she snorted and waved a hand dismissively. "Whatever. It's no surprise, really."

Esmeralda nodded in agreement and returned to her seat.

Estelle turned and sat across from her, then lifted a menu and browsed through the breakfast selection.

Gia looked at Earl, who just shook his head.

Savannah rolled her eyes and poured Earl a cup of coffee.

Well, the sisters could just keep whatever dirt they had to themselves. No way was she going to ask them what they were talking about. She didn't need to know. Sufficiently dried off, Gia rounded the counter and washed her hands. She didn't need gossip spreading through her café, especially the kind that might hinder Hunt's investigation or land her on his bad side.

She grabbed her order pad and approached the sisters. "So, ladies… What's no surprise, really?"

Dang! She'd tried so hard.

Esmeralda perched her reading glasses in her up-do. "Why, because of the blackmail, of course."

"Blackmail?"

"Sure." Estelle lowered her menu to the table. "Barbara Woodhull had dirt on pretty much everyone in Boggy Creek, and let me tell you, that woman was not afraid to use it to her advantage."

"Of course..." Esmeralda shifted her attention back to the menu. "There's always the chance Genny did away with her just to have a shot at winning the Best House Ruffie Award this year."

Estelle snickered. "That could be true, dear, considering Barbara has beat her out every single year since they started doing the Festival. Even on the rare occasions Barbara doesn't win first place, she still always comes out on top of Genny."

Gia bristled. These two hadn't seen Genny last night. The poor woman had been falling apart. That kind of gossip could only lead to trouble. "You can't possibly think—"

"Of course not, dear. Don't be ridiculous." With her menu open on the table in front of her, Esmeralda pointed to the number three special, dismissing any further discussion.

Probably for the best, anyway. Gia remembered, all too well, what it was like to be on the Bailey sisters' radar. Not only did they know everything that went on in Boggy Creek, but they were quick to form opinions and hurl them around like facts with absolutely no evidence to back them up.

"We'll both have the number three, but I want mine with scrambled eggs, and Estelle will have hers over medium."

"I'll get your order right in." Gia jotted the order down and stuck the ticket on the cut-out counter for Cole. She grabbed a couple plates of waffles and brought them to two customers at a corner table.

When she turned and caught sight of the Bailey sisters, they were leaning across the table toward each other, whispering. Their facts were always so accurate, and yet they got so much else wrong, inferring things that didn't even make sense given the information they'd acquired. Could they really be right about the blackmail? The women didn't mean any harm, they were just opinionated, judgmental, and indifferent to the people they enjoyed gossiping so much about. It was as if they were discussing nothing more important than the latest TV series they watched. Who knew? In their minds, maybe it was like that. As long as the misfortune didn't touch them, they could view it as no more than fiction, a story to pass on and ruminate about.

On the other hand, if they were right and Barbara had been blackmailing someone, which had led to her murder, Hunt needed to know about it. And it wasn't like she involved herself in the investigation on purpose or anything. She couldn't help it if information came to her. The responsible thing was to pass that information on to the authorities...after she researched a little, of course, just to be sure she wasn't passing on idle gossip.

Chapter Six

Gia cleared the counter, loaded the last of the dirty dishes into the bus pan, then wiped down the countertop. Rumors of Barbara's death and the potential consequences for the Festival led to a particularly busy breakfast rush, but only a few customers remained. All had been served, their coffee cups topped off. Now she just had to keep an eye out for when they needed their checks.

She lifted the bus pan and carried it back to the kitchen. "Hey, Cole, why don't you take a break?"

"A soon as I'm done here I will." Cole chopped the remainder of the ham on the cutting board, then swept it into an already-half-full stainless-steel bin. "Busy morning, huh?"

"No kidding." While she hoped the lunch rush would be just as hectic, she wished the reason was different, and that everyone was just coming for her amazing food. Technically, the fact that people now gathered in her café to discuss Boggy Creek's dilemmas did bode well for business. And for her. After a rough start, she'd finally started to gain the local residents' acceptance.

Cole covered the bin with Saran Wrap and stuck it in the fridge. "What are people saying?"

With one eye on the dining room, she quickly loaded the few dishes that would still fit into the dishwasher, turned it on, and stuck the pan with the remaining dishes beneath the center island for later. "Why don't you come have something to eat or a cup of coffee while we're slow, and I'll catch you up on the latest gossip? Then, maybe, if we're not busy after, we can talk about a dog treat recipe."

"Sure thing."

He washed his hands while Gia loaded a tray with scones and muffins to restock the cake dishes on the counter then hurried back out front.

Cole followed with refills for the breakfast pie displays. "Leave me out one of those banana chocolate chip muffins, please."

"You got it." After putting a muffin on a small plate for Cole, setting a chocolate, chocolate chip muffin on another plate for herself, and adding a couple cups of coffee, Gia put the remaining muffins in the cake dishes. She brought her last few customers their checks, rang one of them up, and finally took a seat at the counter. She glanced at the clock.

"Willow should be here soon." Cole winked.

She grinned at him. "That obvious, huh?"

"You just look tired."

"Yeah, well. Working this dining room alone is hard work." She sipped her coffee. "I really do have to talk to Willow about Skyla pitching in until I can do something more permanent."

"Why haven't you done it already?"

She shrugged. "Mostly, I think, because I don't want to hurt Willow's feelings. She's a great kid, and she does an amazing job out here, better than me, if I'm honest."

"So?" Cole broke off a piece of his muffin, still warm from the oven, and melted chocolate oozed onto his plate.

She added extra chocolate chips this time, and the muffins looked amazing. The scent of bananas and chocolate made her stomach growl.

"It's not like you're replacing her. You're just trying to add some help, so she doesn't have to do it all alone."

"I know that, and you know that, but every time I approach the subject, she looks so disappointed."

"Then take Skyla up on her offer, at least, for now."

Gia took a bite of her muffin. With running around all morning, she hadn't realized how hungry she was. "I probably will. I'm going to talk to Willow about it when she gets here."

"Good." Cole took another bite, savored it for a moment, then swallowed and washed it down with coffee. "Now, what has everyone been saying?"

He didn't have to elaborate; Gia knew exactly what he meant. "Everyone's shocked that Barbara is gone, but the fact that she was murdered is really what the buzz is all about."

"That leaked already, huh?"

"Seriously? That was all over before my first customer walked through the door." Her first customers of the morning were the Bailey sisters. "You know, the Bailey sisters said something weird this morning."

"The Bailey sisters always say something weird." Cole laughed. "It's kind of their thing, ya know what I mean?"

"Very true." Gia hesitated. Cole was right, those two often got mixed up, if she was being kind and giving them the benefit of the doubt. "But this was even more bizarre than usual."

"Oh?" He lifted a brow and lowered the remainder of his muffin to his plate. "How so?"

"I don't want you to repeat this…" She glanced around the café. Her last couple of customers lingered at a table over coffee. She quickly offered them a refill, which they accepted, then returned to Cole. She was careful to keep her voice low. No sense spreading the rumors those two initiated. "They said Barbara had dirt on half of Boggy Creek, said they thought that might have led to her death."

"Hmm…" Cole ran his hand down the sides of his mouth.

"What do you mean, hmm? Do you know if that's true?"

"I don't. But I do have to say, even though those two rarely get anything right, they usually have fairly accurate information. It's their interpretation that's off."

"I guess." Not that she didn't agree with his assessment—she thought the same thing herself only a few hours ago—but Gia still wasn't convinced they were wrong about Barbara. If they were right, and she was collecting dirt, for what purpose if not blackmail? She corralled her thoughts. What was she doing? The same thing the Bailey sisters did, taking what might be accurate information—or might not—and trying to make it fit the purpose she found made the most sense.

"Good thing you're dating the Police Captain, huh? Makes it easy enough to mention it to him and then forget about it and let the professionals do their jobs." He shot her a pointed glare. "Right?"

"Yes, of course. I just don't want to waste Hunt's time on what is probably just idle gossip."

"Gia…" Cole held her gaze and lifted a brow.

"What? All I'm doing is asking around a bit."

Cole laid a hand over hers. "Problem is, you have no idea who you're asking. Don't forget, someone killed Barbara, and that someone is still roaming free."

That fact was what most of the gossip had centered around this morning. "People are scared."

"Of course they are. And rightfully so."

She had to concede that point. She sipped her coffee.

A gentleman opened the front door and stepped back.

"Thank you, Tom." Savannah smiled as she strode through the door.

"Of course." He followed her into the café.

"Hey there." Savannah kissed Gia's cheek and nodded to Cole, then gestured toward her companion. "This here's Tom Prichard. He's an old friend, a reporter, and a client—since he's gonna be buying the old Haven's Estate out on Route 10."

"Maybe." He pointed a finger in the air. "I *may* be buying the Haven's Estate."

"Yeah, yeah." Savannah waved him off. "He's buying it. We just haven't worked out all the particulars yet."

"Like how I'm going to get a mortgage for that piece of ju—"

"Fixer-upper," Savannah interrupted with a grin.

"Yeah, that." He laughed.

Savannah gestured toward a table. "Why don't you go ahead and grab a corner table, and I'll get us some breakfast pie and coffee. Then we can discuss what might actually be feasible."

"Sounds like a plan." He shook hands with Gia and then Cole. "It was a pleasure meeting you both."

"You too." Gia turned to Savannah. "Go ahead and work, Savannah. I'll bring your coffee and food."

"Nah, I've got it." She rounded the counter, pulled out a serving tray, set a couple slices of meat lovers pie on plates, then added them to the tray with two cups of coffee. "I went by the shelter this morning."

"How's Debby doing?" Gia couldn't imagine. She had to be a wreck. All the Festival proceeds went to the animal shelter, so if it didn't take place, there wouldn't be enough money to run the shelter for another year until the event took place again.

"About how you'd expect. She's in shock over Barbara and scared there's a killer running loose."

"The same thing I've been hearing all morning."

Savannah grabbed silverware from the bin beneath the counter and set it on the tray. "She did say something I didn't quite get, though."

Cole frowned. "What's that?"

"She said she thought it was probably a personal vendetta rather than a random killing."

"Why would she think that?" Gia set her muffin aside, no longer as hungry as she'd thought.

Savannah shrugged. "No idea, and when I tried to question her about it, she just hushed right up."

"Hmm…strange." Gia told her about her conversation with the Bailey sisters. "Something's definitely not right."

"That's for sure." Savannah lifted the tray and started around the counter toward her client. "Of course, if it turns out it was something personal, they will probably let us proceed with the Festival."

"She's going to be crushed if they cancel, you know." Cole watched her go, then pushed his plate aside and grabbed Gia's order pad.

"Yeah, I know." Disappointment surged, surprising her. She hadn't realized how much she was looking forward to it herself. She handed him a pen and cleared their plates. "Hopefully, they'll figure out what happened quickly."

"Let's hope." Distracted, Cole tapped the pen against the pad. "What do you have in mind for the dog treats?"

Gia wiped her hands, rang up the customers who'd lingered over coffee, then leaned against the counter across from Cole. "I definitely want to do a peanut butter treat. If most dogs are anything like Thor, they'll be a huge hit."

"Yeah, that would probably work." He jotted some notes on the pad. "We could even coat some of them with crumbled bacon."

"Definitely. Then, in honor of fall and the Festival," provided Hunt could find Barbara's killer, "We could do a peanut butter pumpkin one."

Cole nodded. "Sure thing, maybe add some cinnamon."

"Mmm…that sounds good. Just make sure you don't use nutmeg. I've researched safe foods and spices for dogs, because sometimes I give Thor a little people food, and nutmeg is toxic to dogs." She liked the idea of sticking with one main flavor and adding to it, at least until she saw how people responded. "Maybe we could do something like that for every season, like almond butter and cranberry for winter and something with strawberries and bananas for spring and summer."

"All right. Let's give it a shot. We have plenty of eggs, but I'll have to pick up whole-wheat flour." He added pumpkin and peanut butter to the list. "When Willow gets here, I'll run out to the supermarket and pick up what we'll need, then we can mix up a small batch later on and give them a try."

The front door opened, and Gia glanced up, then did a double take.

Genny Hart walked in with a woman Gia didn't recognize, though she looked familiar. She'd definitely seen her somewhere before.

Gia grabbed two menus and greeted them by the door. She laid a hand on Genny's arm. "Good morning, Genny. How are you doing?"

"I don't honestly know." Genny shook her head and lowered her gaze. She didn't look much better than she had the day before, her face a red, blotchy mess. If anything, it seemed she was doing worse.

"I'm so sorry for your loss. If there's anything I can do..."

"Thank you." She sucked in a ragged breath. "I don't know what to do with myself. My first instinct is to work on the Festival, but then I think of all the time I spent there with Barbara, and I just...I can't."

"Not that it matters, anyway, since you can't very well work on your house when the police still have the whole area blocked off." Genny's companion slung an arm around her shoulder. "But they'll get it straightened out, and then you'll go back. You know that's what Barbara would want."

This had to be the Kayla Alfie told Hunt about. Despite her words, and her obvious affection for Genny, her tone when she spoke of Barbara held no emotion whatsoever, and her blue eyes turned to ice.

"Thank you, Kayla." Genny patted her hand. "I'm sure you're right."

The door opened again, and three more customers walked in behind them, all wearing business suits. Since they were probably on their lunch breaks, they'd no doubt be in a hurry.

Apparently, Gia's break was over. "Can I show you ladies to a table?"

"Yes, please." Kayla lowered her arm to her side. "Something out of the way, a corner maybe, where Genny won't have to listen to any gossip, if you know what I mean."

"I understand." And so did Savannah and Tom, Cole, the three people who walked in behind them, and possibly anyone who happened to be walking past outside on the sidewalk, thanks to Kayla's loud, brash, completely indiscreet voice. "Follow me, please."

Willow strode through the door and stopped short, just before crashing into one of the businessmen who'd entered behind Genny and Kayla. "Oh excuse me."

They parted so she could slip through.

"Let me show you to a table." Willow grabbed three menus from the stack by the door and led the group toward the front window.

Genny and Kayla followed Gia to the back corner of the room.

She led them to a table for four, the most private she could offer, next to Savannah and Tom.

Now that Willow was there to take care of the remaining customers, and Cole had gone back to the grill, Gia could afford to spend a few minutes chatting with Genny and Kayla. She obviously couldn't ask if Barbara collected dirt on her neighbors, or if she was blackmailing anyone, and she'd have to tread lightly after Kayla's comment about not listening to gossip, but still…

She pulled out a chair for Genny.

"Thank you." Genny sat and pulled herself closer to the table.

Kayla slid past her and took the seat next to her rather than sitting across the table.

Gia handed them each a menu. "Can I start you off with some coffee or fresh squeezed orange juice?"

"Oh yes, coffee would be wonderful, thank you," Genny said. "I don't think I slept a wink last night."

"Who could blame you, Genny? Not for nothing, but you were at the fairgrounds last night, possibly at the exact time Barbara was killed." Kayla browsed the menu as she spoke, not bothering to look at the effect her words had.

A shiver tore through Genny, and she folded her arms across her chest.

She looked up from the menu and pinned Genny with a stare. "Who knows? If it was a random killing, which I doubt, it could have been you the killer targeted."

Kayla seemed so convinced Barbara was the intended victim that the words blurted out of Gia's mouth before her sensor button kicked in. "What makes you think it was anything other than a random killing?"

Kayla shrugged and took her time looking over the menu. "Who knows? Barbara wasn't the nicest person—"

"Kayla…" Genny held up a hand. "Don't, please."

"I know. I'm sorry." She pointed to a drink on her menu. "Could I get a large vanilla cinnamon cold brew, please?"

Gia started to turn then stopped when Kayla spoke again. Loudly.

"Don't get me wrong. I'm not saying anything bad about Barbara. All I'm saying is, it's possible she wasn't killed by a stranger. She did have a way of…shall we say, irritating people."

Savannah's gaze shot to Gia, her eyes wide.

"Maybe she finally pushed the wrong person too far," Kayla finished.

Genny didn't respond.

As much as Gia wanted to find out what she could about Barbara, Kayla's voice carried too far. Gia lowered her own voice in the hope that Kayla would follow suit. "What makes you think that?"

Genny glared at Kayla. "Please, Kayla, enough. I agreed to come in here and eat breakfast because you hounded me about having to eat something, but my stomach is in knots already, and I can't even think about food while you're discussing this."

Gia's cheeks heated. "I'm so sorry, Genny, you're right, of course. Let me get your coffee."

She hurried away, beating herself up over being so insensitive. It wasn't like her to get caught up in gossip like that, but she couldn't help herself. Kayla's insinuation that Barbara had somehow brought about her own tragic demise didn't sit right in Gia's gut, especially after Kayla had asked for privacy. Was she really looking to protect Genny, or did she just want a private place to hammer her? Well, if that was the case, seems she would have done it a little more quietly.

Keeping one eye on the women, Gia poured Genny's coffee and Kayla's cold brew, then added her homemade vanilla cinnamon creamer.

The two leaned closer to each other and spoke too quietly for Gia to make out what they were saying.

So, Kayla did have an indoor voice when she wanted to. That figured, just when Gia wished her words would carry.

Genny frowned and turned away from Kayla, then wiped her eyes with her napkin.

Gia delivered their coffees. "What else can I get you ladies?"

Kayla stared at Genny for a long moment, then finally tore her gaze away and looked up at Gia. "What's in the harvest special?"

Since Kayla's menu sat closed on the table, Gia recited the ingredients. "Scrambled eggs with bacon, thin sliced potatoes, squash, zucchini, peppers and onions, and it comes with home fries, whole grain toast, and orange juice."

"We'll each have the harvest special with whole grain toast and apple butter, if you have it."

"Of course." She started to write their order down.

"Please, don't worry about me." Genny pressed a hand against her stomach. "There's no way I could eat all of that."

Kayla laid a hand on her wrist. "You have to at least try, Genny."

"How about something a little lighter. I have homemade cinnamon apple oatmeal with a fruit cup or maybe a parfait?"

If looks could kill, Gia would have dropped on the spot under Kayla's glare.

"Oh yes, the oatmeal sounds much better, thank you." Genny relaxed against the seat back.

Ignoring Kayla's hostility, Gia changed Genny's order. "Okay, this will be right up."

"Thank you," Genny said.

Kayla simply stacked both menus and shoved them at Gia.

With no reason to linger any longer, and not knowing what she could say to make Genny feel better or regain any kind of good favor she may have been able to achieve with Kayla, Gia took the menus and turned away.

Savannah caught her eye and frowned, and Gia shot her gaze in Genny and Kayla's direction. She and Savannah had been friends long enough that she'd understand what Gia wanted.

As she returned their menus to the stack on the counter, Gia tried to imagine treating Savannah as Kayla had just treated Genny. While the urge to protect her and take care of her would be overwhelming, she couldn't imagine strong arming her like that. Then again, everyone's personalities were different. She didn't know either woman, so who was she to judge?

It seemed Willow had the dining room under control, so Gia focused on the customers sitting at the counter. "How are you today, Sarah?"

"I'm doing well, thank you."

"How did Mason's science project turn out?" Last time Sarah had been in, she'd been a wreck over trying to help her eight-year-old do a project for the science fair.

Sarah shook her head. "Pretty much how I expected. I timed how long it took candy to dissolve in different liquids, while Mason twirled the cups in circles, tipped himself upside down under the counter—don't even ask me how he managed that one—then wrapped my husband's belt around his waist—my Ted is not a small man—hung the slack over the pantry door knob, and pretended to fly."

Gia laughed out loud. Mason was born a few weeks before Sarah's forty-fifth birthday. To say the boy was a handful would be the understatement of the year, but Sarah adored him. As stressed as he could make her, the sun rose and set with him, as far as she was concerned.

Sarah shot her a dirty look.

"What? You have to admit, it's kind of funny. And very creative on Mason's part." Gia wiped a tear from the corner of her eye.

Sarah grinned. "That boy is going to be the death of me. I swear, I'm not sure if he's keeping me young or making me old."

"Nah, I'm pretty sure he's keeping you young, and he's definitely keeping you happy, so that's all that matters."

"That is so true! He's my everything, but that doesn't make him any less exhausting."

"Well, since you have some peace and quiet for a few minutes while he's in school, what can I get you?"

"I'll have hash and eggs with home fries, please."

"Toast?"

"None, thanks." She handed Gia her menu, then fished a paperback out of her tote and set it beside her place setting.

Gia glanced at Genny and Kayla while she crossed the room to put Sarah's ticket up. She'd been hoping for the chance to ask if Genny had given Hunt Barbara's phone, since he hadn't known about it when Gia mentioned it the night before, but she couldn't figure—

Wait. Barbara's phone.

The air shot out of Gia's lungs like she'd been punched in the gut. She stopped dead in her tracks. That's why Kayla looked so familiar. What had Alfie said Kayla's last name was? Claymour? No. Clay...something. Claybourne, that was it. Kayla Claybourne. KC. The woman in the picture, who'd been locked in a steamy embrace when Barbara's phone rang after Savannah fished it out from beneath the bush.

Chapter Seven

Gia bounced back and forth between pitching in with Cole in the kitchen and helping Willow out in the dining room, picking up slack wherever she was needed, chatting with customers, biding her time until Savannah finally finished her meeting with Tom.

By the time Savannah was done, the lunch rush had dwindled. She walked Tom to the door, returned to the counter, and hopped on a stool.

Gia topped off a couple of coffee cups, then held the pot up toward Savannah. "Coffee?"

"Nah, I'm good, thanks. I'll take a Diet Pepsi, though."

She pulled a can of Diet Pepsi from the small fridge and set it in front of Savannah. "So, what's the verdict? Is Tom buying the estate?"

Savannah laughed. "Of course he is. Did you expect anything less?"

"That poor boy didn't stand a chance." Gia couldn't help but laugh. Savannah's confidence and outgoing personality made her the perfect real estate salesperson. That, and her knack for matching the perfect house with its equally perfect prospective owner.

Savannah's grin faded, and she gestured toward the table where Genny and Kayla had sat. "So, what was that all about?"

The two didn't dawdle. When they'd finished eating, they asked for their check, paid, and left, neither looking very happy.

"I don't know. They came in, and Kayla asked for a private table where Genny wouldn't have to hear gossip, then Kayla carried on about Barbara anyway." A pang of guilt surfaced, and she squirmed. "I guess I didn't help matters either, asking about what happened."

Savannah tilted her head to study Gia. "That's not like you. Usually, you're sensitive to people's feelings when it comes to stuff like that."

"I know. I don't know what happened. Kayla was so abrasive and indifferent; I guess I just lost sight of Genny for a moment. I'll have to apologize next time I see her."

"I'm sure she'll understand." Savannah picked up her soda but then put it down without taking a drink. "You're right about Kayla, though. Abrasive is a good word for her."

"If she's like that with everyone, I can see why Barbara didn't like her much. And the way she tries to push Genny into doing what she wants her to would be tough for another friend to watch." Leaning against the counter, Gia tried to stretch her back discreetly. As much as she enjoyed working the dining room and getting to know her customers, lugging heavy trays full of food and bus pans full of dirty dishes was murder on her back. "Anyway, I definitely get the impression Alfie was right. Seems like there was no love lost between Barbara and Kayla."

"Yeah, well, you should have heard Kayla after you walked away." Savannah traced her finger around the rim of the can.

"Were you able to hear what they were talking about?"

"Some of it. Mostly it seemed Kayla was complaining," Savannah said.

"Complaining about what?" Probably Gia changing Genny's breakfast order, if the glare she'd given her was any indication.

"Pretty much everything." She finally took a sip of her soda, before setting it aside and taking her phone out of her oversized bag, rust and gold this time, in honor of the season. "The fact that the police were considering the fairgrounds a crime scene…how dare they even think about not letting the Festival proceed…Genny's husband isn't being sufficiently supportive of her…"

"Really?"

"Mm…hm." She scrolled through her calendar, pausing for a second to glance over her shoulder at the clock, then closed her calendar and dropped the phone back into her bag. "Seems Preston isn't doing enough to help her, didn't even stay home from work today to console her. She doesn't seem to like him very much."

"Kayla Claybourne doesn't seem to like anyone very much."

"Very true." She folded her arms on the counter and leaned forward. "She even had a few choice words to say about Alfie."

"Oh yeah?"

"Yup. She wanted to make sure Alfie didn't think he could latch onto them and participate with their house if the Festival does take place."

"Wow. That's cold." How could anyone act like that? Alfie was so torn up over Barbara's death. Even if she didn't like Barbara or Alfie, you'd think she'd show some kind of compassion, out of respect for Genny, if nothing else. Genny obviously considered Barbara, at least, a good friend. "You don't think Alfie would want to continue Barbara's house?"

"I can't say because I don't know him." She shrugged. "Kayla didn't seem to think so, though."

"Huh…she's a real winner, huh?" That might be more of an understatement than calling Sarah's boy, Mason, a handful.

"Let's just say, I can see why Alfie said the things he did last night."

Two women approached the register, and Gia went to ring them up.

"Hi." One of the women handed her the check and pulled her wallet out of her purse.

"Good afternoon." She took the check and rang the amount into the register. "How was everything?"

"It was wonderful, thank you." The woman handed her a twenty dollar bill. "My sister's been talking about this place for months, insisted that we come here when I visited. I have to say, it didn't disappoint."

"Thank you very much. I'm so glad you enjoyed it." She handed the woman her change. "I hope you'll come again."

"Oh we will, for sure, before I head home." She pulled out a few more bills and added them to her change. "Will you make sure our waitress gets this. She's an absolute sweetheart."

"Yes, thank you." She set the bills aside in an envelope for Willow. "Have a good day."

"You too." The woman walked out and joined another woman, who must have been the sister she was talking about, on the sidewalk.

Gia recognized her, though she didn't recall her name. It always gave her a boost to get repeat customers and customer recommendations.

The second woman stepped up to the register. "How are you?"

"I'm doing well, thank you. And you?"

"Good, good." The woman handed over her check. "You know, I couldn't help overhearing they're talking about cancelling the Festival this year?"

She figured the woman had probably been there while Kayla was carrying on, but that wasn't really fair. Pretty much everyone was talking about the murder. "I don't really know. I guess it will depend on what the police investigation turns up."

"I suppose, but I sure hope they don't cancel. My kids will be so disappointed." The woman held out a debit card.

Gia gestured toward the pin pad. "Do you usually attend the Festival?"

"I wouldn't be able to go this year, because I have a little one at home, but my older kids and their friends all volunteer every year. They usually work in the woods scaring people with Debby from the shelter. It's nice that they get credit at school for community service but, honestly, they'd do it regardless because they enjoy it so much." She inserted her card and punched in her pin.

"I'm sure Debby will reach out to everyone who regularly works with her as soon as she hears anything."

"I'm sure. Or she'll get in touch with the school, since a lot of the kids volunteer, and they'll send out a call." She took her receipt and stuck it into her wallet with her card. "My husband is friends with Mike, who works at the fairgrounds, and he's been trying to reach him all morning to see if he knows what they're going to do, but he hasn't answered his calls."

"I'm sure there's a lot going on out there this morning."

"I'm sure." The woman tucked her purse under her arm. "Enjoy your day."

"Thank you. You too."

Hunt held the door for the woman, greeting her as she passed, then crossed the room, leaned over the counter, and kissed Gia's cheek before taking a seat next to Savannah. "Hey there."

"Hey, yourself." Gia set a mug in front of him.

He held a hand out and shook his head. "Something without caffeine, please. I've been up all night, and I've already drunk so much caffeine I'm jittery. I'm on my way home to try to close my eyes for a few minutes then take a shower. What have you two been up to? Staying out of trouble?"

Savannah answered with a very unladylike snort.

Hunt laughed.

Leo Dumont walked in a moment later, hugged Savannah from behind and dropped a kiss on her head. He sat down on Savannah's other side and leaned around her to see Hunt. "What's so funny?"

He shot him a grin. "Your fiancé doesn't appreciate my sense of humor."

Savannah swung the stool until her back was to Hunt and addressed Leo. "That's because your partner isn't funny."

"Uh oh, I'm not getting involved in any family rift." He helped himself to a blueberry scone from the cake dish closest to him.

Gia grabbed her order pad, intent on curbing any further bickering. "Do you guys want something to eat?"

"Yeah, thanks." Hunt raked a hand through his already disheveled hair. "I'll have scrambled eggs with sausage and home fries."

She jotted scr/s hf. "Toast?"

"Rye, please."

Adding rt, she turned toward Leo. "How about you?"

He wiped the crumbs from his fingers on a napkin. "You can give me the same, but with bacon instead of sausage."

"You got it." She added his order and stuck the ticket on the cut out for Cole.

"So, what's going on?" Hunt asked.

Savannah turned to him, his earlier comment apparently forgotten, or at least forgiven. "You'll never guess who came in a little while ago."

"Genny Hart," Leo said, after swallowing a mouthful of scone.

"Hey." She scowled at him. "How'd you know?"

He shrugged. "Word travels."

She stared at him a moment longer, but when it became clear he wasn't going to elaborate, she continued, "Kayla Claybourne was with her. She's a real piece of work, that one."

To say the least. The image of Kayla on Barbara's phone flashed into Gia's mind. She was going to ask Savannah about it before she had to ring up her customers, but she never had the chance. "Speaking of Kayla… Hunt, do you remember last night when I told you we'd found Barbara's phone?"

"What about it?" He bit into a banana chocolate chip muffin.

Anticipation built while she waited to see if he liked it with the extra chips. "Did Genny give it to you?"

He shook his head. "Nope."

"No?" Gia thought the victim's phone would be an important piece of evidence in the investigation. "Why not?"

He swallowed and wiped his mouth. "She couldn't find it. By the way, this is delicious. Extra chips?"

"Yes. Thank you. I'm glad you like them." Joy swelled, as it did every time someone enjoyed her cooking. But he wasn't getting off the hook that easily. "What do you mean, she couldn't find it? She put it in her back pocket."

He spread his hands wide and shrugged. "Last she remembers, she took it out of her pocket and stuffed it in her purse, which she then left in her house when she went out to see what all the fuss was about—her words. The next time she gave it any thought was after you mentioned it to me and I asked her about it. Seems it disappeared sometime in between."

"Hmm…" She leaned closer to Hunt and lowered her voice. "Do you believe her?"

"No reason not to, at this point." He frowned and straightened. "Why?"

Keeping her voice low, she gestured for Savannah to lean closer. "Last night, right after Savannah found the phone, it rang, and the initials KC popped up."

"Oh right, and there was a background picture of a man and a woman in a pretty hot embrace." Savannah waggled her eyebrows.

When she didn't mention the woman being Kayla, Gia hesitated. She'd hoped Savannah would come to the same conclusion Gia had right away, without having to say anything. Maybe she was mistaken and it was another woman who just resembled Kayla. "Do you remember what the woman looked like?"

Savannah frowned and scratched her head. "She had long dark hair. I remember that. Kind of straight, if I'm not mistaken. I think her eyes were closed, but I'm not sure. Genny snatched the phone before I could see too much. Why?"

"Kayla had her hair up today, but when she walked in, she looked familiar. I'm pretty sure I recognized her from the picture. And the Bailey sisters were in earlier, and they mentioned Barbara may have been collecting dirt on people." Heat flared in her cheeks, her face burning. "Not that I'm passing on gossip, but I thought you guys should know."

"Don't worry about it. Better to let us know; you never can tell what might turn out to be important." Hunt pulled a pad out of his back pocket, then reached across the counter and grabbed the pen she'd left lying there after taking their order. "What about the man? What did he look like? Could you tell who he was?"

She tried to recall as many details from the image as she could, though she'd only seen it for a second or two. No use. She hadn't seen the man's face. "Nah, his back was to the camera. The only thing I can tell you about him was he had plain, probably collar length brown hair."

Savannah jerked back and her eyes widened. "And a tattoo."

Hunt held her gaze, his dark eyes intense. "A tattoo? Are you sure?"

"Positive." She nodded. "A scorpion was tattooed on the back of his right shoulder."

Chapter Eight

As was often the case, late afternoon brought another lull in business. Though her dinner hour had picked up somewhat, with the introduction of a variety of steak and egg dinners to the menu, it was still slower than she'd like. While things were slow, and Willow was refilling and replacing salt and pepper shakers, ketchup bottles, dirty seat cushion covers, and whatever else needed attention in the dining room, Gia headed back to the kitchen.

"Hey, there." Cole untied his apron, balled it up, and shot it through the doorway into the small hamper in the hallway in a beautiful two-point shot. "Nice lunch? Seemed busy from back here."

"I can't complain. Seems our lunch hour is picking up better than dinner." It also seemed Cole had taken care of everything in the kitchen. The empty stainless-steel sinks gleamed, clean dishes were stacked on the shelves above the spotless counters, and a pile of empty bus pans waited on a cart beside the doorway. "You didn't have to do all of this, thank you."

"No problem. I was back here anyway, and you know I hate to walk out of a dirty kitchen." He looked around and scratched his chin. "Now, about dinner, do you want to tweak the menu some more?"

Did she? In addition to her regular breakfast menu, she already added a southwestern dinner menu and a variety of steak and egg recipes. If she kept adding, sooner or later her quality would suffer. Plus, a lot of food would go to waste. Prep work needed to be done ahead of time, and whatever didn't sell would only stay good for so long. "Nah, let's leave it for a while longer and see what happens."

"Sounds like a plan." Cole gestured toward the refrigerator. "Most of the prep work for tomorrow is done, but you are almost out of peppers and onions—a lot of western omelets today—so I'm going to run and pick some up before I head home."

"Thanks, Cole, but you don't have to do that. I can stop on my way home from work."

He waved a hand. "Don't worry about it. I was going to the supermarket anyway to pick up what we'll need for the dog treats. When do you want to give them a try?"

She'd thought about making them at home and letting Thor be her test subject, but Cole seemed so excited about the project she didn't have the heart to do it without him. "You're off tomorrow, so we could do it Wednesday if you want?"

"I don't mind coming in tomorrow, if you want to give it a try. I'm meeting Earl for breakfast anyway."

"What happened to that retirement you were supposed to be enjoying?" Cole was retired and only agreed to come in a few days a week to help her out, so she could have some time away from the grill to get to know her customers. Over the year he'd been working there, his hours had increased gradually until he now worked almost as much as she did.

"Bah...turns out retirement is boring. You can only read so many books, and every hobby I've tried ended in disaster. Some people are just not cut out for rest and relaxation."

Gia laughed.

"You laugh now, honey, but just you wait. I watch the way you run around here; mark my words, you're going to be the same way."

Gia had worked full time since her father put her out the day after she graduated high school. What would it be like to have all day long to do whatever she wanted? She would never set an alarm, which really didn't matter because she usually woke up early without one. Long walks with Thor, kayaking on the river with Trevor, time to hang out with Savannah and maybe pursue more of a relationship with Hunt.

Oh, wait. Savannah and Hunt both worked long hours. So did Trevor, come to think if it. Cole might be right. Aside from having Thor with her every minute of the day, which would never grow old, retirement might not be all it was cracked up to be. "Tomorrow it is."

Cole's deep laughter echoed through the kitchen. "Didn't take you long to figure it out, huh?"

"What can I say? I'm a glutton for punishment."

"See you tomorrow, then. And don't worry about the peppers and onions, I'll take care of having them ready by the time we open tomorrow."

"Thank you, Cole, really." She stopped him on his way out with a hand on his arm. "I mean it. I can't tell you how much I appreciate all that you do for me."

"Any time, dear." He patted her hand on his arm. "Besides, you're going to need all the help you can get if you want to get your house and table set up in time for the Festival."

Yikes! With Barbara's murder, Kayla's odd behavior, and the regular, everyday running around, she'd forgotten she had to put something together. "If they let the Festival go on."

"Oh, it'll go on, trust me."

"How can you be so sure?"

"Because it's never been canceled, even the one year we got heavy rain people slogged through the mud to support the animal shelter."

"Wow."

"Of course, if there was lightning, that would be a different story, but rain wasn't a sufficient deterrent." He pulled his keys out of the pocket of his khaki shorts. "Besides, it's still a couple of weeks away; Hunt and Leo will figure out who killed Barbara before then, she will be laid to rest in peace, and the Festival will go on in her honor."

"You think so?"

"Yup." He kissed her cheek and headed for the door. "If you want to get everyone together and tell them to come over to my house, I have a mostly empty storage shed out back that we can use to build and store whatever you'll need."

"That would be perfect, Cole, thank you." Now if she could just figure out what she needed. Plywood for sure. Tools, nails. Glue, maybe. They'd have to tack the blankets and sheets onto the platforms they were using for beds somehow.

"Any time." He waved as he walked out.

With nothing left to do in the kitchen, Gia returned to the dining room. She hadn't yet told Willow they would be participating in the Festival, and she was hoping Willow, and maybe some of her friends, would want to join them. "Willow, can we talk for a minute?"

"Sure thing," she called from the front of the dining room where she was sweeping the floors. She washed her hands, dried them, and plopped down on a stool at the counter with a huge smile. "So…a table and a house, huh?"

"Seriously? How did you find that out already?"

"What do you mean already? I heard that two or three minutes after walking through the front door." Her expression sobered. "Right after hearing about Ms. Woodhull."

"Did you know Ms. Woodhull?" Gia poured herself a Diet Pepsi and Willow a root beer from the fountain, then set them on the counter.

"Thanks." Willow opened a straw and stuck it in her soda. "Not really. I met her at the Festival—my mom and I volunteer every year—but Mom knows her better than I do. I just show up the night of and scare people. Mom usually helps set up."

"Oh. That was actually one of the things I wanted to talk to you about. I was hoping you, and maybe your mom and some friends would want to work with me on the Festival, but if you already work there with someone else—"

"Oh no, it's not like that. My friends and I started volunteering when we were in high school, and I just kept going afterward because it's fun and it's for a good cause. I usually just show up and go where they need extra help, and Mom works for Debby putting up fliers, pitching in if someone needs a hand and doesn't have everything done. We'd love to do your house."

Relief rushed through her. She needed people she could count on, and Willow and Skyla definitely fit the bill. "Speaking of your mom, I have a question to ask you, but I don't want you to get the wrong idea."

She stirred her straw, clinking the ice against the sides of the glass. "What's up?"

"Your mom and I were talking the other day when she came in for breakfast, and I mentioned wanting to hire a second waitress…"

Willow stiffened.

"Not to replace you or anything, just because it's a lot of work out here by yourself."

Her eyes narrowed.

Maybe Gia was going about this the wrong way. Willow was young but not too young to understand she was running a business and hiring help was just part of that, nothing personal. Not that she expected Willow to argue with her, but she didn't want to hurt her feelings, and she definitely didn't want to lose her. She sucked in a deep breath and braced herself. "And your mom offered to pitch in and work with you during some of the busier shifts."

The air shot from Willow's lungs and she slumped back on the stool. "That would be great."

Wait, what? "It would?"

She sipped her root beer. "Sure. I'd love working with Mom."

Go figure. "So why have you seemed so resistant every time I've suggested hiring another waitress?"

"Well…" Twin patches of red flared on her cheeks, and she played with one of her black stud earrings, twirling it around in her ear. "I love working here, and well…to be honest, your track record for hiring help isn't all that good. I was just afraid you'd hire someone I couldn't get along with, and then I'd have to either suck it up and deal with it or leave, and I didn't want that to happen."

Gia laughed. She couldn't help it, and she couldn't argue. She'd definitely made some hiring mistakes early on but, in her defense, she'd been trying to staff the café in a hurry from New York and hadn't researched references properly. "That's one thing you don't have to worry about. I won't make the same mistake again."

"Great. Now that that's settled, and my mom will be thrilled because she's bored at home, did you choose a theme for your house yet?"

Since the topic had obviously made Willow uncomfortable, Gia let it go. Though she was thrilled Willow had finally opened up enough to share what was on her mind. "The house is long and narrow, so we're thinking maybe a dormitory theme or something like that."

"I love it." She perked up right away. "Are you going to have beds and stuff?"

"Yes, but not real ones. They'll probably be made from wood and have blankets thrown over them."

"That's awesome. Maybe we could put hinges on some of them and make trapdoors, so we can hide inside and pop out." She bounced on her stool.

The thought of walking through a dark house in the dead of night and having someone in a creepy costume and mask pop out of a bed sent a shiver of terror rushing through her. "Perfect!"

"I can't wait." Willow ran around the counter and grabbed her phone from the shelf underneath, then scrolled through and pulled up an internet browser. "I was looking at this before, and this is how I'd like to do my makeup."

She enlarged an image of a girl in a hospital type gown, her eyes rimmed with white makeup, and long lashes painted above and below her lids. Several jagged red splotches, one across her forehead, another running from one corner of her mouth out to her jaw bone, and a couple on her cheeks were painted with stitching surrounding them, as if a random variety of wounds had come open.

"That's pretty elaborate, no?" Gia had been thinking of running to the local Halloween store for a mask.

"Are you kidding? The funnest part of the whole event is everyone getting together during the day to put their makeup and costumes on." She continued scrolling through makeup ideas. "Hey, maybe you could close early that day, and we could all get together here and do it."

Trevor walked in just in time to catch the tail end of her sentence. "Hello, ladies. What's all the excitement about?"

"Howdy, stranger, what are you doing here?"

Trevor had hired a new boy from the local college to work in the shop, but he rarely left him alone.

Gia poured him a pumpkin spice cold brew and set it on the counter. "I thought you weren't coming in until tomorrow morning."

"The town is all abuzz with word of Barbara Woodhull's demise and the pending fate of the Festival. I figured I'd take a quick run down while it was slow enough to leave Matthew by himself behind the counter."

Willow held her phone out for Trevor to see her makeup ideas. "Gia is hosting a house and a table for the Haunted Town Festival, and we're coming up with ideas. I was just telling her we could come early and do our makeup and costumes here, maybe put together one of those four-foot Italian subs with some salads. I know it's not a breakfast food, but that would be easy enough to do ahead of time, and there'd be no real clean-up afterward."

Trevor took the stool next to her, and Willow set the phone on the counter so they could all look.

"Meeting here ahead of time is a great idea. It will make it easier too, since there's never any parking up there. We could all pile into as few cars as possible and head up in groups." Trevor pointed out an image. "I'd love to do that. Does it give directions on how to do it? That can't be real papier-mâché, you'd suffocate."

Willow read the paragraph beneath the picture. "No, it's not, it's just made to look that way."

Gia couldn't tell if the model was a man or a woman, but whoever it was also wore a hospital gown and wrapped their entire head in what looked like papier-mâché bandages and painted black eyes and a black smile on them. The next picture showed the back of the model's head, where an open zipper appeared to be glued on, the inside of which was painted to look as if someone had unzipped the patient's head for a peek inside. "Wow, this Festival is really a big deal, huh?"

"Oh, for sure." Willow scrolled through several more pages of makeup and costumes. "Think of it like a show, with all the preparation—sets, costumes, lighting, sound—"

"Sound?"

"You'll want to put creepy music in your house for sure, just like you'd have if it was in a theater, only it's at the fairgrounds."

Yikes! What had she gotten herself into? This sounded way past her level of expertise.

"Well, count me in, and could you text me that link, please?" Trevor pointed to the image on Willow's phone. "Then, afterward, when we all come back for our cars, I'll treat everyone who worked the house to ice cream at Storm Scoopers. I'm going to be trying out a new flavor, apple cinnamon."

"Woo hoo." Willow bounced up and down. She'd been so mature and responsible since Gia met her that it was nice to see her enjoying something with the enthusiasm of a girl her age. "Kids from school will be lined up out the door to help."

"Apple cinnamon, huh?" Gia's mind raced. "That sounds delicious. Are you going to bring some to the Festival?"

"I was thinking of it, along with the vanilla for the pumpkin spice waffle sandwiches, why?"

"I bet it would be delicious with homemade crumb cake." She could almost smell the scent of apples and cinnamon as she envisioned it.

"Oh wow," Trevor said. "I bet it would be amazing. Want to give it a try?"

Would she be able to get all of this done? After looking at the images Willow, and now Trevor, planned to use for makeup ideas, she wondered where she'd ever find time to do it all. Although, everyone did seem excited about pitching in and helping out. Savannah would do anything she needed, and her brothers would probably help. Earl wanted to join in, along with some of his kids and grandkids, Willow, Skyla, and maybe some of their friends, Cole for sure, Hunt and Leo, if they were able, and Trevor. Maybe even Cybil would want to join them. She'd have to remember to give her a call and ask, if Earl or Cole hadn't already beat her to it. They'd probably be able to get everything done, but she had to get started right away. "Sure thing. That'll be two dessert items for the menu, and then I'll make up a bunch of breakfast pies and home fries. Do you think that'll be enough?"

"It should be. You don't need a huge variety, but you will need a lot of each thing, and don't forget lots of maple syrup for those who want their waffles hot."

"How will you keep the ice cream frozen?"

"There's electricity out there we can plug into, so I can bring a freezer. I just have to get someone with a truck to take it out there."

"That shouldn't be a problem." Willow glanced at the front door when a couple stopped to look at the menu in the window. "A bunch of volunteers with trucks pick up anything that's too big for people to transport within a few days of the event, then they add extra security to deter vandals until the night of."

"Perfect." Trevor stood and lifted his cold brew. "Don't forget to text me that link. By the way, what theme are you doing? Will that makeup work?"

Willow looked toward Gia. "Gia was thinking maybe a dormitory."

The couple entered.

Looked like their break was over. "You know what? In both of those pictures you showed me, the models wore hospital gowns, and it got me thinking, what about a haunted hospital?"

A tremor ran through Trevor, and he shivered. "Hospitals are pretty terrifying in the best of times, and I've spent enough time in and out of them with one injury or another to know."

"And we could still use all the beds like a dormitory, but center it around a hospital theme," Willow pointed out, as she grabbed two menus.

Gia's excitement grew as she warmed to the idea. "What do you think?"

"I love it," Trevor said.

"Me too," echoed Willow. "But first you'll have to run it by the general for final approval."

Gia frowned. "General?"

"Savannah," Trevor and Willow blurted together.

Gia laughed. They were right, of course. "That is, if they let the Festival proceed. Have you heard anything, Trevor?"

Willow hurried off to greet their new customers and lead them to a table. Gia would stop and say hello on her way back to the kitchen.

"Last I heard, they're searching for a person of interest who seems to have disappeared the same night Barbara was killed." Trevor reached into his pocket and pulled out a five dollar bill, but Gia put a hand on his to stop him. No matter how many times she told him he didn't have to pay, and though he refused to accept money from her any time she went in for ice cream, he always offered. When she refused the money, he left it on the counter as a tip. "At least that's the last day anyone remembers seeing him."

"Did they say who it is?" Gia glanced at the clock. Darn, she'd missed the most recent news conference. She'd meant to turn the TV on earlier to catch it, but she'd lost track of time.

"A groundskeeper named Mike Smith."

Chapter Nine

Gia whisked three eggs in a stainless-steel bowl, then added diced ham, and the rest of the peppers and onions Cole left. The evening had flown past, with a busier than usual dinner hour compliments of the mayor's announcement that they might cancel the Haunted Town Festival. Rumors ran rampant about the missing groundskeeper, Mike Smith. He apparently disappeared sometime right before or right after Barbara's murder.

Though no one mentioned it—at least, as far as she'd heard—she clearly remembered Alfie telling Hunt that Mike had been at the fairgrounds when he dropped Barbara off the day she was murdered. Was Alfie the last one who saw Mike? Had Mike killed Barbara, then taken off? Or was Mike Smith buried somewhere alongside Barbara's shallow grave?

Gia shivered and dismissed the thought. She poured the western omelet mixture onto a small dollop of oil on the grill, then cut open a roll and dropped it into the toaster. With that started, she filled a large container with home fries and grabbed a couple cheese slices from the fridge, along with a few pieces of bacon. She tossed the bacon onto the grill to heat and set the cheese aside.

Poor Debby; she must be heartbroken that they were talking about canceling the Festival. What would she do without the donations the annual event would bring?

She flipped the omelet, piled the bacon on one half, and folded it over, then laid the cheese across the top. Gia was thinking about going to the shelter to look for a second puppy, anyway. Maybe she'd stop on her way home and see how Debby was doing.

She pulled the roll from the toaster and loaded it with butter, then put it into a foam tray with the omelet and closed the lid.

Savannah would never forgive her if she went to the shelter and looked at puppies without her. Puppies were pretty much Savannah's favorite thing, which was good, considering she had like four of them. Gia grabbed the phone, dialed Savannah's number, and stuck the phone between her ear and her shoulder.

She loaded the omelet and home fries into a bag.

Savannah answered on the third ring. "Hey, girlfriend, what's up?"

"I was thinking of taking a ride past the shelter after I pick up Thor. Want to take a ride?"

"Of course I do." She laughed. "Do you want to pick me up at home?"

"Sure. I'm just going to put Harley's dinner out back, and I'll get Thor and be on my way." She'd been leaving dinner out for the local homeless man every night since she'd first opened. Harley was one of the sweetest people she'd ever met, and she'd developed a real soft spot for him, but he refused to enter a building, choosing instead to live out in the open. Harley looked out for her all the time, and he had become a good friend. Leaving him dinner was the least she could do.

"Maybe I'll pack an overnight bag and just stay over so you don't have to drive me back home tonight."

"Sounds great. We can pick up dinner at Xavier's on the way home if you want." Maybe Hunt and Leo would have time to stop by.

"Plus, if you bring home a new puppy, I'll be there to help out." Savannah's grin shot through the phone connection as if she were standing in front of Gia.

"I'm not bringing home a puppy tonight."

"We'll see."

"Savannah…" She made her voice as stern as possible, so Savannah would have no doubt she was serious. "I won't have time to take care of a puppy the right way if I'm doing the Festival. I might, and I emphasize *might*, think about it afterward."

"Uh huh. See ya in a few." She hung up before Gia could say anything more.

Maybe taking Savannah with her hadn't been the best idea, after all. She probably should have thought it through a bit more before acting. Story of her life.

She set aside her phone, grabbed Harley's dinner and a large sweet tea, then hit the bar to open the back door with her hip. Though she still parked out front and avoided the back lot whenever she could, she'd gotten better at—

She sensed the man's presence behind the open door a moment too late.

"Hey."

Gia screeched and jerked back, reflexively balling the hand holding the foam sweet tea cup, crushing it. Tea shot everywhere. "Oh man, Harley, you scared the living daylights out of me."

"Sorry. I didn't want you to leave alone." Harley took the bag from her and set it on the table Gia kept beside the door for him. He pulled the wad of napkins from the top of the bag and handed them to her, then held the door open while she wiped herself off.

"Don't worry about it, Harley. It's my own fault. I guess this whole thing with Barbara's murder has me jumpier than I thought." Which was no easy task considering how anxious her ex-husband's crimes, infidelity, and eventual murder had left her. She'd spent years ducking the victims of his theft, avoiding death threats, and enduring a public trial during which his line of mistresses had paraded through for all the world to see. Then, when he'd wound up dead in her dumpster, she'd endured even more.

Harley held the door open, squirming as he stared into the back hallway, clearly torn between helping her and his fear of entering any sort of enclosed structure.

"Why don't you go ahead and sit down and eat. Most of this spilled outside, so I'll just wash up and then hose it down."

"You sure?"

"Positive." She usually just left Harley's dinner on the table, assuming he used the table and chair she left out, but she wasn't sure. And she didn't know how he'd feel about having someone keep him company while he ate, otherwise, she'd make a few minutes to sit across from him. Since he looked to be about two seconds from bolting, she gestured toward his bag. "Go ahead, please. I'm going to go wash up and then I'll grab the hose and clean up out here."

Harley eyed the dinner bag for a moment and then nodded.

Gia hurried inside, washed the tea off herself as best she could, and used spray cleaner and paper towels to mop up the rest of the mess inside and on the back door. Since Cole had finished all the prep work, she'd have time to mop the floor in the morning.

When she returned to the back lot, she found Harley sitting and eating his omelet.

"You cook good."

"Thank you. I'm glad you like it." She unrolled the hose from beside the door and turned it on, then aimed it at the spilled tea, washing it toward a grate in the middle of the lot. The last thing she needed was rats or mice or bugs or whatever else the sugar might attract.

"Can I ask you something?"

She turned to look at him.

He scowled into his container of home fries.

"Is something wrong?" She hadn't had any complaints about the food from any other customers.

"I wanted to know if you'd do something for me." His long, more-gray-than-blond hair shifted from behind his ears and fell into his face. He made no attempt to move it aside.

Gia turned off the hose and returned it to its place, then leaned against the back door. Harley had come that evening, not for dinner, because he usually only picked up his food after she was gone, but to watch out for her because he was concerned for her welfare. It wasn't the first time Harley had looked out for her. There was nothing she wouldn't do for him. "Of course, Harley, anything. You know that. What do you need?"

He set his food aside but kept his gaze steady on the table. "You remember Donna Mae?"

"Yes. Is she okay?" She hadn't spoken to Donna Mae in quite a while. She'd have to stop in the florist and say hello. Maybe she'd like to join them for the Festival.

"She's good." Harley's cheeks flamed red as he finally glanced up at her before returning to staring at the table. "I was hoping she'd have dinner with me one night out here."

Tears pricked the corners of Gia's eyes.

"I thought maybe you had another chair and you'd leave extra for her one night." He lifted his gaze and looked her straight in the eye. "I wouldn't want it for free or anything. I could maybe do some odd jobs for you in exchange for leaving extra."

Gia composed herself quickly so he wouldn't think she didn't want to do it. While she'd have gladly done it for free, she didn't want to insult him by refusing his offer. Besides, sharing dinner with Donna Mae might be his first step toward rejoining society. "I'll tell you what. If you want, you and Donna Mae can come to dinner out here and order whatever you'd like. I'll serve it fresh for the two of you."

Which she would have done for Harley every night, if he didn't always refuse the offer. A nice table cloth, a few good dining room chairs with cushions instead of the folding chair he was currently sitting on. Maybe a centerpiece, though candles might be pushing it too far, would make for a lovely date. Even the view of the wooded area surrounding the parking lot was beautiful, especially at sunset.

"Then, if they let the Festival go ahead, maybe you could help me build some platforms for my house."

"I would like that." Pride shone in his crystal blue eyes. "I'm good with my hands, and it's been a long time since I was able to build anything."

"Good, then it's settled. You just pick a night."

He frowned. "Heard they might not have the Festival, though."

"Don't worry about that. If they don't, we'll find something else for you to do."

He nodded and pulled his food back in front of him, then dug in with gusto.

"Where did you hear they might not have it?" Though Harley didn't usually interact much with Boggy Creek's residents, he had a knack for knowing what was going on.

"Mike out at the fairgrounds told me."

"The groundskeeper?" The same person of interest the police were currently searching for?

"Yup." Harley chewed and swallowed, then wiped his mouth with one of the napkins she'd brought back out with her. "Sometimes the park is crowded, so Mike lets me sleep out there."

"Mike Smith?"

"Uh huh. I don't bother no one, so he doesn't mind."

"Of course you don't. That's nice of Mike. He must be a nice guy."

He finished chewing and swallowed. "Nicer than that other one."

Questions ricocheted through her mind at warp speed. But getting information out of Harley could be akin to pulling teeth. "What other one?"

He sipped his new tea and took another bite. She was beginning to think he wouldn't answer. Then he swallowed and took another long drink. "I have to hide from him."

"Hide from whom?"

"The guard. Or he throws me out."

"Who does? Jeb? The security guard?"

Harley nodded. "He doesn't like anyone around to see what's going on."

"What's going on?"

Harley ate half his roll.

Okay, he was apparently not going to answer that. Either he didn't know, or he was just done talking. Maybe if she changed the subject. "When was the last time you saw Mike?"

"Late last night."

Wait a minute. It was all over the news that the police were searching for Mike as a person of interest in Barbara's death, that he hadn't been seen since the murder. Was that why Harley had come to keep an eye on her? Did he know Mike had something to do with Barbara's murder? "Harley, it's really important that you remember. Are you sure it was last night? After Barbara was found?"

She already knew the truth, though. Harley might not be a chatterbox, but when he did speak, he knew what he was talking about. Hmm…seemed some people could take a lesson from Harley.

He frowned, his face a picture of concentration. "Yup."

"After Barbara was killed or before?"

"After. He was walking around by the hole. Had to move the police tape to go by."

Despite Gia's prodding, changing tactics, and pleading, Harley remained tight-lipped after that, standing to go as soon as he finished eating and thanked her. At least she'd gotten a promise from him that he'd talk to Hunt or Leo if they came to question him, as long as they didn't try to bring him in to the station.

But what on earth could he have meant about Jeb? What would be going on out there that Jeb wouldn't want anyone to see? And did it have anything to do with Mike's disappearance or Barbara's death?

Chapter Ten

Thor poked his head between the seats, furiously wagging his whole back end, the instant Savannah opened the passenger door.

"Hey, there, big fella." She scratched behind his ears in just the right spot to have his eyes rolling back in his head. "You're such a good boy. Are you ready for a brother or sister?"

"Savannah…"

"Oh, quit it." She stuffed her overnight bag on the floor in the back, hopped in, and closed the door. "It's not like he knows what a brother or sister is, since he doesn't have one—the poor only child. Hint…hint…"

"Hey…" Gia shot her a dirty look. "I'm an only child, remember?"

Savannah fluttered her lashes. "Then it seems you, of all people, should understand wanting to have a sibling."

Darn. Point made. When Gia's mother passed away, she had been left with a father who had no interest in her. Growing up with family had been a long-time fantasy.

Her cell phone rang, saving her from continuing the discussion, though she knew Savannah well enough to know it was only a temporary reprieve.

"Sit, boy." She connected the phone to Bluetooth.

Thor plopped on the back seat and rested his head on Gia's shoulder.

"Hey, Hunt." While she backed out, she petted Thor's cheek.

Thor nuzzled closer. She'd missed him. Would getting another puppy make it harder for her to have cuddle time with him? Or would it only add to the joy? Two puppies to snuggle instead of only one. The image brought a smile.

Savannah nudged her with an elbow to the ribs.

"Gia? Are you there?" The tension in Hunt's voice dragged her back to reality.

"She's here, Hunt. Just daydreaming." Savannah gestured toward the speaker.

Hunt must have called to her more than once while her mind had been wandering.

"Sorry, Hunt, I'm here." She backed into the street, then shifted into drive and headed toward the shelter.

"I got your message, but it was cutting in and out, and I couldn't tell what you were trying to say. Something about Harley. Is he all right?"

"Yes, he's fine. Actually, he asked me to cook for him and Donna Mae one night, kind of like a date."

Savannah squealed from the passenger seat. "That's awesome! Good for them."

"Well, he still has to get up the nerve to ask, and then she has to say yes." She hoped for both of their sakes they would work it out.

"She'll say yes," Savannah said with full confidence.

"I hope you're right. I'd be so sad for him if he finally came out of his shell enough to ask, and she turned him down."

Hunt cleared his throat. "Is that what you called for, Gia? I'm a little pressed for time here."

"Oh, sorry." Heat flared in her cheeks. Harley's love life, or lack thereof, probably wasn't at the top of his priority list while he was smack in the middle of a murder investigation. "No, I wanted to tell you when I was talking to Harley, he mentioned seeing Mike Smith, who Trevor said you're looking for as a person of interest, out at the fairgrounds after Barbara was killed."

Dead silence screamed at her over the line.

His number still appeared on her dashboard screen, the seconds ticking slowly by as the silence grew heavier. "Hunt? Did I lose you?"

"I'm still here." He sighed, long and loud. "I thought you were staying out of this?"

"I am staying out of it." Sort of, anyway.

"Hard to tell."

She opened her mouth to argue.

Savannah laid a hand on her wrist. "She is staying out of it, Hunt. As a matter of fact, we're on our way to the shelter right now to look at puppies. Does that sound like something she'd be doing if she were investigating a murder?"

"Gee, Savannah, I don't know. She's on her way to the shelter the woman in charge of the Festival just so happens to run. The very shelter that receives all the proceeds from the Festival. The same shelter I visited this morning to ask questions connected to *my* murder investigation."

"Will ya look at that?" Savannah forced a laugh. "Some coincidence, huh?"

"Gia…I'm not kidding. Stay out of this. And don't drag my cousin into any of your shenanigans."

"Hey," Savannah sat up straighter. "I resent that. I can take care of myself, you know, and any shenanigans I get into are of my own free will. No one is dragging me anywhere."

"All right, both of you knock it off." If Gia didn't interrupt, they'd end up in a full-blown argument.

"He started it." Savannah stuck her tongue out at the phone display. "It's not my fault he's acting like a horse's—"

"Enough! I don't care who started it. If you don't both stop, I'm not telling you what else I learned." That would definitely make Savannah stop. Hunt remained questionable.

"What you learned while not investigating?" Though it was hard to tell through the speaker, she was pretty sure she detected a note of sarcasm.

For the sake of not acting as childish as the two of them, she chose to ignore it. "Harley also told me Mike lets him sleep out at the fairgrounds sometimes, but Jeb doesn't like it, and he chases him away if he finds him out there, because he doesn't want him to see what's going on."

Any hint of sarcasm or playfulness fled from Hunt's tone. "Did he say what's going on?"

"No, he clammed up, and I couldn't get him to tell me anything more."

"All right." He didn't say anything else, the monotonous hum of the tires against the smooth pavement the only sound, other than Thor's panting.

"Hunt?"

"Sorry, I'm here." He sighed again. "Looks like I'll have to go have a talk with Harley. Do you know where he was going?"

"He didn't say, but…" Gia didn't want to anger Hunt, but she'd seen him question people, and he wasn't always the picture of gentility.

"But what?"

She resigned herself to whatever anger she provoked, not only from Hunt, but from Savannah as well, who'd jump to her cousin's defense in an instant, despite bickering with him only moments before. Gia still had to try. She owed Harley that much. "You won't bring him down to the station, right?"

"Of course not, Gia." His voice softened. "I know he's fragile, and I'll treat him with care. I'm glad he's finally looking to spend time with someone."

"Me too. And I don't want to do anything to ruin that." She'd never forgive herself if she interfered with his chances of any kind of friendship with someone. "And also...well...Harley doesn't trust easily, and it means the world to me that he feels comfortable confiding in me. I don't want to betray that trust."

If Harley hadn't agreed to talk to Hunt, she never would have betrayed his confidence. But he agreed because he trusted her, and she valued and fully intended to be worthy of that trust.

"I understand. Don't worry about it."

"Thanks, Hunt."

"Yeah, well, if you want to thank me, just stay out of trouble."

Gia laughed, confident Hunt would take care with Harley. He could be sensitive when he wanted to be. "How can we get into trouble looking at puppies?"

He disconnected without answering, but she was almost positive she heard his eyes roll.

Giant pines towered over the road as she headed toward the shelter. She loved this stretch of highway, lined on both sides by natural Florida wilderness, undisturbed by humanity encroaching. She could almost envision dinosaurs roaming the prehistoric landscape.

Occasional spaces between the trees allowed for sporadic views of a large lake not too far in the distance. Though she'd never have the courage to hike into the dense underbrush herself, Hunt or Trevor might be talked into accompanying her. She squirmed at the realization the alligators that made the lake their home looked suspiciously like the ancestors she'd just been imagining. Granted on a smaller scale, but still...

The memory of ticks crawling over her legs brought an abrupt end to her fantasy. She brushed at her legs, trying to dispel the phantom tingle of tiny legs skittering up her calves.

"What are you doing?" Savannah frowned.

"Nothing, just an itch." No need to listen to a lecture from Savannah, who grew up with all sorts of creepy-crawlies.

She tilted her head and studied Gia for a moment, contemplating something. "So are you going to tell me?"

How could she have possibly known Gia was thinking about creepy-crawly things? "Tell you what?"

"What other interesting tidbits your non-investigation into Barbara's murder might have yielded?" She smirked.

Oh that. "Now that you mention it. I was thinking…"

Savannah opened her eyes wide. "Well, now, there's a surprise."

Gia laughed. Even if Savannah hadn't known what was in her head with the whole tick thing, she always knew the important stuff. "Don't you find it odd both the bloody shovel—"

Savannah held up a finger. "And Barbara's cell phone…"

"Both went missing with Mike Smith?"

"It does look a bit suspicious, if you ask me, which you did." She took out her phone and typed something in, then started scrolling. It didn't take her long to come to the same conclusion Gia had reached when she'd searched earlier. "Do you have any idea how many Mike Smiths there are?"

"Around eight hundred million if my Google search was at all accurate." She'd given it her best shot when she'd gotten a minute to sit earlier, just on the off-chance Mike Smith had collar length brown hair and a scorpion tattoo. Just out of curiosity, not because she was investigating or didn't trust Hunt and Leo to figure it out.

"I should have known." Savannah dropped her phone back into her purse. "I guess that's a dead end."

"At least searching for him that way is, but if we can figure out who knows him, we might be able to search through social media and find him on a 'friends' list somewhere."

"That could work." Savannah scratched Thor's head absently when he poked it between the seats.

Gia gave his side a quick pet. How was she ever going to train him to sit back where it was safer, if she always gave in and petted him when he sat up. She lowered her hand. "Sit back now, Thor, in case I have to stop short."

"Sorry." Savannah dropped her hand into her lap. "Habit."

"I know, for me too." Maybe he wouldn't be as lonely sitting in back if he had a friend back there with him. A friend. Hmm.

"A woman came in this afternoon and mentioned her husband was friends with a guy named Mike who works at the fairgrounds. I don't know who she was, but she did pay by debit card." No matter how hard she racked her brain, though, she couldn't come up with the name that had been on the card. Come to think of it, she probably hadn't even seen it, since the woman hadn't ever handed it to her, had simply inserted it into the pin pad herself. "Hunt spoke to her for a second when they passed in the doorway, but I don't know if he knew her or was just being polite."

"It probably doesn't matter, anyway. Mike is a common enough name. Who knows? There could be ten of them working on the grounds."

"Do you actually believe that?"

Savannah shrugged. "It's possible."

Mmm…hmm. A lot of things were possible; that didn't mean they were going to happen. "What were you saying before?"

Savannah unwound the band holding her hair back and tied it on her wrist, then threaded her fingers into her long blond hair and shook it out. "You're going to have to be a little more specific."

"Oh, sorry." It was easy to forget Savannah's thoughts didn't always wander in the same direction as Gia's. "What you were saying about Debby thinking it might have been a personal vendetta."

"Yeah, but that's all she said. I couldn't get her to elaborate."

"What if the Bailey sisters are right, and she was collecting dirt on people? Is it such a leap to believe she may have been blackmailing them? If the rumors are accurate…"

Savannah chewed on her bottom lip, a sure sign she was mulling the information over.

Gia left her to it for a moment. She hit the turn signal, even though no one was around for miles. The towering trees and endless acres of brush and forest made it easy to lose yourself, forget the outside world even existed. She turned onto a narrow dirt road.

Savannah shifted to face her. "It does make sense. Maybe she stirred the wrong hornets' nest and got stung. But I still don't understand why. Why would she have been blackmailing her friends and neighbors?"

"What if she wasn't blackmailing her friends and neighbors?" What if she was blackmailing people she disliked? Question was; who did she dislike?

Savannah's eyes narrowed. "What do you mean?"

"I'm certain the picture that came up on Barbara's phone, along with the initials KC, was Genny's friend, Kayla."

"Who by all accounts can't stand Barbara."

"Exactly." Which would make sense if the woman was holding something over her head. "So why would Kayla be calling Barbara? And why would Barbara have a picture of Kayla on her phone?"

"I don't know." Savannah shook her head. "I can see what you mean, but it could have been a perfectly legitimate call that had something to do with the Festival. As for the picture; who knows? Maybe Barbara likes to have a picture of the caller so she knows who's calling, even at a quick glance. Maybe she took it from one of Kayla's social media profiles. Maybe it had something to do with the Festival."

"I guess." She had to concede that, since the two did work on the Festival together, and Genny and Barbara pretty much organized everything. There could be a perfectly reasonable explanation as to why Kayla would have called Barbara, though Gia was at a loss about the picture, and she wasn't buying Savannah's hypotheses. "But I sure would love to get my hands on her cell phone records, then maybe we could figure out who she was blackmailing and why."

Who would know that? Anyone? Someone must have said it, if the rumors were to be believed. But who would have talked about being blackmailed? The people she was blackmailing would certainly know, but they'd have kept their mouths shut, for sure. Would Barbara really confide in anyone about something like that? What would she say? Oh, by the way, I'm blackmailing people, which is illegal to begin with, never mind the moral implications. So that raises the question; who would know all of Barbara's deep, dark, dirty secrets?

"Alfie," Savannah said.

Gia glanced at her as she stopped in front of the shelter and shifted into park.

"Just like you and I were both wondering who would have known about the blackmail, besides the killer, that is, close friends often know each other's thoughts. They know each other too well to keep secrets hidden between them. Alfie would have known if something was going on with Barbara. It makes sense."

"It does if they were really as close as it seems." Now she just had to come up with a way to find that out.

Chapter Eleven

Only one other car sat in the small lot as Gia and Savannah climbed out of the car. Gia hooked Thor's leash to his collar and circled the lot with him in case he had to go. When he just stopped and looked up at her, she assumed he didn't and headed for the front door.

Kayla's raised voice brought her to an abrupt halt at the door.

"Is that who I think it is?" Savannah tried to see past the Halloween decorations adorning the window in the door.

"I think so." Gia leaned closer to the door but stopped just short of pressing her ear against it. A witch that appeared to have crashed into the front window blocked her view of the inside. That was okay, though, since it also blocked them from being seen by anyone inside.

"...ridiculous, if you ask me. They should at least let us up there to work on our houses. It's not like she was found dead in a house, for crying out loud."

"I'm sure they'll clear us to go in as soon as they feel they've collected all the evidence they need." Debby's voice sounded strained—not that Gia could blame her under the circumstances. Kayla not only sounded insistent but like she'd been battering Debby for some time.

"Yeah, well, it's not like we can put a house together overnight, you know." She waited a beat. "Oh right. You wouldn't know, would you, since you only haunt the woods. Not much set up involved in that, I suppose."

"Well, I'll be—" Savannah huffed.

"Shh..." Gia leaned closer to hear Debby's response.

"I'm sorry, there's nothing more I can do to hurry—"

"Yeah, yeah. Whatever. Come on, Genny, we can at least start working on costumes—"

The shelter door whipped open, and Gia almost tumbled inside. If not for Savannah's quick reflexes and firm grip on the back of Gia's shirt, she'd have face planted on the waiting room floor at Kayla's feet.

"What are you doing here?" Kayla demanded.

Thor barked.

"Shh…it's okay, boy." Gia petted his head while she composed herself. "I'm sorry. I…uh…we were just stopping in to see Debby."

"About adopting another puppy," Savannah threw in as she guided Gia through the door and past Kayla. She greeted Debby with a hug. "Hey there. How are you doing?"

Debby eyed Kayla from the corner of her eye. "I've been better."

"Aww…" Savannah rubbed a hand up and down Debby's arm. "You poor thing. Don't you worry about anything. I'm sure the Festival will go on as scheduled."

Kayla stepped between them, her face about two inches from Savannah's, and pounced. "How do you know that? Did you hear it from your fiancé or your cousin?"

"Umm…" Savannah took a step backward but lifted her chin in defiance. "No, I didn't hear it from anyone. I just have faith everything will work out."

"Kayla, please, let's go." Genny took her arm.

"In a minute." Kayla shook her off and continued to stare Savannah down. "What *have* you heard then?"

Savannah propped a hand on her hip and waved a finger in front of Kayla. "Now you listen here, honey, with whom I've spoken and what I've heard are none of your ever lovin' business, and furthermore…"

Enough was enough. Gia stepped in front of Savannah. Not that Savannah couldn't hold her own, but no way was Gia going to stand there while someone tried to intimidate her. "You need to back off, Kayla."

Thor growled, a deep rumble low in his throat. His hackles raised. He pressed his body against Gia's legs, positioning himself between her and Kayla.

"Easy, Thor." Gia put a hand on his head.

Thor was the biggest mush going, and no way would he ever attack or bite anyone, but he was a big dog and probably scary if you didn't know him. Still…Gia didn't want him upset by all the animosity.

Thankfully, Kayla backed down. "Look, I didn't mean anything by it. I was just asking. No offense."

Gia stepped aside and looked at Savannah.

She raised her hands to the sides. "None taken. As for the Festival, I understand you're upset. I am too, but getting yourself all in a tizzy isn't going to help anything."

"You're right, of course." Kayla shoved her hands into her hair and squeezed. "It's just a lot of stress not knowing what's going on."

If the deep lines bracketing her mouth, dark, puffy circles ringing her eyes, and iron grip she had on her own hair were any indication, Kayla was most definitely telling the truth about being stressed, but as important as Gia now realized the Festival was to Boggy Creek's residents and the animal shelter, she couldn't imagine that could be the cause of Kayla's obvious tension. There had to be more to it, something in her personal life, maybe.

"It's okay, Kayla." Genny tilted her head and contemplated her friend. "We're all scared. Savannah and Gia understand that, don't you, ladies?"

"Sure thing." Just like Savannah, always quick to forgive. "Everyone's a bit tense under the circumstances."

"See there, Kayla. You're not alone." Genny's eyes held an unmistakable plea. "Now, why don't we head over to my house and work on what we can? Preston's working late tonight, so we—"

Kayla scoffed and muttered under her breath, "Of course he is."

"So we can work in the garage and we won't be bothering him," Genny continued as if Kayla hadn't said anything.

Kayla's jaw clenched, but she refrained from any further comment, instead nodding her head in acknowledgement. "If you'll excuse us."

She and Genny started toward the door.

At that moment, the door swung inward, and Alfie strode through and almost plowed into the two women. "Oh, I'm sorry, Genny. Are you all right?"

She gripped his arms. "Yes, I'm fine. I should have looked where I was going. Forgive me."

"Nothing to forgive." He gave her a quick hug then stepped back. "How are you doing?"

"I've been better. How about you? How are you holding up?"

"I've started planning a memorial, so that's been helping. The police haven't released Barbara's b...haven't released her yet because they are still investigating, but they said I could go ahead and plan a memorial if I wanted. So, I'm doing that. That's actually why I'm here." He held up a small sign and turned to Debby. "Would you mind if I put this up, just to let everyone know about it?"

"Of course not. You go right ahead and put them up wherever you'd like."

He squeezed Genny's arm on his way past, then came face to face with Kayla. "Kayla."

"Alfie."

He side-stepped her and moved on to the window to tape up his sign. Genny and Kayla said their good-byes and made a hasty exit, Kayla pausing just long enough to toss a dirty look over her shoulder at Alfie before following Genny out.

Debby grabbed a handful of tissues and hurried to Alfie's side. "I'm so sorry about Barbara, Alfie. I know how close you two were."

He kept his back to them and nodded.

Gia had no doubt he was crying. "It's nice of you to organize a memorial in her honor."

"Thank you." He sucked in a deep, shuddering breath and turned, then wiped the tears streaming down his face.

"I'd love to come, if that's all right?" Though she'd never met Barbara, she still wanted to pay her respects. With all the tension flying around, she hadn't had a chance to apologize to Genny for her behavior earlier. Maybe she'd get a chance there.

"I'm sorry. I'm such a mess." He let out a shaky laugh and extended a hand. "I'm Alfie Todd."

"Gia Morelli." She shook his hand.

"Hey, I recognize you." He turned toward Savannah. "And you. You were both at the fairgrounds when they found..."

"Yes," Gia answered before he had to finish the thought. "I'm so sorry for your loss."

He lowered his gaze to the floor. "Thank you. That's very kind."

"Please, everyone, sit." Debby gestured toward the seating arrangement in the waiting room. "Wherever are my manners? I'm sorry. That woman rattles me to no end."

Alfie waved her off and went to sit. "Oh, believe you me, I understand completely."

The others followed him and took seats around the coffee table.

"Can I get anyone coffee? Water? Anything?" Debby held a treat out to Thor. "Sit, boy."

He plopped right down and waited patiently, his tail wagging against the floor.

Debby gave him the treat and petted his head. "You're a good boy."

"Nothing for me, thank you." Alfie perched on the edge of his seat with a hand pressed against his stomach. "The thought of eating or drinking anything makes my stomach turn over."

Gia and Savannah declined as well.

"Not to sound as insensitive as Kayla, and I completely understand if you can't discuss it..." Debby glanced back and forth between Gia and Savannah, wringing her hands around and around in her lap. "But have either of you heard anything about whether or not the Festival will go forward?"

"Debby, you could never sound like Kayla." Savannah reached over to her and gripped her hand. "I'm sorry, but I haven't heard. If I do, though, I promise I'll let you know."

"Would you let me know as well? Not that I plan to participate now that Barbara's gone, but I would like the chance to set a small memorial in front of her house, maybe a picture of her from last year's Festival, doing what she loved," Alfie's voice hitched. "So much."

"Of course I will, Alfie," Savannah assured him.

"Why don't you plan to participate, Alfie?" Debby jumped up and busied herself making a fresh pot of coffee, despite the fact they all declined her offer. Who knew? Maybe she wanted some for herself, or maybe she wanted to be prepared in case anyone else dropped by, or maybe she just needed something to do. "I'm sure Barbara would want you to go ahead."

"I know she would. The Festival was so important to her, as was the shelter." A tear tipped over his thick lashes and rolled down his cheek. "I can't work on that house without her. I just...I can't. And Kayla has already made it perfectly clear I'm not welcome to join them."

"Why don't you join us?" Gia ignored Savannah's warning glare. "I'm doing the Festival for the first time this year, and we'd love to have you, if you'd like."

Savannah squinted, her *Hunt's-gonna-kill-you* look firmly in place.

Gia rolled her eyes, continuing the silent conversation. *Yeah, I know.* Not that she could blame him. At this point, everyone was a suspect. She understood that on some level, but she just couldn't imagine this broken man had not only killed his best friend, but then buried her as well.

Whatever. Savannah shrugged. *It's your funeral.*

"You don't have to decide right now," Gia told him. "I own the All-Day Breakfast Café in town. You are welcome to stop in anytime."

"Thank you. That is so sweet of you. I just may take you up on that offer, but right now, all I can think about is finding out what happened to Barbara. I hope you understand."

"Of course I do." She'd feel the same way in his position. "If there's anything I can do..."

"Thank you." He nodded in Gia's direction and stood, then leaned over and gave Thor a quick pet on the head. "Anyway, thank you for letting me put up the sign, Debby. I hope to see y'all tomorrow night."

"I'll be there." Debby saw him out. After watching him get into his car, she closed the door, turned, and slumped back against it.

Gia stood. "Are you okay, Debby?"

She nodded and used her sleeve to wipe the tears from her face. "Yes, I am. I'm sorry."

"No problem." Savannah looked at Gia and shook her head.

Gia nodded. Today was not the day to look at puppies. They'd have to come back another time. Probably for the best, anyway. Knowing Savannah's single-minded determination when she set her mind to something, Gia probably would have gone home with another dog that evening, and that was a commitment she wasn't fully prepared to make, at least not until after the Festival. "You and Barbara must have been good friends."

She looked over her shoulder in the direction Alfie had gone, though she couldn't see out the window, then straightened. "It's not me I'm concerned about, though Barbara and I knew each other for a long time, and I always appreciated everything she did for the shelter. It's Alfie that has me concerned. He's such a gentle soul, and the guilt seems to be eating him alive."

"Guilt?" Had Alfie had some involvement in Barbara's death, after all? "Because he was the one who dropped her off at the fairgrounds the night she was killed?"

"Among other things." Debby sighed and picked up a magazine someone had left open on the coffee table. She closed it but made no move to return it to the rack. "I was out at the fairgrounds the other night. A day or two before Barbara was found. When I arrived, no one else was around, but when I walked past Barbara's house, the two of them were arguing something awful."

"Alfie and Barbara?"

She nodded and sniffed, staring down at the closed magazine in her hands.

"About what? Do you know?"

She shook her head. "Only that it had something to do with Jeb."

"The security guard?" That was the second time his name had come up. First from Harley and now Debby. What in the world was he doing out there?

"Alfie was pleading with Barbara to let the whole thing with Jeb go. She laughed at him, and he got angry, yelled at her that one of these days she was going to get herself killed, and stormed out." Debby rolled the magazine, then unrolled it and started the process all over again.

"Did he see you there?"

"Yeah." She finally stuffed the magazine into an empty space on the rack and cleared two coffee cups from the table. "I just offered him a sympathetic look, and he smiled. But not a genuine smile, you know what I mean? That was a smile filled with pain and sadness. And now she's gone. And he has to live with those harsh words. For a man as sensitive as him…"

"It won't be easy."

"No, it won't. I'm sorry. I just need to finish cleaning up here and get home. Tonight's a night I need to be surrounded by family. I hope you'll understand." She turned and started washing out the cups.

"Of course, Debby. We'll come back another day." Gia hesitated. Though Debby had known Barbara, it didn't seem they'd been very close friends. But still… "Can I ask you something?"

"Sure." She finished washing the cups, dried them, and returned them to their place in the cabinet above the coffee pot, then dumped the potful of coffee she'd just made without drinking any.

"There are rumors flying around about Barbara." She waited, hoping Debby would offer answers without Gia having to ask outright if the rumors were true.

Debby wiped down the counter, her back to Gia.

Savannah shook her head and gestured toward the door. She was probably right; it wasn't the appropriate time for this discussion.

"Barbara worked the Festival every year, despite the fact she never once came into the shelter. Nor did she own any pets. Some of the volunteers used to talk among themselves, though if I overheard them, I did put a stop to it." She grabbed a broom and started to sweep the floor. "They said she volunteered not because she wanted to help the animals, but because she needed to be in the middle of everything. Make her presence known in the community. Let the people she had dirt on squirm while she stood among their families, friends, co-workers, making sure they knew that, at any moment, she could spill the beans and bring their whole worlds crashing down."

"Do you think that's true?" Gia had heard it too many times not to believe there was some truth to the rumors.

She shrugged. "Who knows? Maybe. But I didn't care. She put a lot of time and effort into something good, something that helped these animals. I didn't care why she did it."

"And now? Looking back. What do you think now?"

She stopped sweeping and leaned on the broom, then sucked in a shaky breath and stared Gia straight in the eye. "I think she was seeking atonement."

Chapter Twelve

A quick glance at the dashboard clock told her they'd better get a move on if they were going to get to Xavier's before they closed. "Do you still want barbeque?"

Thor barked from the back seat.

"Not you, silly."

He whined.

"Oh all right, maybe a little." She was going to have to stop giving in to him all the time, or he was going to get spoiled.

His tongue dropped out in the Thor version of a smile, and her heart melted. So what if he was a little spoiled. What was the point of working so hard if she couldn't spoil the people—and animal—she loved?

"Do you have anything in the house to eat?" Savannah had been unusually quiet since they'd left the shelter.

"Not really." Because she owned a café and rarely ate at home, she didn't bother stocking up. "A few boxes of cereal, but I'm pretty sure the milk is past its prime."

She looked out the window. "You'd probably better stop then, just in case Hunt and Leo show up."

"True." By the time either of them took a break, they'd be starving. Dry cereal probably wasn't going to cut it. She headed out of the lot toward Xavier's. "You okay? You seem quiet."

"Just thinking about Alfie." She kept the back of her head to Gia. "I feel his pain. There have been times when I was harsh with you, said things I wished later I could take back. I can't imagine not having had the chance to say I'm sorry."

"Savannah, look at me."

She tore her gaze from the view of the forest. Tears shimmered in her eyes.

"First of all, you've never said anything to me that I didn't need to hear. You're a good enough friend to tell me the truth, even when others might not, and even when it would be easier on you to either lie or not say anything at all." Truth be told, if not for Savannah, she'd probably be sitting in some tiny apartment in New York, keeping a low profile, scraping to make ends meet, and dodging a long line of her ex's investors.

She nodded and lowered her gaze to her hands folded in her lap. "You forgive me?"

"There's nothing to forgive, Savannah." She reached out to her, gripped her hand. "Quite the contrary, you've made everything I've accomplished possible."

"You know I'd never purposely hurt you?"

"Of course I do." Savannah didn't have it in her to hurt a fly. The woman ushered spiders out of the house with patience and a kind word rather than stepping on them or hitting them with a fly swatter attached to a really long pole. "You are my best friend. I've never had a brother or sister, but I'm pretty sure if I did, I couldn't possibly love them any more than I love you."

"I love you too, which is why I might sometimes be a little too honest." A tear rolled down her cheek, and she laughed. "See? That's why it's important to have siblings. So you learn these things. Right, Thor?"

Thor barked twice.

"Ha!" Savannah smiled through her tears. "I told you so. He said, 'That's right.'"

Gia just shook her head and ignored them both. This was obviously an argument she wasn't going to win. "Speaking of honest, it sounds to me like that's all Alfie was doing, giving Barbara a hard truth that she needed to hear. As it turned out, he was right."

"Friends usually are."

Gia pulled her gaze from the road for an instant to raise a brow at her.

"What? Just sayin'." She grinned but sobered quickly. "There's another explanation you're conveniently leaving out."

"Oh, what's that?"

"Alfie knew she would end up getting killed because he knew or suspected he was going to kill her."

"I can't believe that." But Savannah could be right. Even if Gia did hope to ignore the possibility, it didn't change that fact. She hit her turn signal and pulled into the crowded parking lot. "Xavier's sure is hopping for a place that's supposed to close in an hour. And on a weeknight, no less."

"What do you expect? A murderer is on the loose, and most places are closed already. People have to gather somewhere for information as well as the feeling of security that a tight community brings." Savannah climbed out and shut the door.

The downside of living in such a rural area, not much was open past nine o'clock at night, and they would now have to wait in a fairly long line. The upside? The people who came out to support each other no matter what happened. "I'll be right back, Thor."

Leaving the windows cracked open for Thor, she followed Savannah to the back of the line. A rare breeze rustled the trees surrounding the lot as dark clouds built overhead.

"Looks like we're going to get storms," the woman in line in front of them told her companion as she moved forward a step.

He looked up at the roiling sky. "Looks like."

Somehow Gia hadn't expected the weather to top the list of topics the people in line would be gossiping about. She leaned close enough to Savannah that she wouldn't be overheard. "You don't think they'll be bad, do you?"

"The storms?" Savannah shook her head. "I haven't heard they're supposed to be."

The low rumble of thunder still struck fear in her after the tornadoes that had ripped through Boggy Creek last winter. It would definitely take time to get used to such extreme weather. If she ever did. She shivered and shifted her focus to what snippets of conversation she could make out.

A man with a deep, contagious belly laugh was apparently enjoying his meal at a picnic table with a couple of friends. A woman broke up chicken pieces on a foam tray for a little boy. The line inched forward.

"Well, if you ask me, they should be looking a little harder for that guy that disappeared instead of harassing good, upstanding, law-abiding citizens."

Gia froze. There was no mistaking that voice.

"Don't look now," Savannah muttered under her breath.

About five customers ahead of them on line stood Kayla with a small circle of listeners gathered around her. "I mean, why waste time questioning people who obviously don't know what happened, when they could be out looking for the real killer? Just goes to show you how inept our police department is."

A few of those gathered, nodded and murmured their agreement.

Just as surely as Thor's had earlier, Savannah's hackles rose. After all, the people Kayla was calling inept were Savannah's closest cousin and her fiancé.

Though Gia ached to defend them too, confronting Kayla would only draw more attention. She leaned close to Savannah and whispered, "Let it go."

"I will not." She started to step forward.

Gia grabbed her arm. "You won't be helping them. You'll only give her more of an audience if you engage."

Savannah swallowed hard, her gaze narrowing on Kayla…then she nodded.

Gia closed her eyes for a second and blew out the breath she'd been holding.

Kayla continued her rant. "I just hope they'll let the Festival go on. No sense in those poor animals losing out on their funding just because Barbara Woodhull managed to anger the wrong person."

A couple of her listeners shifted and turned away. Seemed not everyone was comfortable publicly bashing a dead woman, no matter what their private opinions might be. Besides, there was absolutely no evidence to back up Kayla's claims, only supposition loosely based on gossip.

The line moved forward, and Kayla lost another supporter.

It didn't even slow her down. If anything, the volume of her voice increased in an effort to gain more attention. "You should all write letters to the mayor, get your friends to write them as well, demand the Festival move forward as planned."

"And if there's a killer out there? What then? Hope he doesn't strike again?" a man yelled. "I don't know about y'all, but my wife and kids will be staying home until they catch this guy."

Nods and murmurs of assent rippled through the crowd.

The counter workers seemed to be moving faster, and the line crept forward again. Maybe they just wanted to get to Kayla and get her out of there before she could stir up too much trouble.

Without another word, Kayla stepped up to the counter and placed her order.

Those who'd been listening to her speech talked quietly amongst themselves, too quietly for Gia to overhear.

Kayla took her tray and turned back to the crowd. "Think about what I said. The shelter needs the Festival to go on, regardless of what else is happening."

Savannah shifted but remained quiet, and they moved through the line and placed their order without incident.

If Gia could get out of there without a confrontation with Kayla, she'd be grateful. She held her breath while they waited for their food. Had she done the right thing? Would it have been better to stand up to her, to defend Hunt and the police department?

"Don't sweat it. You were right." Savannah smiled. "I can see that now that the haze of rage has dissipated. As it was, only a handful of people even paid attention to her, and a number of them disagreed. If I'd have made a big deal of it, more would have taken notice. Thank you."

"Sure thing." Gia paid and took the bags from the girl behind the counter, thanked her, and headed back toward the car. "I was thinking about something."

"Uh oh."

"Don't be a smart aleck."

Savannah laughed. "Sorry, honey, but those words have preceded more than one fiasco that got me into trouble with Hunt."

"While that is technically true, you don't have to keep bringing it up. Besides, this thought won't get you into any trouble." Probably.

"Are you sure?"

Okay, chances were roughly fifty-fifty. Or maybe not quite that good. "Does it matter?"

Savannah laughed. "Not really. I just feel the need to put up a token argument so I can weasel my way out of trouble with Hunt if we get caught. But now I do wish you hadn't stopped me when I went to defend Hunt and Leo."

"Oh, why's that?" Gia hit the button to unlock the car.

Savannah shot her a grin over the roof. "Because then when Hunt starts to ream me over whatever plan you've hatched, I could have led with how I stuck up for him in the middle of a lynch mob."

Hmm...Actually, that was a pretty solid plan. "Maybe it's not too late to go back. Kayla's still sitting at the picnic table over there."

Savannah winked at her and slid into the passenger seat.

With one last, longing gaze at Kayla, Gia gave up and got behind the wheel.

Savannah clicked her seatbelt closed. "Better to get a move on, since I figure whatever you have in mind hinges on the fact that Kayla is here."

"You'd win that bet." Gia set the bags on the center console and petted Thor's head. "Don't eat the food, okay, Thor?"

Savannah rummaged through one of the bags and pulled out a couple of fries. She handed one to Gia.

"Thanks."

"Mm...hm.... So, are you going to share?" She blew on her fry and took a bite.

"Share what?"

"Save the innocent routine for Hunt. It doesn't work on me."

"News flash...it doesn't work on him either." Gia popped her fry into her mouth as she headed out of the parking lot and back down the deserted road. Darkness enveloped them as soon as they left the pool of light surrounding Xavier's. "Anyway, every time I run into Genny, Kayla is with her. I just figured it would be nice to have a conversation with her alone. First of all, to apologize, and second, just to see where her head is at. Kayla is so overbearing; I can't get a feel for Genny at all."

"I know what you mean." Savannah pulled out her phone and started to scroll through her email. She frowned. "Don't you find it strange, though?"

"Find what strange?"

"That Kayla is running all over Boggy Creek carrying on to anyone who will listen about the investigation, Barbara, Preston Hart...I don't know...It just seems inconsiderate, especially since it's obviously upsetting Genny."

Inconsiderate was too kind a word for how Kayla was behaving. Though to be fair, everyone grieved differently. Maybe she was more broken up over Barbara's death than she was willing to admit, even to herself. "You up for a quick side trip then?"

"Sure thing." She closed her email and opened her GPS. "I'll look up Genny's address, but only if you agree that if her husband's home, we won't go to the door. Deal?"

Talking to her with her husband present might not be any better than talking to her with Kayla hovering nearby. If she really wanted to gauge Genny's reactions, she'd have to catch her alone. Genny had said he'd be working late when they'd run into her at the shelter earlier. That didn't mean he was still out but at least there was a chance. "Deal."

"And also, I'm finishing off these fries while you drive." She pulled out another fry. The aroma of seasoning and oil filled the car.

Gia's mouth watered. "Okay, but only if you share."

Savannah handed her another fry, and they ate as Gia followed her directions back into town.

"Up there. On the right." Savannah pointed down a road lined with palm trees. "The third one, with the white picket fence."

Gia crept past the bungalow style home, its front porch elaborately decorated for fall with hay bales, pumpkins, even a giant scarecrow. "Boy, she does get really into the whole decorating thing, huh?"

"Seems like." Savannah studied the house while Gia drove. "There's only one car in the driveway, that white Toyota, but there's no guarantee it's hers."

"It's not the same car that was in the lot at the shelter. That one was black." Of course that one could have been Kayla's, since they hadn't seen who was driving. Gia swung around the block and made a U-turn, then crept back toward Genny's and pulled to the curb in front of the next-door neighbor's house. "What do you want to do?"

Light from the front windows spilled out onto the lawn, casting deep shadows around the porch.

Gia switched off her headlights and cracked the windows open.

Savannah looked over her shoulder down the deserted road and sidewalk, then back at Genny's house. "I don't know. The lights are on, but it is pretty late to just pop in on someone."

"We could call." Though they'd lose the element of surprise if they did.

"For what? You'd have to come up with a reasonable excuse."

Plus, she'd prefer to talk to her face to face. It would be much easier to gauge if she was telling the truth if she could see her facial expressions. Really, though, what reason would she have to lie about anything? Savannah was probably right. Most of the other houses on the block had few, if any, lights shining, aside from their outside lights. It was probably too late to just show up unannounced. Still, she didn't want to wait for tomorrow when Kayla would surely be lurking nearby. She just had to come up with a plausible excuse to call. "We could ask her about changing the theme for our house."

"Why would we change it?"

Uh oh. With everything going on, she'd forgotten to mention the change of theme to Savannah. "Willow and Trevor were looking at makeup ideas earlier, and they found stuff they loved, and the models were wearing hospital gowns, so we started thinking of a haunted hospital theme. We could still use the same idea, the beds lining the ward, and Willow even thought we could put some of them on hinges so people could pop up out of them and scare our guests."

Savannah tapped a nail against her lips.

Gia bit the inside of her cheek to keep from rambling any more. Once she started, she might never be able to stop. If Savannah was insulted, all the rambling in the world wasn't going to change her mind. "If you hate it, we could still do the dormitory. I loved that idea, and it doesn't really matter to me."

"Are you kidding me? I love it. What's creepier than a haunted hospital? I'm just trying to decide if we can get away with bothering Genny about it this late." She held out her phone to Gia. "Can't hurt to give it a shot. The phone number is right there."

Gia took the phone and hit send.

Someone pulled the curtains back from Genny's front window and peered out between them.

Shadows across the window wouldn't allow for a view of whomever stood there.

"Hello?" Genny answered on the second ring.

The curtains fell back across the window.

"Hi, Genny, it's Gia Morelli. I'm sorry to bother you so late, but I was wondering if it would be okay if I changed my house theme?"

"Oh, uh, of course, dear." Genny sounded breathless, winded, as if she'd been running around. "You are welcome to do whatever you'd like as long as no one else is doing it and it's in good taste."

She explained her idea for the haunted hospital.

"I love it! It's even better than the dormitory. You go right ahead."

"Thank you, Genny. I also—"

"I'm sorry. I don't mean to cut you short, but I have to go. I'm exhausted, and I was just going to bed. We can catch up tomorrow." She disconnected the call.

Hard to believe she'd gotten that out of breath getting ready for bed. Gia handed the phone back to Savannah. "So much for stopping by. She rushed off the phone. And I didn't even get to apologize."

"Now what?" Savannah turned the phone over and over in her hand, still studying the house.

"I guess, we go home and eat barbeque." Gia stepped on the brake and started to shift into drive.

"Gia, wait." Savannah slapped her hand off the shifter. "Get your foot off the brake."

She yanked her foot off without hesitating.

Someone cracked Genny's front door open and peeked out. A moment later, Genny stepped out onto the front porch. So much for heading to bed.

Gia and Savannah slid low in their seats.

After scanning the empty street, Genny waved inside, and a man crept out onto the porch. A dark hooded windbreaker blocked any view of his face.

"You get out of here right now, Jeb Hansen. And don't you come back." Genny turned and started back into the house.

Jeb shot an arm across the doorway to block her way. "Oh you can bet I'll be back, as many times as it takes for you to give it up. This isn't over, Genny, not by a long shot."

Chapter Thirteen

"That's the security guard from the fairgrounds. What's he doing here?" Savannah opened the camera on her phone and magnified the image. She snapped a picture.

"Did you get his face in the picture?" The angle Gia was seeing him from didn't allow a clear view of his face.

"No, but I'll try again if he turns around." She held the camera ready.

"No. Wait. Stay quiet." She opened her window a bit more. "And don't take any more pictures. The flash is a dead giveaway."

Jeb strode down the front steps and hurried down the walkway toward Gia and Savannah.

They slid even lower in their seats.

Thor's ears perked, and he sat up straighter.

Oh, please, don't bark, Thor. Not now.

She twisted her arm behind her to scratch his belly.

Jeb climbed into a bright red raised pickup truck with a chrome roll-bar parked across the street from them. He turned on the ignition and opened his window, hooking his elbow over the door frame and holding a phone against his ear. "Yeah, I'm on my way… Says she doesn't have it."

He continued to talk as he pulled away from the curb, but once he hit the gas, his words were lost beneath the rumble of the truck's engine.

"Now what?" Savannah looked back and forth between Genny's now empty front porch and Jeb's truck moving farther away from them.

"Genny already blew me off, said she was going to bed, so we can't very well bother her." Gia checked her rearview mirror and swung the car around, then headed out of Genny's development in the same direction Jeb had. "But we can take a peek at what Jeb's up to."

"What do you think he meant by she doesn't have it?" Savannah enlarged the picture she'd taken. "What could he be looking for?"

Gia shrugged, torn between fear for Genny and curiosity about what her involvement with Jeb could possibly be. "I have no idea. Were you able to get his face at all in the picture?"

"Nothing more than a shadowy profile. At best, it could be any male." She closed the photo screen and opened a search engine. "He could have wanted something completely innocent, you know."

"Yes, it could be, but then why did they seem so..." Genny creeping out onto the porch to look around replayed in her mind. An image of Jeb with the hood pulled over his head on a night that hadn't dropped below seventy-five degrees followed. "Furtive?"

"Who knows? Maybe Genny's husband wouldn't want another man visiting his wife in the middle of the night."

"It's hardly the middle of the night, but I can see your point." Considering a good number of lights up and down the block were already off, it was easy to think it was later than it actually was. "And what about Genny telling him not to come back any more?"

"Lover's spat?" Savannah caught her lower lip between her teeth, searching for something on her phone. "Well, he's not going home."

"How can you tell?"

Savannah held out her phone. "Because Jeb Hansen lives in the other direction."

Gia kept an eye on Jeb's taillights in the distance as she followed him down the long, dark road that led out of town. It didn't take long to figure out he was headed toward the fairgrounds.

"Stay back, Gia." Savannah glanced over her shoulder. "There's no traffic at all on this road. One peek in his rearview mirror, and it won't be hard for him to figure out he's being followed."

Gia pulled to the side of the road, shifted into park, and turned off her headlights.

"What are you doing? You're going to lose him."

She doubted she would, since she thought she had a good idea where he was headed. The question was, why? "What do you want to bet he's headed for the fairgrounds?"

"No way I'd take that bet. There's nothing else out here."

"So we'll wait here for a few minutes, let him think whoever was behind him turned off, and then we'll take a ride past the fairgrounds and see if his truck is there. It's not like that truck will be hard to spot." Which begged the question, why had he bothered sneaking out of Genny's house when he left a bright red monstrosity with all kinds of chrome accents parked right out front?

Gia's cell phone rang.

She jumped, then laughed at herself and checked the caller ID. Unbelievable. The guy had a knack for knowing when she was doing something she probably shouldn't be. Hmm...maybe they should search the car for bugs. She answered on the Bluetooth. "Hey, Hunt."

"Hey, yourself. Are you and Savannah still together?"

Savannah rolled her eyes.

"We are. Is everything okay?"

"Yes, but Leo and I are going to call it quits for a little while in about an hour. Are you going to be up?"

"Sure thing. We're on our way home with Xavier's now." More or less, if you considered heading past the fairgrounds *on the way*, which, technically, it wasn't.

"All right. I'll see you in a few." He disconnected the call.

Savannah turned toward her. "Are you actually going home, or are you still planning to run past the fairgrounds?"

"We're going home." Gia sat for a minute, hands resting on the wheel. She leaned forward and looked up through the windshield. Dark clouds gathered overhead. The last thing she wanted was to get caught in a bad storm at night. Visibility was bad enough sometimes in daylight. "We'll just take the long way."

"By the long way, you mean drive out past the fairgrounds then make a U-turn somewhere up there and head back toward your house?" Savannah grinned.

"Exactly." She shifted into gear and pulled out onto the deserted road. "It sure is quiet up here at night."

Other than the buzz of cicadas and a chorus of croaking frogs, which Gia was proud of herself for recognizing, few other sounds encroached on the silence. A coyote howled in the distance.

As they approached the fairgrounds, Savannah leaned closer to the windshield. "I don't see his truck. Do you?"

Gia squinted to see into the darkened fairgrounds. The only lights shone down on the empty parking lot. "I don't."

Could she have been wrong? What else was up here he could have gone to? "Do you think he could have gone somewhere else?"

"There's really nothing else around." Savannah shook her head, still scanning the surrounding buildings. "I suppose he could have pulled the truck into one of the storage sheds and closed the door."

Gia stopped just short of driving into the parking lot. Not only was there no sign of Jeb, but the entire grounds were deserted. "Do you think I should pull into the lot?"

"I don't see why not. There doesn't seem to be anyone around, and if there is, we can always say we were just running by to see if they'd released the grounds for the Festival."

"Sounds reasonable." She tried to imagine what the fairgrounds would look like with lights, music, tons of people milling around. Less spooky? Maybe. Certainly, less deserted. The low cloud cover would make a perfect backdrop for the Haunted Town Festival. Too bad they couldn't control the weather. "Shouldn't there be a police car around here somewhere? Keeping an eye on the crime scene or something?"

Savannah frowned. "No idea. It seems there would be, but I don't know. Maybe there's one behind the buildings, back where Barbara's body was found."

Gia hit the lock button, just to be on the safe side, and swung a wide U-turn in the empty lot. She slowed to a crawl.

"Or maybe they're done out here." Savannah unbuckled her seatbelt and turned around to look out the back window.

Thor licked her cheek.

She laughed as she flopped back into the seat and reached for the door handle. "Do you think we should take a look around?"

"Not a chance." Gia increased the pressure on the gas pedal. "There's a fine line between being brave and being too stupid to live, and I have no intention of crossing that line. Again."

Savannah shot her a grin. "Afraid Hunt will find out?"

Though she couldn't deny that was a concern, this time it wasn't the most pressing. Nor were the abundance of critters sure to be roaming the forest. "More like afraid we might find something. Do you realize how many acres of wilderness surround this area? Anything could be going on out here, and no one would have a clue. We could probably disappear forever without a trace."

"That could be true." Savannah checked the door lock. "I'm beginning to think Barbara may have stumbled onto something somebody wanted to keep hidden."

Alfie had argued with her over something he was afraid would get her killed, Mike Smith was missing and, by all accounts, Jeb was doing something out here he didn't want anyone to know about. On top of that, general consensus seemed to be Barbara was looking for trouble by blackmailing more than one of Boggy Creek's citizens.

The hairs on the back of Gia's neck stood up, and a chill raced up her spine. With one last look around, she headed out of the lot and back down the long stretch of dark road toward home.

Savannah settled more comfortably in her seat and buckled her seatbelt. "You're sure you don't want to have a look around?"

Thor nuzzled Gia's neck.

"Nah." She reached up to pet him. "We're not investigating this time, remember? We have no personal stake in this case, as Hunt has pointed out more than once. Besides, I want to get home and feed Thor, get him out, and still have time to relax with him for a while."

Savannah tilted her head and studied Gia. "All righty then, let's go eat."

A quiet night with Thor, Savannah, Hunt, and Leo. Perfect. Exactly what Gia needed. Good friends, good food, maybe a movie if anyone could stay awake. The perfect way to spend a night. Cole had taken care of most of the prep work, so she could sleep a few extra minutes in the morning. So, what was nagging at her as she left the fairgrounds behind? And why did she have the niggling feeling something was wrong?

"Cole mentioned something about going out to his house to work on the props for the Festival. He said he's got a huge storage shed out there we can use to build and store stuff in." They should probably go ahead and work on preparing for the Festival. It seemed she was already behind, and if they waited for Hunt to give the go ahead, they might not be able to get everything done in time.

"That'll be great." Savannah dug through her bottomless bag and came up with a pad and pen. "My brother, Michael, works in construction, and he promised he'd get his boss to donate whatever he could. I told him we'd need wood for sure, maybe plywood and two by fours."

"That's awesome. Make sure you tell Michael I said thank you." She could use all the donations she could get.

"Probably paint too."

"Put hinges on the list. Willow seemed really excited about the idea of making something they could hide in."

Savannah nodded and jotted everything down. "We could maybe hit up a few thrift stores for blankets and costumes."

"That's a good idea. I didn't think of that."

"I know someone who works at the hospital too, I could find out if they'd be willing to donate anything, old gowns, scrubs, that kind of stuff."

"That would be great."

"I think I'm going to dress up as a crazy doctor, you know, tease my hair way out, wear scrubs and a mask with maybe some creepy makeup around my eyes." Savannah laughed. "I can't remember where, but I know I saw a glove with syringes on all the fingers somewhere."

Gia hadn't given much thought to her costume. Willow and Trevor planned on being patients, but she hadn't talked to anyone else about it. "That sounds fun. Maybe I'll do that with you. Cole and Earl offered to run the table, though I'd like to be out there some of the time."

"For sure. You can easily bounce back and forth. The scaring usually goes on for a few hours, but that doesn't start until after dark. They have food and music for a few hours before that and for some time after, so you should be good."

The more they discussed their plans, the more excited Gia got. It seemed the entire community took part in some way or another, if not participating, then attending. "Do you really think they'll proceed with the Festival, even after what happened?"

"I really do. But, at the same time, if Hunt doesn't think everyone will be safe, he'll cancel, even if he does take a lot of flak for it."

That was true. Hunt would do what he felt was right no matter what anyone thought. If he even suspected he had a killer targeting random people on the loose, he'd never let the Festival go ahead. "Do you think Barbara was the intended victim and not just a random target?"

Savannah stayed quiet for a few minutes.

The hum of the tires against the smooth pavement lulled Gia, and her mind wandered. What could Barbara have seen or heard that got her killed?

"I'm just not buying Barbara as a random victim. I have a feeling it had something to do with her personally," Savannah said, "though I'm not sure what it could have been."

"Have you heard anything more about Mike Smith?" Gia had a feeling he might be the key to something. Whether or not he had something to do with Barbara's death, or witnessed something happening on the grounds, or knew who the killer was, she had no idea. But if Harley was right, and Mike had been at the fairgrounds after the murder, then at least he hadn't been killed as well.

"Not at all. But I haven't heard any press conferences either."

Gia turned into her driveway, and Thor scrambled to his feet on the back seat.

"I know, boy, you must be hungry." She parked in the driveway, as close to the house as she could, and got out of the car. Not bothering to clip Thor's leash on, she opened the back door for him. "Come on, Thor."

He jumped out of the car and danced around her feet.

Savannah grabbed the food bags.

Still leery of stumbling across snakes or other critters, Gia shone the flashlight she kept on her keychain ahead on the walkway, then opened the front door and held it for Savannah and Thor. "Do you want to go ahead and set up the food while I take care of Thor?"

"Sure thing. The boys should be here any minute." Juggling the take out bags, Savannah grabbed the remote and turned the TV to a local news station.

A commercial was playing, so Gia headed straight for the kitchen. She fed Thor and gave him water. While he ate, she turned on the backyard light and scanned the area as best she could from the window to be sure no bears lurked in the yard before she let Thor out. When he was done, she opened the back door and followed him out onto the deck.

He trotted straight to the section of yard she'd fenced for his potty.

Gia folded her arms and rested them on the deck railing and looked out over the forest surrounding her land. Her land. A couple of years ago, she'd never even have dreamed of owning her own house on an acre of land bordering the Ocala National Forest. Never mind having her dream of owning her own café come true. She inhaled deeply, the scent assuring they'd have rain before long.

She picked up Thor's ball and waited for him to come to her. When he did, she tossed the ball into the circle of light in the yard. "Go get it, boy."

He chased after the ball, then returned to the deck with it and laid down to chew.

"One of these days, you're going to get the hang of playing fetch." She sat on the top step and scooted close to Thor.

He picked up the ball and propped his head on her lap.

"Maybe tomorrow we'll go for a nice long walk in the park when I can take a break." She'd gotten in the habit of sneaking away when the café was slow to pick Thor up from Zoe's and take him for a walk. Sometimes Trevor picked up Brandy and accompanied them.

"Hey there. Am I interrupting?" Hunt closed the back door behind him and sat on the step beside her, tucking her beneath his arm and kissing the top of her head.

"Hey there, yourself. What's going on?" Keeping one hand on Thor's head, she shifted and settled with her back against Hunt.

"Unfortunately, not much." He sighed and petted Thor.

Gia closed her eyes and savored the peace of the moment, wishing the three of them could stay just like that forever. "No new leads?"

"We did get Barbara's phone records."

Gia's heart rate kicked up a notch. "And?"

"For someone who doesn't seem to have been very well liked, she talked to an awful lot of people."

"Really?" That surprised her. Especially since Barbara was mostly described as stand-offish. "From what people are saying, she didn't exactly seem like a social butterfly."

"That's just it, I don't get the impression she was socializing." He shifted to lean against the railing, bringing Gia and Thor with him. "All the calls are short, under five minutes, for the most part."

"Could they have something to do with coordinating the Festival?"

"Possibly. The calls between her and Kayla Claybourne increased to a number of times a day over the past few weeks, so we figured they might be Festival related, but we'll still question Kayla tomorrow."

"Good luck with that." What could two women with such an intense dislike for each other possibly have to talk about several times a day? "We saw her out at Xavier's carrying on about…well, pretty much everything to anyone who would listen."

He groaned. "Savannah told me on my way in."

"Who else did Barbara talk to?"

Hunt peered around her to look her in the eye. "That is sounding suspiciously like an interrogation, ma'am."

Gia laughed. "Sorry. It's my inner detective peeking out."

"Yeah, well, you make sure that inner detective stays in, where she belongs."

"Yes, sir." If she thought he was serious, she might have bristled, but his tone held only humor. This time. Maybe Savannah told him she was staying out of it.

"She talked to Genny a lot. The only calls that lasted more than five minutes were to Genny's phones and to her friend, Alfie."

"Genny's phones? She has more than one?"

"Two different lines in Genny's name, though the calls were more frequent and lasted longer on one of the lines than the other. We have a tech still working on sorting all that out. The records just came in tonight. We'd have been here earlier if they hadn't."

It was probably a good thing for Gia they'd come in, since she'd have had to explain where she was if Hunt and Leo had shown up earlier. She debated telling Hunt about Jeb's visit to Genny and following him to the fairgrounds. But what had she really learned? Nothing. Jeb had every right to visit whoever he wanted, and they hadn't found his car at the fairgrounds. She couldn't say for sure he'd even been up there.

"Hey, you lovebirds. Are y'all coming in to eat?" Savannah called out the back door. "Everything's heated up, and it's getting cold again."

Hunt stood and helped Gia to her feet. "By the way, we spoke to Harley earlier."

"How'd that go?" Gia brushed off the back of her jeans.

"Fine. He was cooperative for a while, even though he didn't seem completely comfortable."

"Was he helpful?" She slid her hand into his as they walked to the door.

Hunt stopped when he reached the door and turned toward her. "He's positive about seeing Mike Smith out at the fairgrounds after the murder."

"Was he able to tell you what's going on out there with Jeb?"

"No, nothing. He shut right down as soon as I asked." He raked his free hand through his already disheveled hair. "So far, he's the only one who seems to know anything out of the ordinary is going on out there, and I can't get him to say a word."

"But you still think he knows something?" Maybe she was wrong and Harley didn't know exactly what Jeb had going on, just that something was.

"He definitely knows something, but whatever it is, he's keeping it to himself." Hunt's phone rang, and he pulled it out of his pocket and frowned at the screen before answering. "Quinn."

The sound of rapid-fire information echoed through the connection. Though Gia couldn't make out the words, the sense of urgency was unmistakable.

"Yeah. No. Tell them to wait. We'll be right there." Hunt shoved the phone into his pocket and kissed her cheek.

So much for a romantic evening.

"I have to go."

"I got that much. Is something wrong?" Probably a dumb question. An urgent phone call in the middle of the night followed by Hunt running out didn't ever bode well.

He yanked open the back door and held it for her and Thor. Despite the direst of circumstances, good old-fashioned manners were ingrained deeply in him. "If you want that food, take it with you, Leo. We have to go. Now."

Leo stared longingly at his full plate for a fraction of a second, grabbed a drumstick, and shoved his chair back. "What happened?"

Hunt grabbed a couple of potato wedges on his way through the kitchen, probably the only dinner he'd have for a long time. "An anonymous call just came in from someone who thinks they stumbled over a second body just outside the fairgrounds."

Chapter Fourteen

"I found something." Savannah held her phone out toward Gia over the All-Day Breakfast Café counter. "At least, I think I did."

The small print on the screen blurred together into a bunch of wiggly lines. After sitting up all night waiting for word from Hunt or Leo, which never came, she could barely function before her first cup of coffee. "What did you find?"

"Breaking news. Apparently, the police have been out at the fairgrounds since early this morning."

Gia paused, coffee pot hovering over Savannah's empty cup. "It doesn't say anything about a body being found?"

Savannah gestured for Gia to pour the coffee, then went back to scrolling. "An ambulance was seen leaving, but they are not reporting what happened. It says there will be more information coming as soon as the police comment and blah, blah, blah…"

Cole frowned. "Who would have even been out at the fairgrounds?"

"As far as I know, the police still have the area blocked off and under surveillance." Earl blew on his coffee and took a sip.

While Gia finished pouring Savannah's coffee then filled a big mug for herself, she told them both about Jeb's visit to Genny and his subsequent trip out toward the fairgrounds. "Do you think that's who they found out there?"

"No idea." Cole tied an apron over his bright blue Hawaiian print shirt. "But it makes sense Jeb might go out there, maybe to talk to the police or take a look around. He did work security, after all."

She brought them up to date on everything she'd heard and her conversation with Harley, only leaving out the information Hunt had shared about the phone records. It went without saying that whatever he shared during an ongoing investigation remained confidential.

"What do you ladies want for breakfast?" Cole asked. He already knew Earl's order since he ate the same breakfast every morning.

Gia pressed a hand against her stomach. After Hunt and Leo left, she wasn't able to eat much, but what she did manage sat in her gut like a rock. "Nothing yet, thanks. Maybe I'll have something in a little while."

"Me neither, but thank you, Cole." Savannah shoved her phone back into her bag and rested her elbows on the counter, then lowered her head into her hands.

Cole started toward the kitchen when someone knocked on the front door. "I'll get it."

"Thanks, Cole." Gia pulled out the cash drawer and put it in the register, then started counting out the change.

Cole opened the front door. "Hey, Leo... What's wrong?"

Gia's gaze shot to the doorway.

Leo stood with his hair sticking up in tufts, dark circles around his eyes, and his mouth firmed into a tight line. His gaze locked on Gia's.

Her breath caught in her throat and she dropped the bills into the drawer and started toward him. "Hunt?"

"No, he's fine. He's at the hospital."

Gia froze. Hospital?

Savannah lurched off her stool. "Is he hurt?"

"No, no. He's okay." Leo crossed the room and squeezed Savannah's arm but didn't stop. Instead, he rounded the counter and stopped in front of Gia. "Gia..."

In her mind, she begged him to stop talking. She didn't know what had happened, but it was obviously bad. And the last time she'd seen him, he'd been running out her front door to the scene of another possible homicide. She braced herself for whatever was about to come.

"Before I say anything, Gia, he's going to be okay."

"Who's going to be okay?"

He blew out a breath. "Harley."

She staggered back, gripping the counter to keep herself upright.

"He's hurt," Leo rushed on as he reached out to her. "He's in the hospital."

The hospital. Hurt. Okay, just hurt, not... The full impact of that punched her in the gut. "He can't be in the hospital."

"He'll be okay, Gia, but he was found unconscious out by the fairgrounds." He led her around the counter to a stool Cole had pulled out for her.

"Someone hit him, knocked him out. He was bleeding heavily when we got to him, but he's okay. They're running tests now."

She ignored the stool, though her legs were so rubbery they might not support her for long. "He can't be in the hospital, Leo. He won't go inside a building."

Sobbing softly, Savannah put an arm around her shoulders. "It's okay, Gia. Leo said he'll be okay."

"I have to get there."

"We're going right now. I came to pick you up." Leo gestured toward the door. "I'm sorry I couldn't get here sooner."

Gia simply nodded, trying to process what was going on in slow motion around her.

Earl stood with his hat on, holding out his hand.

Savannah dug through Gia's bag and fished out her keys then handed them to Earl. She carried hers and Gia's bags as she gripped Gia's arm and led her toward the door.

Willow stood beside the doorway with her hand over her mouth and tears spilling down her cheeks.

Cole held the door open, offering some kind of reassurance as she passed him.

"I can't..." Her breath hitched. Can't what? Can't think. She couldn't think of anything but Harley. Not only was he hurt, but they'd had to take him to a hospital. Her mind raced a million miles an hour. What could have happened? Who would hurt Harley? He was the kindest most innocent soul she'd ever known. Why...She whirled on Leo. "He was hurt because you questioned him. Because I questioned him. It's my fault."

The realization shot through her, numbing every inch of her body, and her mind shut down completely. A wave of blackness encroached in her peripheral vision, threatening to drown her.

"Gia. Gia." Savannah called to her from a great distance. "Come on, Gia, don't do this. Harley needs you right now."

Earl pressed a glass against her lips and tilted it.

She took a sip of water. Her stomach heaved.

"You pull yourself together right now, Gia." Savannah sobbed. "Harley needs you."

She nodded and climbed into the back of Leo's car.

Savannah climbed in beside her, keeping a tight grip on her hand. "He'll be okay."

He had to be okay. She'd never forgive herself as it was.

The trip to the hospital passed in a haze of guilt and regret. Fear for Harley, even though Leo assured them he'd been in touch with Hunt at the hospital and Harley was going to be fine, wouldn't abate. Even if he was fine, what would happen to him? Was he still in danger? Once he was released from the hospital, then what? He lived on the streets. How was anyone supposed to protect him?

When they arrived at the hospital, Leo led them through the crowded emergency department. Patients filled the waiting room, some crying, others staring at the muted television, one man sleeping curled up in a corner chair. The odor of sickness and antiseptic threatened to gag her. Patients spilled out of the cubicles and into the hallways. She skirted several occupied stretchers as she hurried through, following closely on Leo's heels.

He strode toward a small, brightly lit room in the back corner. "You go ahead. Savannah and I will wait here so we don't crowd him."

Gia nodded then stopped in the doorway.

Harley lay on a stretcher, the back raised enough so he wasn't lying flat, a bandage wound around his head. Instead of sitting against the wall, the stretcher had been turned to face a window, the blinds lifted to allow an unimpeded view of the parking lot.

Hunt sat in a chair at his side. He stood as soon as he spotted Gia. "He's okay, Gia. They're not even going to admit him yet. They want to keep him for observation, but they are keeping him here for now where he won't have to feel claustrophobic. No closed in stairways. No elevators."

He put a hand on Harley's shoulder as if reaffirming he'd keep him by the window.

"He's okay?" She'd thought she'd collected herself, but a sob escaped as she crossed the room.

"He's going to be fine." As soon as she reached him, Hunt kissed her head and offered her his chair.

She sat down and took Harley's hand gently in hers.

His eyes opened, and he smiled at her.

All the emotions she'd had such a tenuous grip on burst forth in an uncontrollable rush. She sobbed and lowered her head to their clasped hands.

Harley put his other hand on the back of her head but didn't say anything.

"I'm so sorry, Harley." She had to get a hold of herself, tried to wrestle the tide of emotions back under control. She lifted her head to look into his eyes. "I didn't mean for you to get hurt. I'm sorry."

Harley frowned. "You didn't hurt me."

"Gia." Hunt laid a hand on her shoulder. "It wasn't your fault."

She wasn't about to sit there and argue with him. It didn't matter now anyway. All that mattered was Harley getting well and getting out of the hospital. "Are you okay, Harley?"

He nodded. "Hunt and Leo took care of me. And Hunt asked for a special doctor who helped me. She made them turn me so I could look outside. It's better now."

Gia nodded. The ache in her chest made it impossible to talk. She sat with him, holding his hand, staring out at the palm trees lining the parking lot in the early morning light.

A doctor came in and checked on him, then stepped out into the hallway with Hunt and spoke quietly.

"Can I get you anything, Harley?" She didn't know if he was allowed to have anything, but she was desperate to do something for him.

"No. Thank you."

"I wish there was something I could do to help you."

He squeezed her hand. "You are helping me."

"Do you know who did this to you?" What kind of evil person could do anything to hurt Harley?

Harley's blue eyes glazed over, and he shook his head.

"Could you tell anything about the person?" She prayed Hunt and Leo already had a suspect in custody.

"I didn't see his face. Whoever it was had on a dark blue or black jacket. That's all I know."

An image of Jeb, the hood of his dark windbreaker blocking his face, flashed into her mind. She should have told Hunt they'd seen Jeb at Genny's, that he'd gone out to the fairgrounds. Maybe then Harley wouldn't be lying there.

He shifted and moaned. "I want to go outside."

She wanted to argue with him, wanted to tell him it wasn't safe for him to be out on the streets. "Harley, did you tell Hunt what Jeb was doing out at the fairgrounds?"

He stilled and stared quietly out the window.

Gia reached out and gently turned his head to her until he met her gaze. "Harley, please. You have to tell Hunt what's going on so he can protect you. You won't be safe until they find whoever did this, and the only way they can do that is if they know what's going on. Please, Harley, if you can't talk to Hunt, talk to me."

Hunt met her gaze from the doorway but didn't re-enter the room when the doctor walked away.

"I don't want to hurt anyone." Tears pooled in his eyes.

"You're a total sweetheart, Harley. You could never hurt a soul."

Red patches flared on his cheeks. "It would hurt them if anyone knew and made Jeb stop."

Gia took a deep breath and searched for patience. Harley obviously thought he was protecting someone, but whom? And at what cost? "Do you think Jeb did this to you?"

"I don't know." Harley changed position again and his eyelids fluttered shut.

Gia bit back any further questions. He needed to rest. And for the moment, at least, he was safe.

"Gia?"

She looked up into Hunt's concerned gaze.

Beneath the surface, anger churned in his eyes. His jaw clenched. "Harley has another visitor, and the doctor will only allow one person at a time to come in."

She looked toward the doorway.

Down the hall, Donna Mae clutched a bag to her chest and craned her neck to see into Harley's room.

Gia stood. "Donna Mae is here to see you, Harley."

His eyes popped open, and he tried to smooth his hair around the bandage.

She helped smooth his matted hair away from his face. "The doctor will only let one person visit you at a time, so I'm going to let her come in now, but I'll come back if they don't let you out soon, okay?"

He nodded. "Thank you. You're a good friend."

Hard to tell. What kind of friend was she if she was the reason he was lying there? She kissed his temple, gently so as not to cause him any more pain. *"You're* a good friend, Harley. If you need anything, you just ask them to call me, okay?"

He nodded, but she doubted he'd ever ask for help. She'd come back in a little while. Right now, she had other things to do.

After saying goodbye, she strode from the room without stopping to talk to Hunt, who was caught up in a conversation with another doctor. She reassured Donna Mae he would be okay as she passed her in the hallway.

As soon as Savannah spotted her crossing the small waiting room, she jumped from her chair.

Leo was nowhere in sight.

"If you're coming, let's go." Gia kept walking.

Savannah followed. "Gia, wait. Everyone's waiting to see how Harley is."

Gia paused and looked around the room. She hadn't noticed Earl, Skyla, or Trevor, who all stood staring at her. "He's going to be okay. They're keeping him for observation and waiting for test results, but they expect him to recover. I'm sorry, I have to go now."

She practically ran toward the door. She had to get out of there. Needed air.

"Gia," Skyla called and hurried after her. "Where are you going?"

Good question, but she had no answer. Her mind was too filled with chaos, her heart too filled with pain.

Skyla kept pace beside her. "I already spoke to Willow. With the latest news, the café is packed with residents seeking answers. She and Cole are doing okay, but I'm going to go in and help out, so you don't worry about anything, okay?"

She nodded and whispered a raspy, "Thank you," then continued to the exit. Claustrophobia threatened to suffocate her.

Skyla stopped in the entryway.

Gia paused and turned back to her. "How did Donna Mae find out?"

"I went to her as soon as Willow called."

Gia nodded. "Thank you."

Savannah had to lengthen her stride to keep up. "Where are we going?"

"*We* aren't going anywhere." She held out her hand for her bag.

"Gia, don't do this." Savannah held tight to the strap when Gia tried to take the bag from her.

Gia yanked it harder. When it came free, she headed out the door. "I'll call you later."

Savannah hurried beside her but didn't say anything.

When Gia reached the parking lot, she stopped and stood. Leo had driven her to the hospital, which meant she'd have to get a ride back to the café to get her car. She pulled out her phone.

Savannah dangled her keys in front of her. "Wasn't it nice of Earl to drive your car out here for you?"

"Savannah." The word held a note of warning.

Savannah ignored it. "The way I see it, you have two choices; take me with you and I'll hit the button to find the car, or find another way to get to wherever it is you're going."

"Don't do this, Savannah." Chills tore through her, raising goose bumps. She was shaking and needed to sit down. What she didn't need was Savannah giving her a hard time.

Savannah dropped the keys into her bag and hooked it over her shoulder. "He's my friend too, Gia."

"Don't you get it? Look what happened to Harley because of me." She gestured back toward the hospital where Harley lay hurt. That could easily be Savannah next. She started across the parking lot toward the road. "I'm not putting another friend in danger."

"Number one, you're not putting me anywhere. It's my choice where I go and what I do." She yanked the keys back out and pushed the unlock button.

Two beeps signaled where Earl left the car a few rows over. Savannah went to the car and got in the passenger side.

Fine. She'd drop her off somewhere. Gia got into the driver's side, took the keys from Savannah, and started the car, then just sat there staring out the windshield, her hands shaking too badly to drive. She lowered her head onto the steering wheel.

Savannah laid a hand on her shoulder. "Gia—"

"It's all my fault."

"No—"

"Yes." She yanked her head up and slammed her hands against the steering wheel. "Yes, Savannah, it is. I shouldn't have asked him any questions, should have left him alone, and he'd be okay now."

Tears poured down Savannah's cheeks. "You can't know that, Gia. Leo said they don't know what happened. It could have had something to do with them questioning him, or it might not have. It could be that he was just in the wrong place at the wrong time."

Gia whirled on her. "Do you really believe that?"

"I don't know what to believe, Gia, but I do know there's plenty of guilt to go around. Everyone is feeling it. But it won't change what happened. There's no way you could have known."

"We were there, Savannah. We were right there." As if the guilt of possibly putting him in danger wasn't enough, she had to live with the fact that they were right there. Right there at the fairgrounds. And Savanah wanted to look around. But Gia said no. Then she left. Left him there. What if someone hadn't found him? What if whoever hurt him hadn't left it at that? "We were right there, and if I hadn't been such a coward, maybe I could have stopped it."

"Maybe," Savannah conceded. "And maybe not. Maybe we'd be lying there with him. Or worse. What's done is done. We have no control over the past, Gia."

"Maybe not." She sniffed, stepped on the brake, and slammed the car into gear. "But I most certainly can control what comes next. And now, this is personal."

Chapter Fifteen

"What are we doing here?" Savannah stared at Genny's house but made no move to get out of the car.

Gia swung her door open. "What I should have done last night."

Savannah sighed and reached for the door handle.

Gia stopped her. "Please, Savannah, could you wait here?"

"We've already been down this road."

"It's not because I want to keep you out of harm's way, even though I do. Genny is more likely to open up to me if I'm alone." At least, she hoped that would be the case.

Savannah caught her bottom lip between her teeth, then nodded and slumped back into her seat.

"I'll be right back." Gia shut the door and hurried up Genny's front walk. The same car still sat exactly where it had been parked the night before. Hopefully, that meant Genny was home. She took the three steps up to the front porch and rang the bell.

Genny opened the door, her eyes red-rimmed, bloodshot, and almost swollen shut. She sniffed and wiped her nose with a crumpled tissue. "Gia. I'm sorry, were we supposed to meet?"

"No, Genny. I'm sorry to intrude, but I wanted to know if we could talk for a few minutes?" She tried to look past her discreetly to see if she'd caught her alone.

Genny stepped back for Gia to precede her into the house. The door opened into a small but cozy living room, decorated in a bright, beachy style, predominantly accented with driftwood and fishnets. "Have a seat. Can I get you anything?"

"I'm fine, Genny, thank you. Please." Gia sat on a comfortable couch covered in a navy slip cover. "Sit with me."

Genny took an armchair across the coffee table from her, settling close to the edge, her hands fidgeting in her lap.

Now that Gia had her where she could ask whatever she wanted, she didn't know where to start. "How are you holding up?"

"I've been better." She took a tissue from a half-full box on the coffee table and blew her nose loudly. "Now, is that all you wanted?"

Gia ignored the rude attitude. Clearly, Genny wasn't interested in answering questions Gia had no right to ask. "You and Barbara were close?"

"Very. More like sisters than friends." She pulled out a new tissue and wrung it between her hands. She sniffed and wiped her eyes. "We grew up together on the same block, have...had...been best of friends since childhood."

"What about Kayla? She and Barbara didn't like each other very much, it seems."

Genny's gaze shot to the door, then back to Gia. "What is it you want, Ms. Morelli?"

"Look, I'm not even sure." She needed to find out if Barbara was indeed blackmailing people, and she needed to figure out what was going on at the fairgrounds. Those seemed to be the two major questions that needed answering. At least, for the moment. "All I know is a good friend of mine is in the hospital. He was found out by the fairgrounds last night."

Genny gasped and covered her mouth.

"Someone hit him over the head and either left him for dead or left him unconscious on the ground. Alone."

She shook her head. "No, no, no. This has gone too far. I can't—"

The front door flung open, and Kayla rushed in. She didn't even bother to shut the door behind her. "What's going on here?"

What would she have seen when she'd walked in the door? Two women having a conversation. Nothing more. So, why rush in so confrontational?

Genny averted her gaze. She must have called Kayla when she saw Gia pull up out front.

Savannah sauntered in behind Kayla, pushing the door closed but leaving it ajar. "It's nice to see you too, Kayla."

Kayla glared at her. "Don't play games with me. I don't have the patience for it."

"Well, bless your heart, dear, I didn't realize a friendly conversation required patience." Savannah smiled innocently.

Kayla propped her hands on her hips and glanced down for a second before returning her gaze to Savannah's. "Fine. Why are you here?"

Gia stood. "I'm hoping to find out what happened to Barbara."

"What's the matter?" Kayla smirked. "Your boyfriend can't get the job done without you holding his hand?"

"The police are perfectly capable of finding out what happened, and they will." She tried to inject a threatening tone into the words. A promise of justice. "I'm just looking around for my own answers because a friend of mine was hurt."

She shrugged. "Maybe your friend should stay out of things that don't concern him."

Him? Gia hadn't said her friend was a man. How could Kayla have known? Had the police released the information? Not likely Hunt would ever release Harley's name, but details did sometimes leak, or the press could have picked up on the fact that a man was found injured. "Why did you and Barbara hate each other so much?"

"That doesn't concern you."

Technically, she was right, and yet Gia couldn't let it go. She opened her mouth to ask why they'd spoken by phone so often over the past few months, then shut it again. Hunt would kill her himself if she let that slip. "Okay, then why was your picture on Barbara's phone, and who was the man you were with?"

"Get out." Though Kayla's voice was pitched low, there was no mistaking the threat in her tone.

Savannah shot to Gia's side and whispered in her ear, "That's enough, Gia."

Kayla didn't give her time to respond, simply walked to the front door and ripped it open. "I said, get out. Now. Or the next arrest your boyfriend makes will be yours."

"Come on." Savannah ushered her toward the door. She didn't bother to apologize for Gia's behavior, which Gia appreciated, even though they both knew she was way out of line.

And yet, she couldn't stop herself.

These two were definitely hiding something, and she had every intention of getting to the bottom of it. She whirled on Kayla. "Was she blackmailing you?"

Kayla glanced at Genny, who kept her head down. Leaving the door open, she picked up a phone from a side table by the door. "Last chance. And the only reason you're getting it is that I don't want to upset Genny any more than you already have."

Genny had been about to say something. Gia was certain of it. If Kayla hadn't shown up when she did, Genny would have caved. Maybe that's why she'd called in a reinforcement. Whatever she knew was weighing heavily on her. She wanted to be rid of the burden.

Kayla turned the phone on.

Since Gia didn't know what to ask, and neither woman was likely to answer any more questions anyway, Gia allowed Savannah to lead her to the car. She pulled away from the curb and headed toward town. As soon as she dropped Savannah off, she'd head out to the fairgrounds and see if she could find Jeb.

"Gia…"

She held up a hand. The last thing she needed was someone to point out how wrong she was. "Don't even say it."

Savannah pursed her lips and studied Gia, then let whatever she'd been about to say drop. "Leo called. While you were in with Genny, before her guard dog showed up."

She said a silent thank you that Savannah knew when to let it go. "Did they find whoever hurt Harley?"

She shook her head. "But they did bring Alfie in for questioning. Seems they found him sneaking around out at the fairgrounds."

"When?" Alfie? She couldn't believe he'd have been able to do that to Harley. He seemed so gentle, timid even.

"A little while ago. That's why Leo left the hospital earlier; he got a call from an officer who was out there saying they'd picked him up." Savannah tilted her head back and forth and rubbed the back of her neck. She hadn't slept much more than Gia, and the tension was clearly getting to her. Gia's out of control emotions probably weren't helping matters.

"Did Alfie say what he was doing there?" She still couldn't wrap her head around Alfie as a killer.

"He said he wanted to feel closer to Barbara, so he went out there to walk around."

That made more sense to her than Alfie having hurt his friend. But she didn't know him, and she was going to have to keep that in mind. Generally, trust didn't come easy to her; so what was it about Alfie that made her want to believe him? "Leo wasn't buying it?"

"I guess not." She rolled her shoulders. "But he didn't say. It was the other part of the conversation I found more intriguing."

"Oh yeah, what was that?"

"The cell phone line Barbara spent so much time talking to someone on doesn't belong to Genny." She paused for a beat. "It belongs to her husband, Preston."

"But why would…" Suspicion crept in. "You think Barbara was having an affair with Genny's husband?"

"Leo didn't know what was going on, but I think Genny might have more involvement in this, either directly or indirectly, than Kayla would like anyone to look too closely at."

That would explain her behavior. "You think she's protecting Genny? From what?"

"Who knows? Maybe she's afraid Genny will be next. If she knows why Barbara was killed, who's to say she's not next on the killer's hit list?"

"That would explain why she hovered so closely over Genny, demanded she show up in a public place to eat as if everything were normal, carried on to whomever would listen about how inept the police were and how she thinks Barbara's killing was basically no one's fault but her own. Maybe she's trying to get a message out."

"A message to whom?" Savannah asked.

"The killer? Maybe she's trying to make sure he knows Genny is innocent of any involvement." Even though that theory kind of made sense, it still didn't feel right. But who knew? "Did Leo hear anything about Mike Smith?"

"Nothing." Savannah straightened in her seat and shoved her sunglasses on. "So, now what?"

"Now I head out to the fairgrounds to take a look around."

She looked out the window and frowned. "Then why are we headed toward town?"

"Because I'm dropping you off first."

"We've already had this discussion," she sighed. "And you may as well turn around and head toward the fairgrounds, because if you drop me off, I'm just going to get in my car and head out there, anyway, and then I'll be alone. So, take your choice."

"How'd you get so stubborn?"

Savannah laughed. "I don't know. Maybe it had something to do with growing up in a house full of over overprotective brothers and cousins."

"I'll have to remember to thank Hunt later."

"Is that a note of sarcasm I detect, Gia? Very unbecoming."

"Me? Sarcastic? Never." Though she wasn't happy about Savannah going with her, she couldn't deny being glad for the company. Besides, it was the middle of the day, and the police were probably still out there, so how dangerous could it be? "Has Leo said if they suspect anyone in particular?"

"No."

Not surprising that he wouldn't share with Savannah, even if they did. Though Hunt and Leo never minded talking over pieces of an investigation, some evidence had to remain confidential, even from them.

"But we can try to figure out who the players are on our own." She lowered her sunglasses and waggled her eyebrows.

Just what she needed, her very own George or Bess. But if Savannah was willing to run through scenarios with her, why not take advantage? It's not like she'd be in danger for saying something in a closed car, and she would never share her opinion anywhere else. "We saw Jeb out at the fairgrounds when Barbara was found, so it's possible he was also there when she was killed."

"And Mike Smith was out there when Barbara got there, if Alfie is to be believed."

True. *If* Alfie was telling the truth. So far, no one else that she knew of had mentioned seeing Mike. "Alfie was there too. Plus, he was just picked up for questioning because he was out there again."

Savannah drummed her nails against the door handle. "Do you really think he could have had anything to do with Barbara's murder?"

He'd been so broken up, but still, you never knew. "Not really. Do you?"

She just shook her head. "What about Kayla? Or Genny? According to Alfie, they were both out there when he dropped her off too."

She tried to remember exactly what Alfie said about that. The steady rhythm of Savannah's nails against plastic grounded her, helped her focus more clearly. "Actually, I think Alfie said he saw Kayla. He only assumed Genny was there with her."

Rat-a-tat-tat, rat-a-tat-tat, rat-a-tat-tat. "Okay, so the information we currently have about who's possibly involved does nothing to help us narrow the field. What about physical evidence?"

"If by physical evidence you mean Barbara's cell phone and the shovel we saw at the fairgrounds, they're both missing, so I can't see what good that would do us."

"No, me neither. And we don't know enough about what they found in Barbara's phone records to lead us in any direction."

"Did Leo mention finding any other evidence? Fingerprints maybe? Anything?"

She was already shaking her head before Gia finished. "How about Hunt?"

"No, nothing. But I've barely spoken to him." Gia pulled over and parked on the side of the road just before they reached the fairgrounds.

"Why are you stopping?"

"I figure the police are most likely still out here, securing the scene if nothing else. It's probably better if we walk from here." She wouldn't want to get picked up and have them call Hunt.

Hmm…Just as she was about to go snooping around hoping to find anything that would point toward Harley's attacker, maybe Alfie had been doing the same to find Barbara's killer. That would explain what he was doing snooping around the fairgrounds, and he might not be so forthcoming with the police about it.

Maybe she'd better bump visiting Alfie to the top of her to-do list.

Savannah opened the door then paused. "What if Hunt or Leo drive past and see your car parked here?"

"We'll cross that bridge if we come to it. Hopefully, they'd understand."

Savannah pinned her with a gaze and lifted a brow. "You can't be serious. Has my cousin ever given you reason to believe he's the picture of understanding?"

"He turned Harley's bed to face the window." And that had said everything about why she cared so much for Hunt. He might often get his panties in a twist, but he cared deeply in a way few people in her life ever had.

Savannah took a deep breath and blew it out slowly. "Touché."

They walked up the hard-packed dirt road toward the fairgrounds. Though they didn't see any police cars, the occasional burst of police radio chatter assured them they weren't alone. When they came to a narrow dirt road that split off to the left before they reached the parking lot entrance, Gia stopped. "Do you know where this leads?"

Savannah looked around, then pointed to the right, the direction the main road curved as it led to the parking lot. "The fairgrounds are that way. This looks like it curves to the right a little ways up, so maybe it heads to the parking lot or around the back of the buildings."

"Come on." Gia started down the overgrown path.

Savannah stood at the fork and propped her hands on her hips. The pose was a stark reminder that she and Hunt were related. He used that stance on her more than once. "Where are you going?"

"This way. Maybe we can go around whatever police officers are left up here. If nothing else, we might be able to hear what they're saying."

Savannah dug in her heels. "So now you're resorting to spying?"

"Desperate times and all that…"

She made no attempt to move in Gia's direction, nor did she laugh at Gia's admittedly lame attempt to lighten the situation. "Are you okay, Gia?"

She didn't have time for this. "Sure. Why?"

She threw out an arm toward the path Gia stood on, grass and weeds up to her knees in many patches, though she could still discern a distinct trail. "Traipsing through the Florida wilderness has never been high on your comfort zone list."

"Yeah, well, I'm trying to expand my horizons." And in one minute, she was moving on. With or without Savannah. It was probably safer to leave her behind at the car anyway.

"Whatever you say," Savannah mumbled, but instead of heading back to the car, she grabbed a long stick and shifted a thick patch of weeds aside so she could pass. Then she fell into step at Gia's side.

Tears prickled the backs of Gia's lids. "Thank you."

"What are friends for?" She reached the stick in front of them, careful to poke any thicker patches of vegetation they couldn't see through before walking into or around them.

Gia didn't bother to ask what she was searching for. She was definitely better off not knowing. Though if she did, there was at least a slim chance she'd come to her senses and turn back. They hadn't gone far when the trail split. "Which way?"

Savannah shielded her eyes from the sun and looked down each path. Even with sunglasses, the light was blinding. She pointed to an opening in a patch of woods on the right, where it seemed blue sky met water on the horizon. "It looks like there's a lake down that way."

"Then it makes more sense to head this way." Gia started down the left fork, thankfully the less overgrown of the two.

"What makes you say that?" Savannah stayed put. "If we go toward the lake, I think we'll come to the fairgrounds."

"We'll also come to the alligators and water moccasins." Gia had her limits, even in her current state of mind, and a lake full of predators topped the list.

Savannah laughed. "Now I feel better. I was beginning to think you were going completely crazy."

And just like that she knew she was forgiven. "Who knows? Maybe I am. Just not that crazy."

They walked a little farther. Movement ahead on the path caught Gia's attention, and she held a hand out to stop Savannah, then put a finger against her lips and crept forward.

Savannah moved closer and whispered, "What?"

Gia backpedaled and pointed ahead. In the middle of the trail, a giant spider sat beside a bush eating its prize, some kind of beetle the size of a quarter. Pain squeezed the breath from her lungs. Her unnatural sense of arachnophobia reared its ugly head. She gestured back down the trail and backed away slowly.

"Seriously?" Savannah threw her hands out to the sides. "Why not just go around it?"

Gia kept backing up. "Not a chance. If that thing thinks we're trying to get its food, it just might attack. The other trail seemed like it led more toward the fairgrounds anyway."

"No kidding. Ya think?"

Okay, so Savannah may have pointed that out earlier. Clearly, Gia should have listened then.

"All right. Whatever you say. Gators and Cottonmouths are definitely better than spiders." Savannah shook her head but followed Gia back toward the fork.

In Gia's peripheral vision, something big and dark moved in the brush way too close on their right. Bear? Oh no. She started to hyperventilate, her chest aching as she tried to do so quietly. How far away could a bear smell them from? She grabbed Savannah's arm and dropped below the shrubbery, dragging Savannah with her. Maybe bears relied on sight to hunt, and they could hide from it.

She peeked between the branches, hoping for a glimpse of the bear's back end as it ran in the other direction.

Except it wasn't a bear creeping through the bushes. A man in dark clothing stealthily weaved his way through the brush, not following any discernible trail.

Savannah huffed out a breath. "Let me guess; another spider?"

"Shh," Gia hissed. She put her mouth against Savannah's ear. "A man."

Savannah's eyes widened but she remained quiet and nodded.

Gia released her and they crept closer to the bushes, then took a chance and peered over.

A man in a dark sweatshirt crept through the underbrush and out onto the trail, then stood hunched in the middle of the trail, looking around furtively. Apparently satisfied it was safe, he jogged down the trail for a couple of seconds. He stopped again and looked around, then left the trail, scrambled over a downed tree, and continued deeper into the forest.

"That doesn't look like a cop."

"No, it doesn't." Gia stood. "Let's go."

"Good idea." Savannah jumped up and headed back the way they'd come.

"Where are you going?" It wouldn't be hard for him to lose them if they didn't hurry.

"You said let's go. And it's the first thing you've said all day that makes good sense."

"We don't have time for this, Savannah. Come on. Let's go."

"Go where?"

"I don't want to lose him." Crouching below the brush, Gia scrambled after him.

Savannah grabbed her arm to stop her. "Don't want to lose him? You can't be serious. You just turned around and went down a different path because you were afraid to go around a bug, but you're going to follow a strange man creeping furtively through the forest at the scene of a murder?"

"You're right," Gia admitted.

"Darn right, I am."

"It's dangerous." And she couldn't lead Savannah into danger. Again.

"Darn tootin' it is," Savannah agreed.

"You wait here."

Chapter Sixteen

The stranger stopped in front of a rusted storage shed. He looked around once more then, apparently confident he hadn't been followed, he stood up straight, yanked off his hood, and smoothed back his shaggy brown hair, baring a scar that ran from his ear to the side of his mouth. He heaved open one of the reluctant doors, the loud screech sending several birds flapping indignantly into the air.

Gia pressed herself against a large tree trunk, the bark scraping her cheek, hoping the abundance of moss hanging from its branches would provide enough cover to block her from his view.

Savannah stood behind another tree a few feet away. "Now what, Sherlock?"

The only window visible from her vantage point was covered with what looked like cardboard, blocking any view into the interior of the building. A number of dilapidated buildings stood in various stages of decay throughout the area, any of which could be housing more strangers. A kid's bicycle leaned against a tree beside one of the buildings. A small flower garden sat outside of another. "Now we try to peek inside."

"What! That is so not happening, Gia." Savannah pulled out her cell phone and tapped the screen a few times. "Dang. I still can't get service out here."

"Who are you calling?"

"No one, apparently." Giving up, she shoved the phone into her back jeans pocket. "We're going to have to head back toward the road so I can get service."

"What if he gets away?" Gia couldn't let that happen. For all they knew Harley's attacker could be holed up in that building.

Savannah looked back the way they'd come, then toward the building again. She tapped her nails against her belt buckle. "We are not going down there, Gia."

"No, we aren't." No way was she putting Savannah in harm's way any more than she already had. "You're going to go back to the road and wait for me. If I don't come back in a few minutes, you can call for help."

"Forget it. Not happening." Sweat dripped down the side of her face, dampening long tendrils of her hair. She shoved it behind her ear.

"Then keep watch from here. I'll be right back." Ignoring Savannah's frantically whispered protests, Gia left the cover of the tree. She crept closer to the shed, her gaze riveted on the rusted doorway, ready to duck at the first sign of movement.

A nearby rattling sound made her pause. She scanned the ground around her.

"Gia, don't move," Savannah called, heedless of how her voice carried in the still wilderness.

Gia froze.

A large, brown snake with a diamond pattern covering its skin, poised to strike no more than a few feet away.

The man with the scar stuck his head out the door, met Gia's gaze, then took off running deeper into the forest.

"Back up," Savannah hissed. "Slowly."

Another man peered out the window of a rotted wooden building, then he bolted in the opposite direction.

Gia did as Savannah ordered, inching backward one step at a time, barely lifting her feet, keeping as quiet as possible with her breathing so ragged. Her heart hammered so hard her chest ached, as she put as much distance between her and the snake staring her down as possible.

The snake rattled its tail once more, then slithered beneath a rock.

The instant the snake disappeared, Gia shifted her gaze to the man with the scar crashing through the overgrown brush, the shaggy brown hair brushing his collar bringing back the image of the man Kayla had been with in the picture on Barbara's phone.

Giving the rock a wide berth, Gia started after the man with the scar.

Savannah grabbed her arm and yanked her back. "That's enough, Gia. You're not thinking clearly."

"But you saw him. He had on a dark hooded sweatshirt. Harley said whoever attacked him was wearing a dark jacket."

"And Jeb had on a dark jacket last night too. A lot of people wear dark jackets, Gia."

"Yeah, but how many of them are creeping around the deserted fairgrounds where Harley was attacked?" She turned again, intent on finding out where he was going. "Besides, did you see his hair? What if it's the man from the picture with Kayla?"

Savannah grabbed her wrist, digging her nails in hard and spinning her back around. "So what's your plan, huh? Chase him through the woods, somehow avoiding getting bitten by something venomous until you catch him? And then what? Tackle him to the ground and rip his shirt off to see if he has a scorpion tattooed on his back? Or maybe you could just ask nicely and hope he tells you the truth, and maybe offers a full confession while he's at it, instead of killing you and dumping your body in the swamp."

"He's getting away." What if the police weren't able to find him and he want after Harley again? Or Savannah?

"Then the best thing you can do is run back to the road with me so we can call Hunt. I am not leaving you alone out here, and I am not allowing you to take so much as one step farther into this forest, so if he gets away, it's no one's fault but your own."

The thought of having to tell Hunt she was snooping around the fairgrounds and trying to go after a possible killer was enough of a slap in the face to snap her back to reality. The thought of Harley's attacker getting away because she didn't get help in time prodded her into action. She started running back the way they'd come.

Savannah ran at her side, her phone held out in front of her. The instant she got service, she stopped, bent at the waist, and dialed Hunt. Between huffing and puffing, she quickly explained the situation.

Though she could hear Hunt yelling, Gia didn't bother to listen to what he was saying. She didn't have to. He couldn't be any angrier with her than she already was with herself.

She'd almost gotten herself hurt, if not killed. She'd put Savannah in danger, not only from a possible killer, but from all kinds of venomous creatures. What on earth had she been thinking?

She hadn't been. She'd been so consumed by the need to keep Harley safe, and so blinded by the guilt that he'd been hurt because of her, she hadn't thought at all.

Savannah hung up, then looked around. "Come on. We have to get back to the car. Hunt is sending a couple of officers from the fairgrounds to meet us. Look for landmarks so we can tell them how to get back out here."

Forest surrounded them, encroaching from every side, closing them in and cutting them off from civilization. Even the ramshackle buildings disappeared from view. The full force of the danger they'd been in slammed through Gia.

She'd lost all sense of direction. If left to her own devices, she'd probably wander through the Florida swampland indefinitely without ever finding her way out.

Apparently satisfied she could find her way back to the car, Savannah started forward down a barely discernible trail.

"Wait," Gia sobbed. "Oh man, Savannah. I am so, so sorry. I messed up. I can't believe I did that."

"Me neither." She sucked in a deep, shaky breath. "But I understand."

"How could you understand that?" Gia pressed a hand against the ache in her chest. How would she ever ease the pain? She bent over and propped her other hand on her knee, desperately sucking air into her starving lungs.

Savannah laid a hand on her back. "You're worried about Harley, afraid whoever attacked him is going to try to finish the job once he's released."

As usual, Savannah did understand. But still…"That's no excuse for my behavior."

She pried Gia's hand away from her chest and held it tight. "It's okay, Gia."

"No, it's not. I put you at risk." She straightened and looked around the deserted woods. "That's inexcusable."

Savannah rubbed a hand up and down her arm. "You didn't put me at risk, Gia. I could have walked away and sought help at any time."

"But you didn't. You chose to stay."

"Of course I did. You're my best friend. I'd never walk away from you. And Harley's my friend too. He didn't deserve what happened to him, and whoever did it needs to be found. And punished."

"But not by us."

She released Gia's hand and tucked some of the damp tendrils clinging to her face behind her ear. "No, not by us. Hunt will find him."

Gia nodded and looked at her feet.

"It's okay, Gia. Just like I told Hunt, we're both fine."

"Yeah, but are we now on a killer's radar too?" Just what she needed, more guilt.

Savannah pursed her lips. "I don't know, and right now it doesn't matter. The best thing we can do to keep everyone safe is, first, get out of here and then, help the police catch this guy."

Gia nodded. Savannah was right. They had to figure out where they were so they could tell the officers how to get there. Gia followed Savannah back toward the car, careful to memorize any distinguishing features that would give the police a trail to follow.

They emerged from the woods to find several police vehicles lining the road.

A small group of officers jogged toward them.

One of them stopped, while the others continued down the trail. "Are you ladies all right?"

"We're fine." Savannah gave him directions as best she could, pointing out the way the man had fled.

Gia stepped forward. "I can go with you, if you want, show you the way back to the storage shed."

"No, you can't," the officer said. "Sorry, ma'am, but no way am I earning the captain's wrath. You two go back to your car, turn on the AC, lock the doors, and wait for Captain Quinn. He's on his way."

Great. Just what she needed. Hunt on the warpath. Not that she could blame him. She'd put Savannah in danger again. "I'm sorry, Savannah, I don't know what came over me."

"It's okay." She opened the car door and looked over the roof at Gia. "Trust me, I know you weren't thinking clearly."

"What makes you think that?"

She grinned. "Because not only did you try to run through the Florida wilderness after a possible killer, you barely batted an eye at a rattlesnake a few feet from your foot."

"Rattlesnake? Is that what that was?"

"Mmm-hmm..."

"That one's venomous." She knew that much from the social media groups she'd joined to learn more about Florida wildlife.

"Yup." Savannah slid into the car, pulled the door shut, and fanned herself with a pamphlet she yanked from her bag.

Gia got in and cranked the air conditioning. Sweat ran down her back—more from the realization a venomous snake had almost bitten her than her run through the forest. "You saved my life. How can I ever thank you for that?"

"For starters, you can tell Hunt it was all your fault." She lowered her sunglasses and waggled her eyebrows.

"Oh yeah?" She slumped back in the seat, rested her head against the headrest, and closed her eyes. "What happened to you can make your own decisions and no one can make you do something you don't want to do?"

"That goes out the window when my friend manages to get herself into trouble."

Gia reached across the center console and squeezed Savannah's hand. "Thank you, Savannah. And I really am sorry."

"I know. It's okay. My first instinct was to run after him too. If not for the snake, I would have been right behind you."

"A sobering thought." Gia lifted her sweat soaked hair off the back of her neck and tied it in a band she kept on her wrist. "How angry was Hunt?"

"Better not to think about that right now, honey, but it's been nice knowing you."

Gia laughed, and tears streamed down her cheeks.

"Aww...sweetie, are you okay?" Savannah handed her a tissue.

"Thanks." Was she okay? She honestly had no clue. The attack on Harley had her on an emotional roller coaster; upset, relieved, angry, grateful. Afraid. That was the worst of it; an overwhelming sense of fear for the people she loved.

A knock on the window beside her head made her jump. She looked out the window to find Hunt staring back at her. She might have been better off taking her chances with the killer. Resigned to her fate, she sighed and got out of the car, then lifted her chin and faced him head on. "I'm so sorry, Hunt. I messed up."

He ran a hand through his hair, then propped it on his hip, staring hard at her. Beneath the harsh scowl, his eyes filled with something else. Concern. And the same fear she'd just been thinking of. "Are you all right?"

"Yes, I think I am."

He pulled her into his arms.

She rested her cheek against him, losing herself in the sense of security his presence brought.

He set her back too soon. "I need you both to look at a few pictures, see if you can recognize the man you saw. Did you get a good look at his face?"

Gia nodded. "We weren't right on top of him, but I could make out a scar running down the side of his face."

"Which side?"

"The right, I think."

"I think so too." Savannah frowned and looked at Gia. "Do you really think he was the guy in the picture with Kayla?"

"I don't know. I got caught up in wanting to catch him because he seemed to be acting suspicious." A dull throb started at her temples. "Other than having shaggy brown hair, there's nothing else I could say was the same."

Hunt jogged back to his car, which he'd parked on the shoulder behind her, and returned with a stack of pictures. He shuffled through them, then handed one to her.

She recognized him instantly. "That's him."

"Are you sure?"

Savannah looked over her shoulder. "Yes, I'm sure. That's him. Who is he?"

"The elusive Mike Smith." Hunt stood staring at the picture. "At least, now we have confirmation he's alive."

"And you probably would have caught him if I had just gone back to the car and called you instead of making a scene and letting him know we were there." That was something Gia would beat herself up over for a long time, especially if it turned out he was the killer and anyone else died. In that case, she would never forgive herself.

Hunt put a finger beneath her chin and lifted, forcing her to meet his gaze. "As much as I hate to admit this, and trust me, it pains me, if it wasn't for you, we wouldn't even have a clue where to look for him. There are enough acres of wilderness out there for someone to disappear for a very long time if they wanted to. At least, now, we know he's there and have a direction to look."

"Thank you for that." It couldn't have been easy for him to admit, especially when he had to be harboring a lot more anger than he was showing. Seems Captain Hunter Quinn was developing a sensitive side.

He tapped her nose with his finger. "Mmm-hmm…just don't let it go to your head."

"Nope. Not happening." She held her hands up and backed away. "From now on, I'm out of your investigation."

He rolled his eyes, reminding her of Savannah. "I'll believe that when I see it."

"No, for real. Savannah and I are going to hit up a thrift store and maybe a flea market if we have time, then I'm going to stop by the café and see what's going on, then I'm heading over to Barbara's memorial." She held up her hands before he could protest. "Just to pay my respects. If Harley's still in the hospital after that, I'll go visit him. If not, I plan to pick up Thor and head out to Cole's to work on props for the Festival. Do you think it will go ahead?"

Hunt took a deep breath and let it out slowly. "We're under a lot of pressure to make sure it does, but I just don't know at this point. It can't hurt to go ahead and work on getting ready, though. At worst, I think it'll probably just be postponed, not canceled, though it's tradition for it to take place the last Saturday in October."

"Better late than never, I guess." Savannah pointed at him. "If you and Leo get time later, you could stop in at Cole's and help out."

"We'll see."

"Oh, I should have thought to ask before, have you released Alfie yet? I don't imagine the memorial service could go on without him, since he organized it all." And she wanted to stop in and see him, see how he was holding up, and she couldn't very well do that if he was in police custody.

"We let him go." He leaned his back against the car, crossed one leg over the other, and folded his arms. "We had nothing at all to hold him on."

"Because he's innocent? Or because you just can't prove he's guilty?"

"Gut instinct? I don't think he killed her, but don't go getting too friendly. While I have no way to prove his guilt, I also can't prove his innocence."

Gia nodded. "Fair enough."

Hunt's phone rang, and he straightened and checked the caller ID before pressing it to his ear, switching from semi-relaxed mode to cop mode in a fraction of a second. "Yeah? Okay…I'm on my way."

Whatever had happened just decreased the chances of him and Leo making it out to Cole's. "Is everything okay?"

"They've got Mike." He kissed Gia's cheek, then Savannah's, started across the street, then looked back. "Get in your car and lock the doors, then head back to town. I'll catch up with you later."

Chapter Seventeen

Cars crowded the small parking lot behind Auntie Em's Closet, trucks backed up to the delivery doors, and people milled about, chatting, most with coffee cups in hand, some even bearing the All-Day Breakfast Café logo.

Gia wedged her car between a pickup truck and a palm tree. "Why's it so crowded?"

"The Festival. People are looking for costumes and props." Savannah got out, propped her sunglasses on top of her head, and shut the door. "Emma knows that, and she keeps an eye out for stuff all year long."

"Look out!" a man yelled from behind a truck by the back door.

Gia whirled toward him in time to see the couch he was trying to load onto the bed of his pickup truck topple over.

Several people ducked out of the way. Others stopped and turned toward the commotion.

"Sorry." The teenage boy trying to help him load it offered a sheepish smile and struggled to help him get it upright.

Two men who'd been crossing the lot toward their cars ran to help.

An undercurrent of anxiety cut through the buzz of excitement. Most of Boggy Creek's residents were on edge with a killer on the loose.

Savannah held the door open, and Gia walked into chaos.

Clothes were strewn everywhere, and people dug through tables and racks crammed full of garments. The majority of the crowd gathered around a section toward the back of the store.

Gia hesitated. "Let me guess, that's where we're headed."

"Yup." With a smile, Savannah bounced right into the pandemonium.

Gia hung back.

Laughter filled the store, the sense of community palpable.

"Hey, Gia." Savannah held up a yellowed tunic style top that had probably been white once upon a time. "What do you think of this? Someone could wear it as a scrub top."

Gia moved closer. "That could work."

"Go check the back table. Someone said they had sheets and pillow cases back there." She gestured toward a less crowded section of the shop near the back corner.

Gia sent her a silent thank you and took off in the direction she'd indicated. She rounded a section of floor to ceiling shelves stuffed full of bottles and jars, old bowls, vintage tea cups, and stenciled tin serving trays with scalloped edges. Not one bare inch of space remained.

She paused for a minute to admire a tray with blue roses painted on the bottom, then continued to the back table. She made a mental note to come back in one day and browse when she didn't have a hundred-mile-long to-do list. Auntie Em's Closet seemed like a treasure trove worth exploring, and Gia had a weakness for anything kitchen related.

Stacks of sheets and blankets that were much less pawed through than the clothing filled a long table. A sign in the center read "Sheets $1."

Gia took a deep breath and dove in. Seemed bedding was in less demand than vintage clothing for the Festival, and she had the corner to herself. She set the fitted sheets aside in a neat pile. Since their beds didn't have mattresses, there would be nothing to fit the corners around. She ignored floral and print sheets—though they would have worked for a dormitory, they didn't seem right for a hospital.

She picked up a scratchy, thin white blanket and checked the price. Two dollars. "Perfect."

She looked around for a cart. When she didn't see one, she set the blanket atop a smaller pile, then dug back in. Before long, she had a stack of flat sheets, mostly white and cream, but a few tan, and one faded yellow and an olive green. She piled pillow cases beside them, but she couldn't find any pillows.

"You hiding too?" a man's voice asked from right behind her.

"Ahh…" She spun toward him. "Oh…man, Alfie. You startled me."

"Sorry." His cheeks flamed red.

"No worries." Who needed the ten years he'd just scared off her life? Though her heart still raced, she tried to soothe her inner turmoil. Hunt needed to get this case solved. Or she needed to start paying closer attention to what was going on around her. "Actually, I'm looking for stuff for the Festival. We're doing a haunted hospital theme, and I need bedding."

"Oh, I'm sorry. I figured you were hiding from the mob."

She grinned. "That too."

Alfie sorted through a stack of sheets Gia had set aside. He opened a fitted sheet then folded it in half, lining up the gathered elastic corners and tucking them into one another. "I was at the police station earlier."

"Oh?" No sense letting on she already knew. Maybe he'd tell her something she didn't already know.

"I heard you and Savannah found Mike."

Uh oh. If Alfie had heard that when he was there to be questioned and definitely not considered trustworthy, who else was privy to the information?

"Where'd you hear that?" Not Hunt or Leo, that's for sure.

He folded the sheet in half again, once again tucking the corners inside of each other. "Around. Do you mind if I ask where you found him?"

Gia squirmed. No way did she want to share information with someone who still remained on the suspect list, even if Hunt didn't think he was the killer.

"Out by the fairgrounds." True enough, without giving too much away.

"Past the fairgrounds? In an old storage building?" He kept his head tilted down toward the sheet he was folding but peered up at her from beneath his lashes.

A quick glance around assured her no one was listening, yet she still lowered her voice. "How'd you know that?"

"Kind of reminds you of a little town out there, doesn't it?" He tugged at his collar, then set the folded sheet aside and started on the next.

"What are you saying, Alfie?"

"Saying?" Sweat beaded his brow. "Nothing. I'm not saying anything."

She waited him out.

"Really. It was just an observation." His hands shook as he tucked the corners of a pink calico sheet together. "But I think they are barking up the wrong tree with Mike. I don't think he killed Barbara, and he would never in a million years have hurt Harley."

"How do you know that? Do you know him?" If she remembered correctly, Alfie had told Hunt he didn't really know Mike when he'd questioned him the night Barbara was killed.

He shrugged and set the sheet aside. "I know him a little. Enough to know the police shouldn't waste their time with him. Maybe you could let Captain Quinn know that?"

"Alfie, you're going to have to be a little more specific. If Mike's not guilty, and you know that for a fact, you should tell the police that. Do you know where he was when Barbara was killed?"

He bit his lip and shook his head.

"Then how can you be so sure he wasn't involved? And why did he hide from the police and run from me?" Oops. She hadn't meant to let that slip.

Alfie glanced around the store. He started to say something, then froze, his mouth hanging open as he stared toward the front of the store.

Gia looked over her shoulder but couldn't pick out whatever had caught his attention. "How could you know he isn't the killer?"

"Not everyone has the courage to risk everything, not even for someone they love," he whispered and shook out the next sheet, casting a pointed glance from the corners of his eyes toward an over packed shelf unit not far from them.

Someone moved on the other side of the shelf.

Gia let the question drop and raised her voice. "And where did you learn how to fold those things? I can never get them folded and usually wind up settling for sort of folding them in half then rolling them up in a ball."

Alfie laughed and wiped the sweat from his brow with his sleeve. He gestured toward the leaning pile she'd accumulated. "Want me to grab you a cart?"

"Would you mind?"

"Not at all. I saw one by the books a few minutes ago. I'll see if it's still there." He ran off, and Gia returned to her search, keeping a close watch to see who emerged from behind the shelves.

A woman with a nametag that read EMMA approached the table. "Can I help you find anything?"

"Umm…" She looked around, trying to figure out what she still needed, still a little shaken by Alfie's attempt to…To what? To share some sort of information, she was pretty sure. Now if only she could find a decoder ring to figure out what it was. Emma probably didn't have one of those on hand. "Actually, I could use some pillows, if you have any."

"Hmm…for the Festival?" She turned in a circle, quickly scanning the packed shelves.

"Yes, we're doing a haunted hospital theme, and I wanted them for the beds. I found cases, but no pillows."

"The only pillows I have are throw pillows, and they're a few dollars apiece. Or…" She lifted a finger in front of her, then grabbed a pillow case. "Come with me."

Gia followed her to a section dedicated to bath stuff, not only towels and washcloths but vintage scales, copper garbage pails, and beautiful old mirrors.

"These towels are only fifty cents each." She loosely folded a towel and stuffed it into the pillow case, then fluffed it a bit. "Or, if you prefer it a little thicker, you could use two towels, and it would still only be a dollar a pillow, plus the cost of the case. And, since it's for the Festival, you get a twenty-five percent discount off your entire order."

"Oh, wow. That's really nice of you, but you don't have to do that." The prices were already so low; she couldn't understand how they were making any sort of profit as it was.

"No problem." She smiled and started sorting through and picking out light colored towels. "I take a lot of donations for the Festival of things I wouldn't normally be able to sell, so I don't mind helping out as much as I can."

"Thank you."

"Of course." Her smile faded. "It's just a shame Barbara won't be here to enjoy it. She always came in for a truckload of items."

"She really enjoyed the Festival, huh?" Gia grabbed a white towel wedged beneath a stack of washcloths and added it to the pile.

Emma shrugged. "She always seemed to in the past, but the last time I saw her she seemed strange."

"Strange?" Gia folded a washcloth in half, then folded it again the long way. If they got medical tape, they might be able to use the washcloths for bandages. She started digging for more white ones. "What do you mean strange?"

"Well, she was very agitated, and kept looking over her shoulder, not at all like she usually acted."

Gia added several washcloths to the growing pile. "What do you mean?"

Emma shrugged and folded a white towel.

"I'm sorry. I didn't mean to intrude. I just didn't know her."

"Oh no, it's okay." She pulled a couple of gray washcloths out and held them up. "Would these work?"

"They'd be perfect, thank you."

Emma added the washcloths to the pile then turned and rested a hip against the table, arms folded across her chest. "Barbara was a very confident woman. She always knew exactly what she wanted, always thought she was doing things the right way, because it was her way. You know what I mean?"

Gia nodded, scanning past Emma for Alfie. She didn't want him to walk up as she was talking about Barbara. He'd be hurt if she said anything negative, and everyone knew what good friends Barbara and Alfie had been. If she saw him, Emma might stop talking. "I do."

"Oh my." Emma laughed. "Why am I even trying to put a kind spin on it. The woman was stubborn as a mule. And then some. She was often abrasive, tended to keep to herself, and didn't seem to bother with many people."

Nothing new there. Most everyone shared the same opinion of her.

"But that last time I saw her, she seemed different. Nervous and, I don't know..." She shook her head and frowned. "More than that. She seemed anxious and jumpy when she first came in but then, after she got into that argument, she got even worse. So bad, her hands were shaking when she pulled the money out of her wallet and handed it to me for her purchase."

Still no sign of Alfie. "What argument?"

Emma looked around and lowered her voice. "She had a terrible argument with Kayla Claybourne."

This was the first she'd heard about that. "About what? Do you know?"

She shook her head and leaned back, resting her hands on either side of her on the table. "I don't. I was working the register that day, and the mad rush hadn't started yet, so I didn't have a ton of help."

Gia could certainly relate to that.

"But their raised voices carried, and it was clear from their postures they weren't happy with each other, but Kayla seemed to be the more intimidating of the two. Barbara seemed to be backing down, if you can believe it. I never thought I'd see that day."

"What happened after the argument?"

"Kayla stormed out, and Barbara came to the register. But, like I said, she seemed jumpy and downright scared by that point, so I watched the surveillance camera as she left, just to keep an eye on her, ya know?"

Gia nodded.

"And, sure enough, Kayla was outside waiting for her. When Barbara got to her car, Kayla waylaid her, pointed a finger in her face, said something very brief, and walked away. I grabbed the phone, but before I could even dial, Kayla was gone. Who knows? Maybe if I had called the police, things would have turned out differently." She stood and shook off her melancholy, then offered a semi-smile. "Anyway, I have to get back to work. Is there anything else I can help you with?"

"Oh, there you are, Gia." Savannah balanced several garments over one arm, carried a long lamppost in the opposite hand, and pushed a carriage in front of her. "Hi, Emma."

"Hi, Savannah. Do you need help with that?"

"Nah, I got it, thanks." She held up the garments. "Here, take a look and see what you guys think."

Gia sifted through the frocks and aprons. "I think they'll work."

"Great. We'll toss them into the accessories box, and whoever wants can grab them." Savannah gestured toward the piles of towels and washcloths. "Are these yours?"

Gia nodded.

After laying the garments over the carriage handle and propping the lamppost against the table, Savannah scooped a bunch of towels and washcloths into her arms and deposited them into the carriage.

"Thanks, Savannah. I have a bunch of sheets over on the other table too." She surveyed the crowded shop but found no sign of Alfie. "Alfie was supposed to get me a carriage, but he disappeared."

Savannah gestured over her shoulder. "He took off out the front door when Kayla came in."

"I didn't see her come in." Gia didn't blame him. Barbara was his friend; no reason for him to listen to Kayla badmouth her.

Emma grunted. "Looks like it's time for me to get back to work, see if I can keep that one from making a spectacle of herself in here like she did yesterday."

"I'm good now, Emma, but thank you so much for all your help."

"Of course, anytime." She started away.

"Oh, wait," Gia called after Emma. "One more thing. Do you remember what Barbara bought that day?"

"Hmm…let me think a minute." She tilted her head and narrowed her eyes, her focus turning inward. "She bought a bunch of stuff. Tarps, clothing to use for costumes, a shovel, a candelabra, a couple of—"

"Wait. Back up. A shovel? What kind of shovel?"

"Just a regular shovel, the kind with the handle on one end, but not the pointy kind, like a spade, the kind with the squared off edge. I'm not sure what it's called."

"That's okay, I know which one you're talking about." Because she was pretty sure she'd seen it lying in the storage shed the night Barbara was found.

Chapter Eighteen

Cole and Earl, their self-appointed bodyguards for the evening, hovered over Gia and Savannah in the small hall Alfie rented for Barbara's memorial service. He'd spared no expense when it came to the flowers, which overflowed from the room out the door and down the wide staircase.

Gia kissed Alfie's cheek. "It looks beautiful, Alfie."

"Thank you. It does, doesn't it?"

"I'm sure Barbara would have loved it."

Alfie let out a half-laugh, half-sob. "Actually, she'd hate it. She'd say it was wasteful. But it was important to me, so she'd have understood."

"I'm sure she would have." Gia wanted to ask him about why he'd taken off from the thrift shop, but it didn't seem like the right time. After the service, maybe she could get him alone.

Alfie used a crumpled tissue to wipe his eyes. "By the way, I've decided I'd like to take you up on your offer, if it's still valid."

"Yes, we'd love to have you work with us. We're getting started tonight after we leave, if you'd like to join. You're always welcome."

"Thank you." He glanced past her. "If you'll excuse me."

"Of course." She let him go. If he wanted to speak to her in private, there'd be plenty of time at Cole's. At least there, they'd be surrounded by friends. Whatever had him so spooked might seem less intimidating. Maybe he'd share whatever was on his mind.

Savannah looked pointedly across the room toward a man standing off by himself staring at a picture of Barbara that Alfie had set on a table. It was a head shot from a previous year's Festival, and Barbara's expression was stern in the zombie makeup she'd donned for the occasion. "That's Preston Hart, Genny's husband."

"Why does he look so angry?"

Preston Hart's expression hardened even more, his jaw clenched as he ground his teeth back and forth. After a quick look around, he laid the picture face down on the table, then walked away.

"No idea, but I've been watching him for the past fifteen minutes or so, and all he does is wander around staring at pictures like he'd kill her all over again if he could."

Gia scanned the room for Genny and found her seated on a small love seat in a front corner of the room, a box of tissues on a table at her side, and a small garbage pail discreetly tucked beneath the table. She stared at a picture collage set on an easel beside a large vase filled with lilies.

Kayla approached and handed her a foam cup, then sat next to her and gently brushed a loose strand of hair behind her ear. She leaned close and whispered.

Genny nodded and handed the cup back to her without taking a sip. She started to stand but swayed.

Kayla immediately reached out a hand to steady her, then helped her return to her seat. After another hushed conversation, Kayla walked out.

If Gia was going to talk to Genny alone, this might be her only chance. "I'll be right back, Savannah."

"Sure thing, but Gia…"

She paused.

"Stay out of trouble."

Since she clearly deserved that, she let it drop. Leaving Savannah with Cole and Earl, Gia approached Genny. "Excuse me, Genny."

Genny looked up and sighed.

Gia couldn't blame her. "I just wanted to tell you how sorry I am, both for your loss and for my behavior. A friend of mine was hurt, and I let my emotions dictate my actions. I never meant to hurt you, and I apologize."

Genny studied her but didn't say anything.

"Well, that's all I wanted to say." Not wanting to intrude, Gia started to walk away.

"Alfie says lilies suggest the soul has returned to a peaceful state of innocence." Genny spoke so quietly, Gia could barely hear her.

She turned around and moved closer.

Genny continued to stare at the pictures and the flowers. "Do you think that's true?"

Taking that as an invitation, Gia sat beside her on the love seat. "I'd like to believe it is."

"Me too." She absently shredded a tissue.

"I'm sure Barbara is at peace now, and soon they'll find whoever did this to her." From the agony in Genny's eyes, Gia doubted it would matter much to her if they found Barbara's killer. It wouldn't bring her friend back.

Genny's breath hitched, and she lowered her gaze to the tissue on her lap.

"Is there anything I can do for you, Genny?"

"She just needs time to heal." Kayla's voice from just beside her startled Gia.

She stiffened, waiting for the assault she was sure would come.

Instead, Kayla pulled up a chair and sat across from them. Her gaze met Genny's for a split second before she shifted her focus to Gia.

This apology stuck in her throat for some reason, not because Kayla didn't deserve it; it just wasn't as easy to admit she was wrong to Kayla as it had been with Genny. Either way, she'd treated the woman with complete disrespect, and like it or not, that behavior was inexcusable. "Kayla, I just want to offer you a sincere apology, whether or not you accept it is up to you, and I'll certainly understand if you don't, but I was completely out of line, and for that I'm truly sorry."

She waved a hand. "Don't worry about it."

Gia tried, and probably failed, to keep her expression from betraying her surprise. She hadn't expected Kayla to be the forgiving type. "Thank you. I appreciate your understanding."

"Of course." Her gaze touched on Genny's again, then skittered away just as quickly.

"If you'll both excuse me." Genny stood and dropped her shredded tissue in the garbage pail. "I need to get some fresh air."

Gia started to stand, expecting Kayla would accompany Genny outside.

But Kayla laid a hand on her arm. "Please, stay."

"Sure." Gia sat back down, curious to see what Kayla wanted with her. Maybe she'd only acted forgiving for Genny's sake. If that was the case, she was probably about to get a major tongue lashing.

Kayla watched Genny cross the room.

Preston watched his wife leave, then flopped onto a chair, folded his hands between his knees, and studied the floor.

"She's fragile, you know," Kayla said, in a much softer tone than Gia would have thought possible.

"I realize that, and I'm so sorry for hurting her."

"I believe you." She waited a beat, then continued. "You seem like a kind woman, Gia. I'm sorry your friend was hurt. I hope he recovers quickly."

"Thank you." She'd spoken to Hunt just before she headed to the memorial, and he said Harley had been released. Donna Mae promised to keep an eye on him overnight, so she'd have to remember to give her a call later.

"Being that you were willing to go to such great lengths to defend your friend, I hope you can understand I feel the same way about Genny. There's nothing I wouldn't do for her. I hope you'll forgive my earlier behavior too. I'd like to be able to work together on the Festival, if it goes forward."

Maybe she'd rushed to judge Kayla too quickly. Gia certainly hadn't put her best foot forward of late. Perhaps Kayla hadn't either. "I'd like that too."

Kayla started to stand, then sat back down and looked around. "You asked earlier why I disliked Barbara so much."

Gia held her breath, hoping she'd continue.

"Barbara Woodhull was not a kind woman." She paused, studying Gia as if waiting for her reaction.

"You're not the first person to say that."

Kayla nodded. "Most people would rather bury their heads in the sand than face the truth, but you don't strike me that way. I respect that."

"Thank you." Why was she starting to get the feeling Kayla wanted something from her?

"Genny is my best friend, and Barbara treated her so badly." Tears shimmered in Kayla's eyes, and Gia imagined they were for Genny, not Barbara. "Let's be honest, we all do things sometimes to hurt one another, no matter how close we are. But Barbara was different. She treated Genny like competition. Whatever Genny had, Barbara wanted. Only she wanted more or better, anything to outdo Genny. But Genny was too kindhearted to see the truth."

Gia bit back the question she wanted to ask—why was Kayla telling her all this?

"This Festival means the world to Genny. She loves helping the shelter, loves organizing the event, loves the sense of community the event brings. Joining together for a helpful cause always—well, usually—brings out the best in people. She would be devastated if it was canceled."

"I imagine a lot of people would be."

"Yes, exactly." She slid to the edge of her seat and sat up straighter. "So you can certainly see why it would be good for everyone if the Festival were allowed to proceed."

"Of course."

"Oh, great." She patted Gia's clasped hands and smiled. "Since you agree, I assume you'll speak to Detective Quinn about releasing the crime scene and letting us get back to work."

Uh oh. Gia squirmed beneath Kayla's steady stare. How had she managed to get roped into that so easily?

Kayla stood and held out her hand. "Thank you, Gia, I appreciate your help. I hope to see you around the fairgrounds, and if there's anything you need, just let me know."

"Uh…" What could she say? Nothing really. She shook her hand. "Thank you."

Seriously? Had she really just thanked this woman for manipulating her into trying to talk Hunt into releasing the crime scene? Not that he'd listen to her; he'd release the crime scene when he'd found all the evidence he needed, and he'd allow the Festival to proceed only if he felt his community would be safe if he did so. Besides, technically, she hadn't agreed to anything. Kayla just assumed once she planted the seed Gia would do her bidding.

Kayla headed out of the room in the same direction Genny had gone without stopping to speak to anyone else.

"You okay?" Savannah asked.

Gia hadn't heard her approach, though she wasn't surprised she'd showed up the instant Kayla left. She'd probably had a close eye on her the whole time they were talking. "Somehow I get the feeling that can be a very dangerous woman."

Savannah frowned after her. "Did she say something to you?"

"That's just it, she was nice as could be, forgave me for beating her up earlier, even understood the desire to do anything for a friend. Then she told me I should talk to Hunt about releasing the crime scene."

"Hmm…are you going to do it?"

Was she? "Nah. Hunt knows how important this event is for the community and the shelter. If he feels it's safe, he'll release it. If he doesn't, he'll take enough flak without me adding to his stress."

"Come on." Savannah gestured toward a podium at the front of the room. "Alfie's going to say a few words, and then we're all going to head out to Cole's to work for a couple of hours."

"But it's dark out?"

"He has lights, Gia."

She laughed and massaged the bridge of her nose. Of course he did.

"Zoe is going to meet you out there with Thor." Savannah gestured for Gia to precede her toward the back of the room. "She's bringing Brandy too."

"Okay, thanks."

"Sure thing." Savannah followed her to the back row where Cole, Earl, and Skyla all waited.

"Hey, Skyla." Gia sat down next to her. "I just wanted to thank you again for jumping in for me today."

"Of course, anytime."

"How'd it go?" She needed to get back to the café, needed her life to get back to normal.

"Great. I love working with Willow, and she's a great teacher." She smiled, her eyes filled with pride.

"She's a great person." One of the kindest Gia knew, just like her mother. "You've done an amazing job raising her."

"Thank you."

She remembered Willow saying Skyla worked more closely with Barbara than she had. "Did you know Barbara well?"

Skyla shrugged and kept her voice low. "I knew her from volunteer work, but I steered clear of her as much as I could."

"You didn't like her?"

"More that I didn't trust her. I don't mean to speak ill of the dead, but Barbara was known to dig up dirt better left buried and, well, with the situation with Willow's father, I thought it best to stay off her radar."

Gia nodded and dropped the subject. She understood Skyla's decision.

Alfie took his place behind the podium and waited for everyone to settle down. "First, I want to thank all of you for coming to honor a woman who was a pillar of this community, a woman who always put others ahead of herself..."

While Alfie droned on with a long list of attributes no one but him seemed to have seen in Barbara, Gia studied the crowd. Genny and Kayla sat together in the front row. Jeb Hansen leaned against a wall at the back of the room, constantly scanning the crowd as if searching for something. Preston Hart sat alone at the side of the room, shaking his head as Alfie spoke.

"He's not very attentive, is he?" Savannah whispered. "Seems maybe Kayla had that one pegged."

After a few minutes, Preston got up and walked out without so much as a goodbye to his wife.

Chapter Nineteen

When she could finally tear herself away from helping Cole at the grill the next morning, Gia ran through the list of ingredients on her recipe and started setting everything she'd need on the center island. "I'm glad you came in this morning, Cole, though I'd have understood if you wanted to take a day for yourself after taking care of everything for me yesterday when you were supposed to have a day off."

"Don't worry about it. I'm enjoying myself." Cole flipped three pancakes then poured warm maple syrup into a small carafe.

"Well, I really appreciate it, thank you. I don't know what I'd have done this morning without you."

"Any time." He put the pancakes on a plate and slid it onto the cutout for Willow to pick up, then started on the next order. "So, what are you doing there?"

"I decided to tweak the pumpkin spice waffle recipe. I want to make sure it's perfect before the Festival and then add it to the menu for the fall." She pulled a dozen eggs from the refrigerator. "I was thinking of doing a seasonal menu with a few specials for each season. I'll do the pumpkin spice waffles with warm maple syrup and maybe cinnamon apples for the fall."

"The dog treat idea inspired you, huh?" He winked.

"Exactly," she laughed.

Cole cracked a dozen eggs into a bowl, then turned to face her as he scrambled. "What are you doing different?"

"I want to try it with homemade pumpkin spice instead of the store bought one."

"You think it'll make a difference?"

"I don't know, but it can't hurt to try." She set out nutmeg, cinnamon, cloves, and ginger.

Cole looked over the ingredients. "You use pumpkin puree instead of pie filling?"

"Yup." She ran through her list. "I was thinking of trying almond milk instead of regular this time. What do you think?"

"That might be good. Seems a lot of people prefer it, nowadays." He turned and poured the eggs onto the grill, then sprinkled in precooked crumbled sausage and shredded potatoes. "I want to try making the dog treats when we slow down after breakfast too."

She would have done those first, since she'd never tried them before and they'd probably require more tweaking than the waffles, which would be good to go if not for her love of trying new things, but Cole wanted to help with them, and one of them had to man the grill until they slowed down. *If* they slowed down. News of Harley's attack had made it through the rumor mill, and they'd been swamped all morning. "I told Zoe we'd bring some by after lunch for the dogs to try. She was going to check with each of the owners when they dropped their pups off this morning to make sure it was okay with them."

"I already know Trevor's in." He flipped the eggs and sectioned them into four omelets. "He said so last night."

"Are we getting together again tonight?" Even though they'd only been able to work for a couple of hours after the memorial the night before, she'd had a great time. Cole ordered pizzas, and a good number of people showed up to help.

"That's the plan. Since we don't have the memorial tonight, everyone's planning on heading out right after work. I left a key to the shed under my door mat in case anyone gets there before me. Hope you don't mind pizza again."

"Are you kidding me? There's no such thing as too much pizza. Besides, that was especially good. Where did you get it?"

"The new place down the road by Trevor's."

She was going to have to start going there. It was the best pizza she'd had since moving, by far.

Savannah poked her head through the kitchen doorway. "Hey, Gia, got a sec?"

"Sure. What's up?"

"Check this out." She held her phone out to Gia.

Gia took it from her and looked at a picture of a young man with his arm around a woman, both of them dressed in pirate costumes.

"Look familiar?"

Gia enlarged the picture, focusing on the woman. Even though she was much younger in the picture, it was easy enough to recognize Barbara Woodhull after looking at all the pictures of her displayed at the memorial the night before. "The woman is Barbara, but I don't recognize the man."

Savannah leaned back against the counter. "Look closer."

The man's arm was slung around Barbara's neck, her head tilted into his shoulder. Gia definitely got the impression the two were more than just friends.

She swiped her finger to get a close-up of the man's face. He had short brown hair, brown eyes, and a serious expression. She held out the phone for Cole to see. "I don't know. Who is he?"

Cole shook his head. "I don't recognize him either."

Savannah smirked. "None other than the elusive Mike Smith."

Questions erupted in Gia's head. An overflow of thoughts ricocheted in a million directions, all at once. Mike and Barbara? "Are you sure it's him? I thought Mike had a scar down the side of his face."

"Yes, it's definitely him. Once I knew what he looked like and that he got the scar in a motorcycle accident back a few years ago, it wasn't all that hard to find him, thanks to my reporter friend." She tapped the phone. "He's got a number of social media accounts, though none of them have been used recently, and despite the fact that, according to Tom, he has no known address and hasn't had a paycheck in years."

How could that be when several people said he worked at the fairgrounds? "That doesn't make sense."

"No, it doesn't, and it's possible Tom just hasn't found all of the information on him yet, but he'll keep looking and let me know whatever he digs up."

Gia nodded absently as she took a closer look at the picture. Though Mike was sporting a huge smile, Barbara gazed into the distance as if she were a million miles away. "How'd you find out about Mike's accident?"

"Leo called a little while ago."

Though they'd waited up most of the night, they hadn't heard a word from Leo or Hunt after Mike had been taken into custody.

"He said Hunt will call you in a little while, but he was bogged down with paperwork at the moment."

"So, what does this mean?" Gia returned the picture to normal size, then scrolled through the rest of Mike's social media posts.

"Apparently, he and Barbara were a couple at some point."

"Do you think that has anything to do with what happened to her?" She knew from experience a years' old grudge could sometimes come back to haunt you.

Savannah shrugged and shook her head. "I don't know."

"You don't think it's too much of a coincidence that they dated at one time, then Barbara was murdered, Mike was possibly one of the last people to see her alive, and he ran from the police in the area where she was found?"

Cole piled home fries into a bowl and put it on the cutout. "In a town this size, with even fewer people back when those pictures were taken, it's not that much of a coincidence that two people who dated back in the day would end up having some sort of overlap in their lives at some point in the future."

"Besides," Savannah was quick to point out. "Mike didn't run from the police; he ran from you."

Cole laughed out loud.

Heat crept up her cheeks. "Ha ha. Very funny."

"Funny or not, it's still true," Savannah said. "Maybe he thought you were a reporter or something."

Gia had to concede the point, even if she didn't want to. It wasn't like she'd identified herself in any way, and Mike probably had no clue who she was. Savannah and Cole were both right. "So, we don't know anything more now than we did befo— Hey, wait a minute."

"What's up?" Savannah moved beside her and glanced over her shoulder at the new picture she'd enlarged on the screen.

Cole joined her over Gia's other shoulder.

In the picture, Mike sat amidst a group of six boys, all around his own age. "Look at the guy with the long, dark hair."

Savannah squinted at the phone. "He looks familiar."

"He should." She focused on one guy in particular, enlarging the screen to show his features more clearly. "You just spoke with him the other night."

"Jeb Hansen," Savannah blurted.

"So, Jeb and Mike hung out at some point." Cole returned to the grill and checked the next order in line. "What could that have to do with Barbara's murder?"

"And what could it have to do with whatever Jeb is doing at the fairgrounds now?" Probably nothing, but you never could tell. It still seemed a little too coincidental.

"I don't know." Savannah took the phone from her and pointed through the cutout into the dining room where Hunt had just walked in. "But I'm going to show Hunt the pictures, just in case."

"Good idea. Could you tell him I'll be out in a minute, and see if he wants something to eat?" Gia set the recipe aside and stuck the eggs back into the fridge. She'd have to tackle this later, probably after the lunch rush at this point. "Are you okay for now, Cole?"

"Sure thing, ma'am."

Sometimes, she worried he was beginning to work too hard, but he seemed happy enough, humming a tune as he worked. "Thank you."

"Let me know what Hunt says," he called after her.

She shot him a thumb's up on her way out the door, then made a quick pit stop in her office to run a brush through her hair and tie it back up neater. When she reached the dining room, Savannah was already on her way back to the kitchen with Hunt's order.

She hooked a thumb toward the dining room and scowled. "The brat confiscated my phone."

Gia laughed as she passed her, then stood across the counter from where Hunt sat scrolling through Savannah's phone. "Howdy, stranger."

"Howdy, yourself." He stood and gave her a quick kiss, then returned to scrolling.

"Anything interesting?"

"Not really." He darkened the screen and set the phone aside. "Anything going on here?"

"Lots of gossip, but that's about it." Since Hunt didn't have coffee in front of him, and Savannah would have offered as soon as he walked in, he'd probably already overindulged on caffeine. "Do you want something to drink? Orange juice? Water?"

"Savannah's getting me something with my breakfast, thanks." He looked around the café, crowded for this time on a weekday morning. Everyone was focused on their meals and their companions. Still, Hunt leaned forward and spoke quietly. "How was the memorial? I was hoping to make it, but I couldn't get away, and my officers didn't report anything."

"Interesting." Gia bent close and rested her forearms on the counter, hands clasped in front of her, shooting for a casual pose that would bring her close enough to talk to Hunt without being overheard. "I apologized to Genny and Kayla, and they were both very forgiving. Of course Kayla's forgiveness came with a…request, demand, whatever."

"Oh? What's that?"

"She wants me to talk you into releasing the fairgrounds and allowing the Festival to proceed."

Hunt laughed and propped a finger beneath her chin. He waggled his eyebrows. "Well, dear, let's see how persuasive you can be."

She gave him a quick peck on the cheek and pulled back. Though the desire to kiss him was strong, she was standing in the middle of her place of business.

"Not very persuasive, Gia." He feigned disappointment, though he would have already known what to expect. "In that case, no Festival."

"Yeah, right," she laughed.

But his expression remained somber.

"Seriously?"

He sat back, all signs of playfulness gone. "What do you expect, Gia? A woman was killed out there, a man was attacked and hurt, and I'm supposed to allow most of the town to go out there and traipse around after dark?"

Well, when he put it like that. "Are you announcing it yet?"

"No." He rolled his shoulders, and the full weight of his fatigue hit Gia. "We'll wait and see. We won't cancel until the last minute and, hopefully, even if we do, we'll be able to just postpone it until we catch the killer. In the meantime, we still have a couple of weeks to work on it."

Gia didn't push it further. The last thing he needed was her harassing him. "I take it you didn't learn anything new?"

Though she'd kept her question vague so as not to be overheard, Hunt understood she was asking about Mike. "Looks like a dead end."

Gia sighed. "What about Alfie?"

"What about him?"

The words stuck in her throat. With Kayla, Gia had felt she'd been manipulated into doing her bidding. Alfie, on the other hand, had seemed genuinely dismayed over whatever information he had that he refused to share, for whatever his reasons. She sighed. "I ran into him in the thrift shop, and he said I should let you know Mike didn't kill Barbara or attack Harley."

He raised a brow and waited for her to elaborate.

Keeping her voice low, she relayed the conversation she'd had with him. Hunt ran a hand over his chin. "That's all he said?"

"Yes."

"Seems I'll have to have another chat with Alfie." He frowned.

"What?"

"Look, Gia, that's two people who have asked you to intervene in this investigation because of your relationship with me."

Uh oh. Even though they didn't get to spend a lot of time together at the moment, since both of them had demanding careers, their still developing relationship worked for them. And she hoped it would evolve into something more as time went on. But if Hunt went into protective mode now, he might well decide it wasn't safe for her to be associated with him. "Enough, Hunt. It's a small town. What are you going to do, sacrifice having a wife, a family, because people know you're a cop?"

Resting his elbows on the counter, he lowered his head and clasped his hands over the back of his neck. "I just don't like that fact that you might be on a killer's radar because of our relationship."

Her relationship with Hunt had nothing to do with her coming to a killer's attention, though her trip to the fairgrounds had most certainly been a catalyst. Gia laid a hand on top of his and leaned close. "Let's face it, Hunt, my relationship with you probably has little or nothing to do with me being on a killer's radar."

His sort-of-laugh held no humor, and he sat up straighter, pinning her with steel in his dark eyes. "Gia, I don't need to talk to you about what happened yesterday, right?"

"Nope, I'm good." She squirmed beneath the intensity of his stare. "I'm sorry, Hunt. It won't happen again. I just lost it a little seeing Harley lying there in that hospital, feeling like it was my fault. I'm glad they let him go. Have you talked to him this morning?"

He studied her for another moment, then sighed and slumped against the seat back. "No, but I spoke to Donna Mae. They spent the night in her yard, a campout of sorts. Though Harley drew the line at a tent, he did accept a sleeping bag, open, not zipped, and spread on the grass."

"Oh good, I'm so glad."

"Me too."

Savannah returned and set Hunt's breakfast and orange juice in front of him, then took a seat on the stool next to his and grabbed a muffin out of the cake dish closest to her.

"All right, guys. You enjoy your breakfast. Time for me to get back to work." Gia went to ring a customer. "Good morning, I hope you enjoyed everything."

"Oh, it was wonderful, thank you." The woman handed her the check and two twenty-dollar bills. "Could you be sure to give the change to our waitress, please?"

"I will. Thank you."

Gia rang the purchase and put Willow's tip into her envelope, as the next customer stepped up to the register. "Hi, can I help you?"

"I'd like a banana muffin and a vanilla cold brew, please. To go."

"Of course." Gia packaged the order and rang her up, then handed her the bag and cup and turned to the next customer. "Gouh...oh...Kayla. Good morning."

"Good morning, Gia."

Genny stood beside her, shoulders hunched, eyes ringed by dark purple circles.

"Good morning, Genny, how are you doing?"

"Fine, thank you."

Gia looked to Kayla, who only shook her head.

Collecting herself, despite her mounting concern for Genny, Gia took the check from Kayla and set it aside. "Breakfast is on me."

"You don't have to do that," Kayla said.

"Don't worry about it. It's the least I can do after the way I acted."

Kayla smiled. "Thank you, Gia. It's not necessary, but we truly appreciate it."

The drastic difference in Kayla's behavior was throwing her off. Perhaps her concern for Genny had made her act the way she had. Gia's cheeks heated. She could certainly relate. "Is there anything else I can get you?"

"No, thank you." She started to turn away, but then turned back. "Oh, by the way, are you still doing the hospital theme?"

Genny's shoulders slumped even further, her gaze fixed in the distance.

"Umm…" Gia dragged her attention back to the conversation. "Yes, that's the plan, anyway."

"Good. I spoke to a friend of mine who works at a medical supply company in Orlando, and they are willing to donate supplies for the Festival, if you're interested."

"Are you kidding? That would be great." She grabbed a pad and pen. "Who do I have to contact?"

Kayla waved a hand. "Don't worry about it. We have to run to Orlando to pick up a few larger items this afternoon, anyway, and we're taking Preston's truck, so I'll stop and pick up whatever they're willing to donate."

Genny sucked in a deep shaky breath, nodded, and offered a half smile that didn't come close to touching her eyes. Apparently, she was more tuned in to the conversation than Gia realized.

"Thanks, Kayla, that would be great."

"No problem." She looked around then gestured toward Hunt, who was still sitting beside Savannah at the counter. "Any news about the Festival?"

"Nothing new." True enough. And she wasn't about to repeat anything Hunt had said.

"All right, then. Where will you be later so I can drop the stuff off to you? Since we obviously can't get into the fairgrounds to leave it there." A bit of the old Kayla crept into her tone.

For some reason, that seemed more natural to Gia than this new Pollyanna version. "Oh, you don't have to do that. I can come pick everything up from you when you get back."

"I don't mind. Besides, I don't know what he has for us, so it may not fit in your car. I know he had some IV poles."

"That's awesome." Despite the circumstances, Gia's excitement grew with each new piece that came together. Maybe this whole thing wouldn't be as difficult as she'd thought. If it went ahead, of course. She wrote Cole's address on the back of an order slip and handed it to Kayla. "Right now, we're working out of Cole's house, so you can bring everything there if you'd like."

Even if the Festival was postponed, it seemed like it would probably go ahead at some point. Besides, she'd gotten a late start, so a postponement would only buy them more time to prepare. And if it wasn't postponed, they'd need every second they could get.

"Perfect." Kayla tucked the slip of paper into her bag. "Isn't it, Genny?"

Genny stared at her and sobbed. Then she nodded and walked away.

Chapter Twenty

"Hey, Gia, could you hand me a couple of those hinges?" Cole held a piece of plywood against the box he'd built to look like a small bed.

Gia grabbed three hinges from the bag the hardware store had donated. "Can I hold something for you?"

"You know what?" He set the plywood aside and scratched his head. "This isn't going to work."

"Why not?" The box looked great. It would definitely pass for a small bed once she made it up with sheets and blankets. They'd already figured out they could cut the blankets and staple them to the door so it would look made when it was closed and not fall off when it opened for someone to jump out.

"It's too heavy. And when the hinges are on, whoever's jumping out of it has to be able to push it open, and the plywood is just too heavy."

"What about using something lighter for the door?" Earl gestured toward a pile of wood scraps in the corner.

"Nothing big enough." He propped his hands on his hips and stared at the offending box.

"I'll tell you what." Earl took off his fishing cap and smoothed his hair. "My boy, Jackie, has a pickup truck. I'll drop him off at work tomorrow, take the truck, and we'll run out to the lumber yard and pick up something lighter. Paneling, maybe?"

"That might actually work. And we don't need many pieces. I can probably get two doors out of each piece, so two sheets oughta be enough." Cole returned the piece of plywood he'd been trying to attach to the woodpile, then stretched and rubbed his back. "I'll tell you what; it sure feels good to be doing physical labor again, but I'm not gonna lie, I'm gonna be feelin' it tomorrow."

"You can say that again." Gia stood and stretched, then looked around the shed. Props stood in various stages of construction, fabric lay strewn about for costumes, a couple of masks sat on a table in the corner. She studied her friends, all gathered, working together to do something good and having a blast. While at one time she may have enjoyed the anonymity of living in a big city, she'd never again want to be without the sense of community and friendship living in Boggy Creek had brought her.

Thor nudged her with his nose.

"Hey there, boy, are you having fun?"

He barked once and sat.

His thick coat was damp, probably drool from wrestling around with Brandy and Caesar, Cybil's beagle mix. "Eww…I love you, Thor, but you are a mess. You're going to need a bath later."

"Hey, I think he wants another one of those treats," Cole yelled.

Gia had a feeling it was probably water he needed, but she didn't dash Cole's hopes. The dogs had all loved the treats they brought down to Zoe's that afternoon. "I think you might be right, Cole."

She grabbed what was left in the bag of treats and gave one to each of the dogs, then filled three bowls with water.

Cole petted Thor's head, despite the drying drool that stiffened the thick fur around his head and neck. "You know, I have to say I miss having a dog around."

"Want to take a ride out to the shelter with me after the Festival and take a look around?" Gia grinned. If she could sic Savannah on Cole, maybe she'd cut Gia some slack.

"Hmm…" Thor nuzzled his hand, then went back to drinking his water. "Cybil asked me the same thing. I think I might just do that. An early Christmas present to myself. You're thinking of getting another too, right?"

"I'm thinking about it. I'm just not quite sure I'm cut out to own multiple dogs." She took a quick glance around to be sure Savannah hadn't heard her.

Cole waved off her concerns. "Once you have one, the rest are easy."

"Oh? Then why don't you have a dog?"

"I always had dogs when I was younger, but when I lost my last two within a few weeks of each other, I decided to wait a while before getting another." He smiled. "I think maybe I've waited long enough."

"Oh no. I'm so sorry." Having never owned a pet before Thor, she couldn't imagine how he'd suffered. It was no surprise to her he'd waited so long. Her plan for the night now involved a very long snuggle with Thor on the couch. Maybe she'd watch a movie. Thor always perked up when she watched anything with a dog in it, his head tilted as he studied the screen.

The shed door swung open, and Donna Mae waved to Gia from the doorway.

"Excuse me, Cole. I'll be right back, but when the Festival is over, we'll pick a day to go to the shelter."

"Sounds good." He stood and twisted from one side to the other. "Time for me to go back to work, anyway. Don't tell anyone, but my boss is a slave driver."

Gia laughed as he walked away.

She crossed the large space quickly, hoping Harley had come with her, and gave Donna Mae a hug. "Hi there, how are you doing?"

Donna Mae stepped back and gestured toward the door. "I'm doing well thank you, and I brought someone to see you."

Gia hurried outside and found Harley standing on the walkway, gazing up at the moon. "Harley?"

He turned. "Gia."

A clean bandage was wrapped around his head.

She hugged him quickly, then stepped back, choked back tears, and forced words past the lump in her throat. "How are you doing?"

"I'm good. Donna Mae took good care of me."

"But now he doesn't want to stay with me again," Donna Mae scolded playfully, but there was no mistaking the worry filling her big green eyes.

"Why not?" Gia glanced at Harley.

Harley fidgeted beneath her gaze. "I don't want to be a bother."

"You could never be a bother, Harley." Donna Mae slid her hand into his. "I already told you that."

Harley nodded but didn't say anything else on the subject, so Gia let it drop.

Harley took a deep breath and squared his shoulders. "You said I could come out here and help."

"Of course you can. I'm thrilled to have you, both of you. Give me a sec." She hurried inside and found Cole soldering metal pieces together to make a headboard. She tapped him on the shoulder, and he lifted the mask he was wearing.

"Harley's here, and he'd like to help."

"That's great." Cole turned off the flame, and set his mask aside. "He's feeling better, I take it?"

"Seems like. Can we find something for him to do outside? Maybe painting or something?"

"Absolutely. I have those signs stacked over by the door to paint."

"Oh right." They'd decided to make signs pointing to different places in the "hospital." The morgue and the lab were two of Gia's favorites. She'd already sketched the words with blood dripping from them. "That's perfect."

She gathered the signs, a couple gallons of paint, and a package of different sized brushes and brought them outside.

Cole followed with a couple of saw horses. He set them side by side. "Here you go, Harley. You can lay the signs across these while you paint and then just leave them to dry. We're not supposed to get any rain before tomorrow."

"Perfect, Cole, thank you." Gia set the paint and brushes on the ground, then balanced the signs across the saw horses.

"Any time." He shook Harley's hand. "I'm glad you're feeling better, man. Just have Donna Mae come get me when you're ready for more work. What do you enjoy doing? Anything special?"

"I like painting. I can also build and solder. I learned it in school and I was pretty good."

"Sounds great. I have a ton of stuff for you to do, then."

"Gia," Kayla called from the side of the house.

"Will you guys excuse me for a minute." Gia headed toward her.

"You sure have a ton of help here." Kayla gestured toward the open shed door. "Things are looking good."

"Thanks." Though Kayla seemed to be in a good enough mood, Gia couldn't help but wonder if she had something up her sleeve. She didn't like feeling that way about anyone, but Kayla just rubbed her the wrong way.

"I have the stuff in the back of the truck for you." She gestured toward the front of the house. "If you want to give me a quick hand."

"Sure thing. Should I grab a couple of people to help?"

"Nah. Don't interrupt anyone, it's not more than the two of us can handle, and you guys need to keep working if you're going to get done in time." She started across the yard.

Gia fell into step beside her. "Where's Genny?"

She shook her head. "She wanted to go home, so I dropped her off on my way here."

Gia laid a hand on Kayla's arm to stop her. "Is she all right?"

Kayla shrugged. "She's taking it hard, harder than I would have expected, but she'll be okay. Come on, though, I want to get this done so I can get back to her. She'll need me tonight."

"Why? Is something wrong?" She hadn't looked good the last few times Gia had seen her.

"No, nothing more than has been wrong anyway, but I don't like to leave her alone."

She'd been alone the night Jeb had been at the house. Where had Kayla been then? "Where's her husband?"

"He's home right now, but I'm sure he'll be out later."

Gia wanted to question her, but she'd already pushed things too far with her and had somehow earned her forgiveness. No way did she want to mess that up. At the same time, it didn't hurt to feel her out if she was being talkative. She walked with her toward the house. "You can tell me it's none of my business if you want to, but I'm curious; do you know if the rumors about Barbara are true?"

They followed a walkway that led around the house to the circular driveway out front. Kayla remained quiet until they reached a pickup truck parked beneath a lamppost in the driveway, and Gia figured she wasn't going to answer.

Then she stopped and turned to lean her back against the truck's tailgate. "I told you before, Barbara was not a kind woman, and she did treat Genny badly. But truth is, she treated everyone badly. She enjoyed seeing people squirm. Mike Smith, person of interest, is a perfect example. Even after her death that woman is still ruining that poor guy's life."

Gia leaned next to her, settling in for what she hoped would be a long talk. "What do you mean?"

"She and Mike had an affair, what seems like a lifetime ago, now. At the time, Mike had been married to his high school sweetheart for about three years. That was Barbara's way, you know. She had a long list of lovers, every last one of them married. Seems not only did she enjoy making people squirm, she also enjoyed the challenge of conquering a married man, getting him to cheat on his wife, then dumping him and holding it over his head for the rest of his life."

At the end of the day, each of those men had made a choice, and any or all of them could have said no, but Gia remained quiet. No way did she want to do anything to make Kayla stop talking.

"Anyway, that's how she could afford to stay home without working, the long line of men she blackmailed into supporting her. But with Mike, she messed up. Social media was new at the time, and she didn't really know what she was dabbling in. Supposedly, she posted a picture of her and Mike on his account by mistake."

"Supposedly?"

Kayla shrugged. "Who knows? Maybe Mike wouldn't go along with whatever she was demanding of him. Or maybe she just enjoyed hurting him. Or maybe it really was an accident. Whatever the truth is, probably no one will ever know, but it doesn't matter. What matters is Mike's wife saw the picture and threw him out. She'd been the love of his life, and he'd lost her. I'm not sure if it was losing her that destroyed him, or the guilt of having betrayed her. Either way, he was never the same again. Then he had a motorcycle accident a few years back, and rumor has it he tried to contact her afterward, tried to apologize and make amends, at least, get her forgiveness if nothing else."

"And?"

"She blew him off. Told him to go jump in a lake, preferably full of gators, or words to that effect."

Gia's heart ached. If he'd tried so recently to contact his ex-wife again, was it possible he'd killed Barbara after she rejected him? He obviously still had feelings for his ex and had harbored an incredible amount of regret for a long time.

Kayla straightened. "So, anyway, now you have a glimpse of the kind of woman Barbara was. And now I have to get back to Genny, and Preston needs his truck back, so why don't we get this stuff unloaded?"

"Did she know? Genny. Did she know what Barbara was doing?"

Kayla contemplated for a moment before answering. "Genny is the kind of person who only sees the best in people. It's not always a virtue."

It seemed Gia's first impression of how Kayla treated Genny might have been mistaken. She'd thought Kayla was bullying her, pushing her around, but maybe she'd just been trying to do right by her, to protect her.

What lengths had Gia gone to when Harley had been hurt? She run off half-cocked ready to find the person who'd hurt him, even though she'd put not only herself in danger, but Savannah as well. Savannah, who was the best friend she'd ever had, and yet, she hadn't been thinking clearly enough to protect her at all costs. "Genny must be a very good friend."

Kayla caught her gaze and held it. "She's my best friend in the world, and there's nothing I wouldn't do for her."

Gia wanted to keep her talking, but Kayla opened the tailgate and pulled out a box. "There are scrubs in here, masks, those paper bootie things surgeons wear on their feet, even a couple of clipboards you can make charts for, if you want."

That might be a fun idea. Maybe they could come up with some corny sayings for the charts, like people sometimes did with gravestones, then hang them on the bottoms of the beds. "Do you want me to take that?"

"I've got it, but there's another one in there, the long skinny one. That's got the IV poles and I think he said some crutches." She started back toward the house, leaving Gia to grab the other box.

"Kayla?" Gia called.

She stopped and turned.

"Was she blackmailing you?"

"Let's just say I had an affair I wasn't proud of, and she found out."

The man in the picture with her on Barbara's phone. Now it made sense. So did the phone calls Hunt had found in the phone records. "Did you give her what she asked for?"

Her lips firmed into a thin line. "She left me no choice."

Gia watched her walk away, shoulders slumped with the weight of whatever guilt she held, then turned to the truck.

As Gia slid the box toward her, it caught on something. Great. She climbed into the back of the truck. A metal pole sticking out of the box had caught through a loop on a canvas drop cloth. She unwound the cloth and slid the box toward the edge of the truck bed.

When she started to move around the box, her foot caught in the cloth, and she tripped. She reached out a hand and caught the side of the truck to keep from falling, then stopped and bent to disentangle her foot.

The edge of a shovel, its blade covered in some kind of brown rust, stuck out from beneath the cloth. Once she untangled her foot from the cloth and set the cloth aside, she pulled out her phone and shone its flashlight at the shovel, which appeared to be the very same shovel she'd seen in the storage shed the night she and Savannah had gone out to the fairgrounds to meet Barbara.

Chapter Twenty-One

Gia fumbled her phone, and it dropped. If not for the flashlight still shining, she'd have never found it in the dark. She snatched the phone up, her only lifeline if the wrong person caught her in the truck, and lurched toward the edge. Just as she was about to jump out, her foot caught the drop cloth again, and she tumbled out onto the ground. She hit the driveway hard. Pain rocketed through her head.

"Gia? Are you okay?" Harley ran toward her, then yelled over his shoulder to Donna Mae. "Go get help."

Gia tried to warn him off, but her vision blurred.

"What happened?" Harley looked around, then squatted at her side. "You're bleeding."

It didn't matter. She had to get help. They were sitting ducks out there on the driveway. She tried to sit up.

Harley held her in place. "Don't move. Donna Mae went for help."

She fought back the eddy of darkness threatening to overcome her. "Have to move."

"What?" Harley's expression twisted in confusion. "Why?"

"Dangerous." She had to get up. Had to fight to stay conscious. "Need Hunt. Now."

"Hold on." Harley pried the phone she was clutching in a desperately tight grip from her hand and scrolled through the names, then hit Hunt's. "I'll get him."

Hunt answered right away, his voice carrying in the still quiet of the night. "Sorry, love, it doesn't look like I'm going to make it out of here any time soon."

"Gia's hurt," Harley blurted.

There was a pause on the other end, a fraction of a second. "Who is this?" "It's me. It's Harley."

"Gia, what happened?" Trevor reached her first. He dropped to his knees at her side. "Let me see your head."

A light shone in her eyes.

The chattering of voices moved closer as word must have spread about her fall. She had to get up. Had to get everyone inside where they'd be safe. Had to keep anyone from touching the truck. "Move."

Someone held out a rag, and Trevor pressed it against her head. "No, Gia, you have to stay still."

She clawed her way through the encroaching darkness. She had to make him understand. No sense. He wouldn't listen. How could she get through to him? She couldn't. But Savannah would understand. She used the last of her strength to whisper, "Savannah," then her body went limp and she surrendered to the dark.

"Gia, wake up." Savannah's voice cut through the haze of blackness. She tapped her cheek lightly. "Come on, Gia. Can somebody get a wet rag so I can clean some of this blood off. Keep holding that compress tight, Trevor."

The wail of sirens moved closer.

Gia struggled back toward consciousness and croaked, "Savannah."

"It's all right, honey, I'm here." She smoothed Gia's hair away from the cut on her head. "You'll be okay. Just lie still."

"Can't."

"What?" Savannah took a wet rag someone held out and wiped her forehead and down the side of her face.

Gia used all of her strength to reach up and push her hand away.

Savannah studied her for a moment, then frowned and leaned over her. "What's wrong?"

"Not safe."

Savannah froze. She lifted her head and looked around at the gathered crowd, then leaned closer. "Did someone do this to you?"

"No." Frustration built. She needed to get Savannah to understand, but she couldn't seem to get her brain to connect to her mouth. "Shovel."

Kayla leaned over her. "Is she all right?"

"She'll be fine. I think she fell out of the truck." Savannah sat up straighter. Gia could tell she didn't fully understand, but at least she realized something was off. "Why don't you help get everyone to back away a little and give her some air?"

Cole stepped in. "All right, let's all back away. The EMTs will be here any minute, and we want to give them room to work."

Gia looked up into the concerned faces of all her friends surrounding her. She'd tried to protect them, tried to make them move away, tried to make them realize they could be in danger.

Blue and red light flashed on and off through the night.

She closed her eyes to reduce the dizzying effect. No use. Even through her closed lids, the strobe effect assailed her. Her stomach turned over.

Savannah turned her head to the side and covered her eyes. At least she'd understood that much. Most likely when Gia's face had turned green.

As everyone moved back, a cool breeze washed over her.

"What happened?" Hunt fell to his knees on her side, opposite Savannah.

"No one's sure. Donna Mae came in and said Gia was hurt, then we all ran out and found her lying on the driveway."

Kayla stepped forward. "She was helping me get boxes out of Preston's truck. She was fine when I walked away a minute or two before Donna Mae came in."

"All right." He turned his attention to Gia. "Gia, can you hear me?"

She started to nod, then thought better of the idea. At least, the cool breeze was beginning to wash away some of the brain fog.

Savannah feigned hovering over her to whisper in Hunt's ear. "She said something about a shovel."

"Did someone hit you, Gia?" The insistence in Hunt's tone helped her focus.

"No. I fell." She sucked in a shaky breath. "Out of truck. Found shovel."

"All right. Okay." Hunt squeezed her hand. "Savannah, you stay with her. The paramedics are right behind me."

"You're okay, now. Hunt will take care of it."

Knowing Hunt understood enough to figure out what had happened, Gia relaxed into Savannah's arms. "I'm sorry I put you in danger."

Savannah hugged her tighter. "You didn't put me anywhere, Gia. And I'd never want to be anywhere else but at your side, no matter what."

"Me too." She reached up to hold Savannah's hand, the warmth of friendship embracing her.

The next few hours passed in a haze of activity as they took her by ambulance to the hospital, and the doctors ran a gazillion tests before deciding she had a mild concussion and, basically, according to Savannah, a good ole knock to the head. They stitched her up and said she could go home as long as someone stayed with her.

Of course Savannah obliged. "You sure you don't feel sick anymore? I love you dearly, but you are not throwing up in my new car."

Gia started to laugh, then stopped when it sent a jolt of pain shooting through her head.

"That bandage is a good look, though." Savannah lifted her sunglasses and peered at her. "But you might have to be a patient now instead of a doctor."

"If the Festival isn't postponed."

Savannah propped her glasses back in place, opened the passenger door for Gia, then gave her a hand in. "At least now it's looking a little more likely it'll go ahead."

"Oh yeah?"

"Hunt called. A million times, actually." She shut the door and went around the back of the car before sliding into the driver's seat and continuing without interrupting her flow. "He said he'd be by later."

Gia nodded. He'd stayed behind after finding the shovel in the back of the truck, but she'd spoken to him once or twice between tests. "Did they find anything?"

"First, do you want to go to my house or your house?" She adjusted her rearview mirror and shifted into gear.

"Where's Thor?"

"Cole took him, remember?"

Did she? Oh yes. Savannah had said that the last hundred times she'd asked.

"He's going to drop him off wherever you want to go."

What she wanted more than anything was to snuggle up on her couch with a soft blanket, a cup of hot tea with honey, and Thor at her side. "I'd like to go home, if you don't mind staying with me."

"Of course I don't. I didn't claim your spare bedroom for no reason, now, did I?"

Gia laughed. Savannah wasn't lying. She'd not only claimed the spare bedroom but moved so much of her stuff in it was hard to tell she didn't live there. "So, what did Hunt say?"

Savannah sighed and looked over at her before making the turn to head out to Gia's house. "He found the shovel, and it was used to kill Barbara."

Even though she'd had a feeling that was the case, the news still came as a shock. "Kayla?"

"No. Since they narrowed down the time of death, Genny swears Kayla was with her during the time Barbara was killed. Preston, on the other hand, seems to have no alibi for the time in question." She flipped the radio on to a soft rock station and turned the volume low.

Gia relaxed back in the seat. "Preston Hart? Genny's husband? I don't understand."

"The shovel was found in his truck, and his prints were the only ones found on it. Seems he must have missed one and a partial when he wiped it down."

Gia tried to picture Preston as the killer. He'd definitely seemed to be harboring a good amount of anger when she'd seen him at the memorial. And it seemed he was spending an awful lot of time away from home of late, especially strange considering his wife was going through a traumatic experience.

Plus, Genny's deteriorating condition made a lot more sense if she knew her husband had killed her good friend. But what reason could he have had to kill her? And why on earth would he leave the shovel lying in his truck? "Why didn't he just get rid of the shovel?"

Savannah shrugged and hit her turn signal. "No one knows, and he's not talking."

"They brought him in for questioning?"

"Actually, they just arrested him." She turned onto the long stretch of road that would lead out to Gia's development and settled in for the ride. "Seems the numerous phone calls back and forth between him and Barbara, his print found on the murder weapon that was found in his truck, and his lack of an alibi for the time in question were enough to bring him in."

"What did he say?"

"I told you, nothing. That boy clammed up tighter than my granny's girdle at an all you can eat breakfast buffet."

What more could she ask? She didn't know Preston Hart, so she had no way to know if it was out of character for him. Maybe he was jealous of his wife's relationship with Barbara. He didn't seem to have much involvement with Genny. Come to think of it, with all the talk of Genny and Barbara and the Festival lately, Gia hadn't heard his name mentioned once. Did he even participate in the Festival?

But then, Kayla seemed to be the one Genny spent the most time with. If he was going to be jealous of any relationship, it seemed it would have been the one with the woman who seemed to have the most control over Genny. "What about Kayla?"

"They questioned her for a few hours, then let her go. She says she never saw the shovel. It must have been under the drop cloth, and they just threw the boxes in on top of it without looking. Her friend at the medical supply house who helped her load the truck confirmed her story."

She couldn't begin to imagine what kind of pain Genny must be going through. Had she known? As torn up as she was, Gia found it hard to believe she wouldn't have turned him in if she'd known. "How's Genny doing?"

"By all accounts, she hasn't left the house. Kayla went back there as soon as she left the police station."

Gia's head throbbed, and she closed her eyes and massaged her temples. "Do you think she knew?"

Savannah turned into Gia's driveway but left the car running with the AC on. "No one knows, but there's plenty of speculation running around."

"Like what?"

"Seems the general consensus is Barbara and Preston were having an affair, then she tried to blackmail him and he let her have it."

That made sense, especially considering Kayla said Barbara often went after married men, but her good friend's husband? "Is that what Hunt thinks?"

"He's reserving judgment."

He would. No way he'd let wild conjecture or gossip dictate what avenues he pursued. "What do you think?"

"I honestly don't know. For argument's sake, let's say Genny knew."

Gia opened her eyes and sat up straighter. "It would make sense that she was such a mess if not only was her husband having an affair with one of her best friends, but he'd then killed her."

"True." Savannah turned toward her and ticked off one finger. "And if I were Genny, and that was the scenario, the first thing I'd do is talk to my best friend about it and ask your advice."

"So, you think that's what happened with Genny and Kayla? Why Kayla was sticking so close…"

"And why Preston kept his distance at the memorial and seemed to be spending his nights elsewhere…"

"And why Kayla was running around town trying to cast suspicion everywhere except close to home." Everything added up in Gia's mind, yet in her gut, something still felt off.

Cole's jeep pulled in the driveway behind them. He hopped out and opened the back door for Thor.

Gia opened her door and stood tentatively, waiting to make sure she was steady on her feet before moving away from the car.

Thor bounded toward her.

"Easy, boy." Leaving the door open, she perched on the edge of the passenger seat to pet him. "Were you a good boy while I was gone?"

"Are you kidding me? He was an angel. Made me know for sure I'll be getting one of my own soon." Cole held up two bags. "Now, come on in. Thor and I made you some nice chicken soup with homemade biscuits."

She pressed a hand against her stomach and realized she was hungry. "That sounds perfect, Cole. Thank you. For everything. I was worried sick about Thor until Savannah told me you took him."

"And then she was worried sick again every time she couldn't remember that I told her you took him." Savannah reached out a hand to help her up. "Come on. Let's go get you comfortable."

While Savannah settled her on the couch, despite numerous protests that she was perfectly capable of coming to the table and helping set up, Cole fed Thor and took him out.

"There, how's that?" Savannah fluffed the pillow behind her back one more time, then guided her against it and tucked a fleece blanket around her.

Thor wandered in, jumped onto the couch she'd given up on trying to keep him off of, and settled his big head in her lap.

Cole followed right behind him with a steaming bowl of chicken soup, the aroma surrounding her in comfort.

"Everything's perfect, now, Savannah, thank you."

Chapter Twenty-Two

"Can you grab the other end of this platform, Savannah?" Gia held up one end of a bed platform, the other end still balanced on the edge of Earl's son Jackie's pickup truck.

"I've got it, Savannah." Alfie scrambled into the truck and lifted the other end, then held it as he climbed down.

"Thanks, Alfie." Gia walked backward toward her "house." With Preston in custody, Hunt had finally released the fairgrounds so everyone could get back to work. With only two days until the Festival, they didn't have much time. "Just let me know if Thor gets behind me."

The last thing she needed was to fall over him while backing up.

"Why didn't you pull the truck closer?" Alfie shifted his end to get a better grip.

"I wasn't sure how far we were allowed to pull up." She adjusted her grip. Even with the lightweight trapdoors Cole had managed to make, the boxes were still heavy to carry. The bedding tacked to them didn't help matters, as it made them slippery.

"Oh, you can pull all the way down the road to the house while you're working."

"Thanks." That would have been good to know sooner. She probably should have asked. "I'll back it up before we unload the rest."

"Is this one of the ones with the trap door? Willow said I could have one to jump out of. I can't wait. It's going to be so scary." Trevor's excitement level was pretty much through the roof. He'd been texting her costume ideas non-stop for days.

"It would definitely scare the living daylights out of me." Admittedly, she scared easier than most people.

They had to tilt the platform to get it through the doorway, and then Gia needed a break. Her hands ached and her back was on fire, but in a good way. "Let's put it down here for now. We can worry about getting it into place later."

"Go ahead and put your end down first," Trevor said.

Gia lowered her end to the floor, then stood and brushed her hands off and shook out her arms. "They are definitely heavier than they look."

Alfie let his end drop with a thud. "That's for sure. But look how great it looks."

He was right. The beds looked great. "We still have to make up the charts."

He rubbed his hands together. "That should be fun."

"We're going to meet early at the café tomorrow morning if you'd like to join us. We'll have breakfast and toss around ideas."

Alfie lowered his gaze to the floor. "I can't thank you enough for letting me join you, Gia. You can't imagine how much I appreciate it."

"Any time, Alfie. I hope you'll stay in touch afterward too." She sat down on the platform to catch her breath for a minute before moving on to whatever detail awaited her attention next. "How are you doing?"

He shrugged and sat next to her. "Some days are better than others. It helps that they caught her killer, but it doesn't bring her back. You know what I mean?"

"Yeah, I do."

He clasped his hands between his knees. "Who'd have thought Preston could do something like that?"

That seemed to be the general consensus throughout the community. "People can do things that seem out of character when they're backed into a corner."

She hadn't discussed the case with Alfie since Preston's arrest. She'd wanted to give him time to heal in peace. "Did you know what she was doing?"

Alfie studied a small cut on his palm. "Yeah, I knew. Some of it anyway, just not all the details or all the people involved. And her affair with Preston came as a complete shock."

"You tried to stop her." Debby had said as much, but after getting to know Alfie a little better over the past week while they worked on the house for the Festival, she wouldn't have expected any less.

"I did. For years. It was the one and only thing we ever argued about. And we argued about it all the time."

"Do you mind if I ask why you stayed friends with her, knowing what she was doing?" Gia held up a hand. "Don't get me wrong; I'm not judging, just curious. It doesn't seem like the kind of person you'd befriend."

"I don't blame you. And I wouldn't blame you if you judged me for it, but Barbara and I had been good friends, the best of friends for a very long time before I found out what she was doing. By then, I'd already loved her dearly, and she didn't have anyone else—no surprise, really, considering what she was doing. She needed me."

"I can understand that, Alfie."

He looked her straight in the eye. "Can you?"

What would she do if she found out tomorrow that Savannah was doing something that immoral? She didn't know. Maybe the same thing Alfie had done, fight with her, try to make her stop, and at the end of the day, accept her for who she was. Because she didn't have it in her to walk away from her best friend. "Yes, I really can. There's nothing I wouldn't do for Savannah, no matter what."

"Maybe you really do get it then." He smiled, reached over, and squeezed her hand. Then he jumped to his feet. "Speaking of Savannah, we'd better get back to work before she finds us sitting here and hits us over the head with that clipboard she's carrying around."

"You go ahead. I'll be right there."

He pointed a finger at her and grinned. "Don't take too long, if you know what's good for you."

She laughed. It hadn't taken him long to figure Savannah out.

"Come on, Thor. I'm sure Savannah will forgive me one little break to give you water." She filled Thor's bowl from the water bottle in her bag and set it on the floor, then sat on a chair someone had left by the door.

Thor lapped his water like he hadn't had a drink in days. Seemed scrambling around trying, and failing, to stay out from under foot made him thirsty.

Gia sipped her own water bottle, waiting for him to finish. When he was done, he laid his head in her lap, and she weaved her fingers into his thick fur. "You're having fun out here, aren't you?"

He looked up at her, his brown eyes wide and filled with love.

"Come on, then. You can only run around a few more minutes, because it's almost dark." Once it was dark out, she kept him on his leash. No sense taking any chances. Even a big black dog wouldn't be hard to lose in all this wilderness, especially in the dark.

She headed out the door and paused to watch the sun set on the horizon, the brilliant hues painting the sky a vibrant pink and orange. The colorful

Florida sunsets still amazed her. Watching the sun set behind the skyscrapers in New York just didn't compare. "All right, this time the break's really over. Come on, Thor."

She strode down the dirt road with Thor at her side.

"Come on, Gia. Everyone headed back to Cole's for one more trip. If we get all that done tonight, we can start bringing the tables and stuff out tomorrow. We'll store it all in the house until Saturday, then set up in the morning." Savannah walked back toward the parking lot with her. "What did you decide to do Saturday? Close early?"

"I think I'm just going to close for the day. Willow invited everyone to the café to get dressed and do makeup, and I ordered a big hero and some salads, so I figured why not just close and enjoy the day?"

"I think that's a great idea. And people will certainly understand. Most of the businesses that participate do close for the day. Some even close Sunday too, so they can sleep in and then clean it all up."

She'd considered doing the same, but Sundays were a busy day in the café. "I can't afford to close for two days, though it does sound appealing."

Thor stopped at her side and perked his ears up.

"Thor?" She patted her leg for him to heel.

He started to trot at her side, then stopped again and glanced behind him. He barked at something, though she had no clue what.

"Do you hear anything?" Savannah looked in the direction he was facing.

Gia squinted into the last of the setting sun and listened closely. "Nothing. What about you?"

Savannah shook her head.

Thor bolted.

"Thor, no!" Gia reached for his collar but missed. She ran after him.

Savannah kept pace with her. "Thor, come back."

"Thor." Pain tore through her. What if he didn't come back? "Thor, come. Now, Thor."

"I don't see him, do you?" Savannah stopped and scanned the area. "Do you have your cell phone? I left mine in the car."

She patted her pockets, then racked her brain trying to remember where she'd left it. No use. She couldn't even think with Thor missing. She bent over and wrapped her arms around herself. She had to think. Go back to the car for Savannah's phone and call for help, or keep searching for him? "No. I don't have it."

"Okay." Savannah covered her eyes with her hand, but tears flowed from beneath it. "All right. Let's not panic."

"I have to find him, Savannah. I can't leave him out here."

"No one's leaving him." She grabbed Gia's hand and tugged her forward. "Come on. We'll look a little more and call him. Maybe he'll come back on his own, but if we can't find him in a few minutes, we'll run back to the car and call for help."

Unable to speak, Gia nodded and started jogging in the direction he'd gone. Darkness covered any trail he might have left when he ran, and most of the dirt on the road had been kicked up with everyone moving stuff into their houses.

"Don't worry, Gia. Everyone's coming back. They were just going to Cole's and heading right back out here. We'll have help in a little bit even without stopping to call anyone."

She nodded again. Tears impeded her vision.

Savannah cupped her hands around her mouth and screamed. "Thor!"

Gia sucked in a breath and yelled, "Thor! Come!"

"Cookie!" Savannah yelled. "Thor! Do you want a cookie?"

When they reached their house, Gia took a quick look inside. "Thor? Are you in here?"

She waited, straining to hear even the slightest indication he was in the building. Nothing.

Savannah circled the building, calling his name over and over.

Gia joined her on the dirt road out front. "Which way?"

"Shh..."

Gia froze.

"Did you hear that?"

No matter how hard she listened, she didn't hear anything out of the ordinary. "What?"

"I'm not sure. It came from that way." She pointed toward the woods.

"Do you think he'd have left the trail?" Gia looked the way Savannah had indicated, then back the way they'd come. "Wouldn't it make more sense he'd have stayed somewhere familiar?"

"Unless something piqued his interest. It'll be okay, Gia. We'll find him. Trust me. It's not like none of my guys has ever taken off before. It's normal, and we'll get him back."

Gia only nodded, the ache in her chest making it too painful to talk.

"Look." Savannah gestured the same direction she just had again. "Is that a light?"

Deeper in the woods, in the same direction they'd chased Mike Smith, a light flickered.

"Come on." Gia started toward the light. If that rattlesnake was still out there, it might hurt Thor.

Savannah grabbed her arm. "Maybe we should leave a note in the house saying where we went. That way, as soon as the others get back, they'll be able to help us search."

The light flickered once and went out.

"No way. Thor!" Gia started running in that direction, heedless of whatever obstacles blocked her path. She dodged branches, skirted bushes, and scrambled over a fallen tree. "Oh, Thor, where are you?"

Savannah fell behind, but Gia kept going. She had to find him. "Oh please," she prayed. "Thor!"

A dog barked in the distance.

She sucked in a shaky breath. Okay. He was okay. She just had to get ahold of him now. "Thor! Come!"

Thorns scratched her arms and face. Pricker bushes grabbed her bare legs.

She plowed through and stumbled into a clearing. An old camper, set on cinder blocks and tilting dangerously to one side, blocked her view of anything past the clearing. Not that she would have been able to see much, anyway. Full dark had fallen, and even the bright moon couldn't penetrate the thick canopy of pines above her.

Movement from inside the camper caught her attention. Something glowed inside.

She crept closer, curbing the urge to scream Thor's name until she knew what she was up against. She looked over her shoulder for Savannah, then started back. She had to find Thor, but she was not leaving Savannah alone in the dark forest to look for him, when she had no idea who might be hiding out in any of the outbuildings nearby. She'd find Savannah first, then they'd continue the hunt for Thor.

"Psst." Savannah crouched a few feet away from her, pointing at the trailer.

Gia squatted next to her. "Are you okay?"

"I'm fine. Are you?"

"I will be once we find Thor."

Savannah started to stand. "Maybe we should head back and get help."

It was too dark to see anything past the clearing, and falling in a lake or stepping on a rattlesnake wasn't going to help Thor.

"He may have already gone back to the house or the car looking for you."

Savannah was right. They weren't going to find him this way. "I'm pretty sure I heard barking in this direction. Let me just check inside, then we'll go back."

Savannah nodded. "But stay quiet. We have no idea what's out here."

"You wait here."

Savannah grabbed her arm. "No, I'm not—"

"I'm serious, Savannah." Gia shook her off. "You wait here, and if anything happens you run for help."

"Gia—"

"If you won't wait here, I'm not checking."

"Go. But hurry." Savannah crouched lower and slid back closer to the bushes.

Gia crept across the clearing, keeping her full focus on the camper. Savannah would keep an eye out for everything else. The hard-packed sand absorbed the sound of her footsteps.

A soft whimper came from inside the camper.

Thor! She bolted across the remaining few feet and through the open doorway.

Chapter Twenty-Three

A woman sat cross legged in the middle of the room, staring intently at her cell phone and crying softly.

Gia crept closer. The rotting floorboards squealed in protest. "Genny? Is that you?"

She rocked back and forth, keening. "Why? Why? Why?"

She had to find Thor, but she couldn't leave Genny here like this.

Savannah approached quietly and laid a hand on Gia's arm. "Come on, Gia, we have to go. We'll take her with us."

Gia nodded and started forward, then stopped when Genny started to speak.

"How could this have happened? I don't understand. I was so sure it was her."

Gia doubted she even realized they'd come in. "Genny, are you all right?"

"Genny," Savannah called softly. "Come on, now. You have to come with us."

"Right after the Festival, I was supposed to start planning his surprise birthday party. It was going to be a huge bash, and I only had two weeks to pull it off. But I could have done it. And now he's sitting in jail." She sobbed and stared at the phone, continuing to rock back and forth, back and forth.

Gia and Savannah moved up on either side of her. They'd get her up off the floor and take her with them, but they didn't have time to mess around here with Thor missing. Did that make her a terrible person? She hoped not, but... She caught a glimpse of the picture Genny was staring at—the picture from Barbara's phone of Kayla locked in a man's embrace—just as Savannah gasped.

"Oh no. Gia, we have to get out of here," Savannah whispered urgently and tugged on Gia's arm, then looked around wildly. "Come on. Leave her here, and we'll get Hunt to come back for her. It's not like she's hurt or anything."

Gia looked around but couldn't find whatever had Savannah so panicked. "What's wrong?"

Savannah pointed at the picture. "She said she was planning a birthday bash for her husband two weeks from now. That makes him a Scorpio."

The full implication slammed through Gia like a ton of bricks. The breath shot from her lungs. "It wasn't Barbara he was having an affair with…"

"It was Kayla," Savannah finished. "And that's not Genny's phone."

The phone Genny held in her hand had the same blue rhinestone studded case as Barbara's. Coincidence? Probably not. "It's Barbara's. The one Genny supposedly lost."

"I didn't know," Genny said quietly. "I thought it was her. It was an accident. I didn't mean it. Oh no, what have I done. I can't take it back. Oh no, oh no, no, no, no…"

Genny rocked and rambled, giving no indication she even suspected she wasn't alone.

"We have to go, Savannah." Gia started backing toward the door as quietly as possible, keeping a death grip on Savannah's hand. They'd have to get Genny help and find Thor as quickly as possible.

"I didn't know. Then, when I saw them, I knew, and it was too late." Genny sobbed and babbled incoherently.

When she reached the door, Gia turned to run and plowed smack into Kayla.

"Sorry, ladies, but I don't think so." Kayla caught her balance and held a gun pointed at Savannah's chest.

Gia froze and shot her arms into the air. "Look, Kayla, you don't have to do this."

Savannah backed away, her hands held high.

Kayla stepped forward, keeping pace with Savannah. "One more step, and I'll shoot right now."

Savannah stopped moving.

Gia had to get Kayla's attention off Savannah. If she could just get her to turn the gun toward her, Savannah might get a chance to run. All she'd have to do is make it out the door. Once she was outside, the darkness would swallow her up. As long as she moved quietly, she'd have a good chance of getting away.

Gia took a deep breath and tried to regain some sense of control over her emotions. Her voice shook despite her best efforts to sound confident. "Genny killed Barbara, didn't she?"

Kayla turned her head the slightest bit toward Gia but kept the gun firmly trained on Savannah. Her hand was rock steady. "It was an accident. You don't understand."

If Gia could keep her talking, stall until someone got back to the fairgrounds and realized they were missing, maybe they'd make it out of there. "So explain it to me. I want to understand. Honestly, I do. I like Genny. Who knows? If you tell me what happened, I might even be able to talk Hunt out of pressing charges."

Okay, that was a whopping lie.

"Don't be ridiculous, Gia. You weren't even able to get him to release the fairgrounds so the Festival could proceed, but I'm supposed to believe you're persuasive enough to talk him out of arresting Genny for murder?"

"It wouldn't be murder charges." Savannah inched forward...one millimeter at a time.

Gia looked at her, pleading with her eyes for Savannah to stay still, to stay quiet, inconspicuous, invisible. "No, not if it was an accident. The charges wouldn't be that serious. Manslaughter, maybe—"

Genny sobbed.

"And I think I could talk him out of that." Gia slid a fraction of an inch toward Savannah. "Please. You're going to kill me anyway, and it's not like anyone's going to stumble onto us out here, so why don't you just tell me what happened? Let me see if I can help."

Kayla frowned, but at least she didn't pull the trigger.

Gia shifted, barely moving, but still inching closer to Savannah. She had to get between Savannah and Kayla.

"It was an accident." Genny stood behind her. She slid between Gia and Savannah to stand next to Kayla.

By the time Gia considered grabbing her and using her as a bargaining chip, she'd already stepped out of reach.

Genny swiped both hands over her swollen, blotchy face. "I didn't mean it."

"You don't have to do this, Genny," Kayla growled.

"Yes, I do." She turned to face Kayla, who kept the gun leveled in Savannah's direction. "I have to at least try to explain. Right now, you haven't done anything but try to help me."

Kayla's jaw clenched.

"If you do this..." Genny gestured toward the gun, then at Gia and Savannah. "You're guilty of murder. I already have enough guilt to last a lifetime; I don't need two more deaths and you in prison to weigh me down further."

"Fine. If you feel the need to explain, explain. But I'm not lowering the weapon, and if either of you move, I'll end the conversation once and for all." Kayla mopped her brow.

"I was doing the bills one day, and there was a discrepancy in the amount on the phone bill. I ran through the call logs to see if maybe we were charged for a call or something, and I saw call after call after call between Barbara and Preston. Don't you get it? He was mine..." She screamed and fell to her knees. "He was mine. She always had to have everything I had, always had to be one step better than me, always wanted more and more and more. It was never enough."

"Genny, please..." Tears flowed down Kayla's cheeks. The thought of killing two women hadn't brought an ounce of emotion to her face, but Genny's pain obviously touched her in a way nothing else did. So why would she have had an affair with Genny's husband? What could have brought more pain than that?

Genny didn't even look up. "I confronted her. And of course she denied it. I was so angry, blind with rage, and I grabbed the closest thing to me and swung..."

"That's enough, now, Genny." Kayla laid a hand on her shoulder.

Genny yanked away and tipped to the side, then scrambled to her feet and faced Kayla head on. "No, it's not enough. How could you do that to me? I killed my best friend—"

"I'm your best friend." Kayla's jaw clenched.

"No." Genny shook her head wildly, her hair tumbling into her face. "My best friend wouldn't have had an affair with my husband."

"Oh really?" Kayla whirled on Genny, her eyes wild, the gun aimed directly at her. "Answer me this..."

Gia froze in place, praying Savannah would do the same.

Kayla moved closer, stalking Genny, an inch from her face, gun held between them. "If it had happened the other way around, would Barbara have covered up the fact that you'd killed me? Would Barbara have stood by your side and tried to make everyone believe it was my own fault I'd been killed? And when all that failed, and the investigator still kept asking questions and pushing for the truth of what happened, and the Festival you loved so much was in danger of being canceled, would Barbara have framed the man she loved to let you go free?"

Genny lowered her gaze to the ground and stepped back.

Kayla spun back toward Savannah, gun held out in front of her in a tight two-handed grip. "And you! You had to go and pick up her phone, right! Another couple of minutes, and I'd have found it. If not for that, Genny would never have seen that picture, would never have known it was me and not Barbara fooling around with Preston."

Gia stepped between them just as Kayla pulled the trigger. Pain tore through her shoulder.

"Gia!" Savannah gripped both her arms from behind.

A low growl from the corner made Kayla pause. Her attention shifted toward the sound.

"Thor! No! Stay!" Gia pounced on Kayla. She grabbed Kayla's fists, both clenched around the gun, in both hands and shoved them up toward the ceiling, then slammed her head into Kayla's face.

Blood spurted from her nose. Kayla shook it off, recovering quickly, and tried to wrestle the gun back under her control.

Gia shoved her shoulder into Kayla's chest. If she could just back her against the wall.

Thor barked frantically, bounding back and forth, searching for an opening.

Thor, please stay back. She couldn't let Kayla regain control of the gun.

Kayla's rage strengthened her, fueled her power.

Gia backpedaled, desperately trying to maintain her fragile grip on the weapon.

Savannah moved in behind Kayla, lifted a half-rotted piece of wood, and slammed it into Kayla's head.

She dropped like a stone and smacked her head against the floor.

A sob tore through Gia as she fell back, landing hard on the floor.

Thor skidded to a stop at her side, his gaze riveted on Kayla even as he pressed himself against Gia.

"Oh, Thor, thank you, boy. You are such a good boy." She petted his side with one hand, while keeping pressure on her bleeding shoulder with the other.

"Gia..." Savannah grabbed the gun from Kayla's hands and patted her down, searching for any other weapons, then pressed her fingers against her neck and breathed a sigh of relief. Apparently, she was still alive. Satisfied she didn't have any other weapons, Savannah scooted to Gia's other side. Tear tracks stained her cheeks. "Are you all right, Gia?"

"I'm okay. Thanks to you and Thor."

"Are you sure?" She tucked the gun into her waistband and pulled Gia's hand aside to check her shoulder. "Okay. Okay, it doesn't look like it's that bad. I think it just skimmed your shoulder. Are you sure you're okay?"

Gia nodded. Some of the pain had subsided, Thor was pressed against her, and Savannah was okay. "Genny?"

Savannah pointed to the corner where Genny sat sobbing, her face cradled in her hands.

"Can you walk?" Savannah started to help her up.

"Wait."

She let go immediately. "I'm sorry. Did I hurt you?"

"No. I'm all right, but we can't both go. One of us has to stay here." No way could they leave Genny alone with Kayla.

"You are clearly not thinking straight."

"Listen, Savannah," Gia hissed between clenched teeth as she bit back a stab of pain. "We can't very well carry Genny out of here, and I don't think she's in any shape to walk out."

"So we leave her here until we get help."

"We can't."

"Why not? Even if she gets Kayla up and they run, Hunt will find them."

"It's not that." The memory of the fierce determination in her eyes when Kayla had turned on Genny brought a bolt of fear. "I'm not sure what Kayla will do to her if she wakes up. She's going to know we got away, and there's no telling how she'll react."

"We're not leaving her with the gun," Savannah pleaded.

"I know. But whatever she does, Genny's in no condition to defend herself."

"All right. Okay. Let me think for a minute." Savannah looked around the room then scrambled to her feet. "The phone."

"What?"

"Barbara's phone." She grabbed the phone from the middle of the room where Genny must have dropped it and looked at the screen. "Dang."

"No service?"

"None." She stuffed the phone into her pocket.

About what Gia had expected, given they hadn't had service in the area when they'd chased Mike Smith out there. "Listen to me, Savannah, and don't argue. There's no time."

"Why do I have a feeling I'm not going to like this?" Savannah shoved her hands into her hair and squeezed her eyes closed, then shot them open and stared at Kayla.

Gia sat up straighter and scooted back until she hit the wall. "It doesn't matter if you like it or not, it's what has to be done. I'm not leaving you here alone with them, and I can't let you go running through the dark woods alone at night, so that only leaves one choice."

"Oh? And what's that?"

Gia hugged Thor close. "You're going to give me the gun in case Kayla wakes up, and you're going to take Thor and go for help."

Savannah bristled, caught her bottom lip between her teeth and shook her head. "No. Not happening. No way I'm leaving you here alone. We'll wait for help. Someone is bound to find us."

"Come on, Savannah. Even though that *might* be true, though you know as well as I do it's not very likely, and when will they get here? Kayla is going to wake up, and if help hasn't arrived, I'm going to have to stop her from coming after us again." Tears threatened, but Gia held them back. If Savannah thought she was falling apart, she'd never leave her. "I don't want to have to hurt her, Savannah. Please…"

She blew out a breath, glanced at Kayla and then Genny, and nodded. "Okay, Gia, I'll go."

Relief coursed through her. "Thank you."

Savannah handed her the gun, then bent over and hugged her. "I'll be right back. But, Gia…"

"Yes?"

"If you ever step in front of a bullet meant for me again, I'll kill you myself."

Gia half-laughed half-sobbed, despite the stab of pain it brought, and dropped her head back against the wall. She let her eyes flutter closed for just an instant. "I love you, my friend, and there's nothing I wouldn't do to protect you."

Savannah hugged her again, then stood.

Gia struggled upright and hugged Thor once more. "Please make sure you hold onto his collar. Don't let him get lost again."

"I won't. I promise."

Chapter Twenty-Four

Gia rearranged the table one last time, pulling a stack of paper plates more toward the front corner and pushing a cake dish filled with mini breakfast pies farther back. They had plenty more in the warmers, but she liked how the display looked with the rust, gold, and burgundy flannel tablecloth and fake brown, orange, red, and yellow leaves scattered over the table.

Savannah laughed. "It's the same stuff, Gia, no matter how many times you rearrange it."

"I can't help it. I want everything to be just perfect."

"And it will be, my friend. Now, come on. They're going to be opening the gates in about half an hour, and we still have to drop Thor off at Zoe's building."

"I'm coming, I'm coming." She switched the muffins and scones one more time.

Savannah rolled her eyes.

"Okay. I'm done now." She unclipped the extra-long leash she'd gotten Thor especially for the fairgrounds—wouldn't want him to get lost again—from around a nearby tree and swapped it for his regular leash, then ruffled the fur on his head. "Don't worry, boy, I promise you can run around again as soon as we get home to the fenced yard."

He barked once, then trotted beside her toward the building Zoe had set aside for pet sitting.

Savannah hooked her arm through Gia's as they walked. "Have I thanked you again for saving me?"

"Not in the last five minutes."

Savannah laughed. "Well, thank you. Again. And I'll probably say it a million more times after this, so get used to it."

Gia stopped and faced her.

Tears shimmered in Savannah's eyes.

"You don't have to keep thanking me, Savannah. I don't know what I would have done through the whole Bradley situation without your help. You may never have stepped in front of a bullet for me, but you saved me just the same, more than once, in a million different ways. And then again when you knocked Kayla out. I was losing, then. If not for you, she most likely would have overpowered me. And if you hadn't gone for help and brought Hunt and Leo back with you before Kayla woke up...well...I don't even want to think about what might have happened, to me or to Genny."

"Thankfully, Cole had already realized something was wrong when no one could find us and called Hunt and Leo. If they hadn't already been close, she'd have woken up before I made it back." Savannah sniffed and wiped her eyes. Then she hooked her arm through Gia's again and rested her head on her good shoulder as they walked. "You are my best friend in the world, Gia. There's nothing I wouldn't do for you."

"Can I ask you something?" As they moved closer to the road, the sounds of a large crowd talking and laughing reached them, adding to Gia's growing excitement.

"Of course."

"We haven't had much time alone to talk about it, but Kayla rambled on and on to Genny about how Barbara wouldn't have covered up the fact that she'd killed someone, wouldn't have stood by her side and framed someone else for her mistakes." As much as Gia loved Savannah, and wanted with all her heart to believe she'd do anything in the world for her, she wasn't sure she could go to the lengths Kayla had, even to protect her. "What would you have done? If it was me and you found out I'd killed someone?"

Savannah took her time thinking about her answer. She clearly understood Gia was seeking an honest answer, maybe even doing a bit of soul searching herself.

"Hey, you two, get ready. Debby's gonna open the gates." Cole waved as he hurried across the freshly mown field toward the table where he and Earl would serve their guests while Gia worked the house.

A roar went up from the crowd.

"Sounds like Debby already opened the gates." Gia picked up the pace. Maybe this conversation was best left for another time, anyway. "We'd better hurry."

"We still have a few hours before they open the houses, but we'll be back in plenty of time for you to work the table for a while too." But Savannah quickened her pace too. "And in answer to your question. I've given it a lot of thought, especially while I was running back through the woods with Thor to get help, after I had to leave you there, injured, and I'm sure scared. And I don't think Kayla did what she did out of friendship. I think she did it out of guilt. Her affair with her best friend's husband was the catalyst that set all the events that followed in motion, and I think the guilt became too heavy a burden for her to bear."

"You're probably right." She petted Thor's head while they walked, comforted to have her hero beside her. "I'd been thinking all along about Alfie, and how he stayed friends with Barbara even after he learned what she was doing, and I honestly believe I would have done the same thing. I realize now that I would have stayed friends with you, but I would have handled the situation differently."

"Sometimes, enabling someone to hurt themselves isn't the kindest option. It is however the easiest. It's never easy to watch a friend go through a difficult time, or to make choices you can clearly see are going to hurt them, but in the long run, there are only two options. You can either wait it out, let them make their own bad decisions, and then be there to help them pick up the pieces—which I honestly believe is most often the right choice."

And she was probably right, because that's exactly how she'd handled the situation with Gia when she'd chosen to marry Bradley.

"But there reaches a point where the friend goes too far, as in Barbara's case, and at that point, I think you need to intervene and try to get your friend the help they need."

"Tough love."

"Exactly, but love all the same." Savannah reached over and squeezed her hand. "No one ever said it was easy."

Gia hoped if the time ever came, she'd have the same strength and courage Savannah had and would be able to do right by her.

"Hey, there's Zoe." Savannah pointed in the direction of what looked like a large stable.

Zoe hurried toward them. "Here, I've got him. I was waiting for you."

"Sorry, Gia got held up rearranging her table ten thousand times." Savannah laughed. "I think that bullet in her shoulder slowed her ability to make a decision."

"Ha ha." Gia petted Thor again and held the leash out to Zoe. "You be a good boy, now."

Zoe took Thor's leash. "Come on, boy, the other dogs are waiting for you. I have lots of fun activities planned, including an obstacle course some of the kids helped me set up out back. Say goodbye to Mama."

Gia gave Thor a big hug. "Have fun, boy. You'll keep a close eye on him, right?"

Zoe rubbed a hand up and down Gia's good arm. "You know I will. We fenced the corral out back with chicken wire so no one can escape. He'll be safe. I promise."

Gia did know that, or she wouldn't be leaving him with her, but it didn't make it any easier.

"Go on, and have fun. Your table should be gathering quite a crowd by now. Time for you to go mingle." Zoe turned and jogged toward the building with Thor.

"Come on." Savannah tugged on her arm. "There's Hunt and Leo."

They crossed back over to Gia's table, where she resisted the urge to rearrange everything once more. Not that she could have, even if she'd wanted to, since it was packed with customers.

Cole and Earl seemed to have a good rhythm going behind the table, and Willow and Skyla both moved through the crowd taking orders to hurry things along.

Hunt sat at a picnic table with Leo, their plates piled high with pumpkin spice waffles and breakfast pies.

A little more tired than she'd like to admit, and slightly winded from setting up and walking Thor to Zoe's tent, she sat beside Hunt. "Hey there. Hi, Leo."

"Hey." Leo wrapped an arm around Savannah when she sat next to him. He'd been hovering ever since he'd found out she'd almost been shot. When she told him Gia had saved her, he sent the biggest bouquet she'd ever seen to the house.

"How're you feeling?" Hunt kissed her cheek.

"A little tired, but doing okay." As much as she wanted to greet everyone, the doctor had told her to take it easy when she needed to. And if she didn't take a moment to rest now, she'd only become more uncomfortable as the night wore on.

"These waffles are delicious." Hunt added more syrup to his plate.

"Thank you." She'd barely had a moment to see Hunt since he'd lost it when he found out she'd been shot. "Have you heard anything about Genny?"

She hadn't resisted when Hunt had arrested her and, thankfully, Kayla had remained unconscious until Savannah had returned with Hunt and Leo.

"She's still undergoing evaluation to determine if she's even fit to stand trial. We should have some news in the coming weeks." Hunt finished eating and pushed his plate aside. "When she met with Barbara at the fairgrounds, she'd intended to confront her about the affair but hadn't planned to harm her."

"What about Kayla?"

"Apparently, she and Preston had been seeing each other for quite some time—not that there's any crime in that no matter how immoral it might be. And Kayla is perfectly fit to stand trial, which she will, not only for her role in covering up Barbara's death, but for kidnapping and attempted murder as well." He wrapped his arm around Gia and pulled her close. "Honestly, she seems to be more at fault for the whole thing than Genny. If things actually played out the way Genny is saying, it was more or less an accident. She lashed out without meaning to kill Barbara, not even really meaning to hurt her, just so beside herself she lost her temper. It would have gone better for her if Kayla hadn't come along and talked her into covering it up and then framing Preston."

Gia settled against Hunt, enjoying the warmth of his arm around her, the woodsy scent of his aftershave enveloping her. "Where is he?"

"Don't know. He disappeared as soon as we released him."

"He knew Genny killed her?"

Hunt shrugged. "He never said, and we can't prove it, but I think he did. I think the weight of his guilt made him keep his mouth shut instead of turning her in."

"That's understandable," Leo said. "If not for him betraying her by having an affair with her best friend, none of the rest would have happened."

Savannah took a bite of Leo's waffle. "Mmm...these really are good. By the way, did you guys ever find out what was going on with Mike and Jeb out at the fairgrounds?"

"Yeah, Jeb came in after we picked Mike up and confessed. Said he didn't want Mike in trouble because of him. Plus, he felt guilty for hitting Harley when he found him walking around out there. Seems emotions were running out of control for everyone, and he was desperate to find Barbara's phone to get rid of the evidence Barbara had been blackmailing him with," Hunt said. "Apparently, Jeb's been renting out the rotting storage buildings to people who had no place to live. Mike included. He was also paying Mike cash, under the table, to keep up the grounds all year."

"How'd he get away with that?"

"He's been doing it for years. Whoever owns the land let it sit there and was happy enough to have Jeb keeping an eye on it."

"Is he going to be in trouble?"

Hunt shrugged. "That's up to the DA."

"Come on, guys, it's almost time." Alfie plopped on the end of the bench closest to Gia. He wore surgical scrubs, with a stethoscope draped around his neck. A zipper started at his nose, just above his surgical mask, and opened as it went up to his forehead. "We have to go through the house and make sure everything's set up. And I want to stop at Barbara's house and add some more flowers."

Two houses would stand empty at this year's Festival, Barbara's with a picture, candles, and flowers in memory, and Genny's, with nothing but darkness to mark her absence.

Gia stood and stretched, then pushed Hunt playfully. "So, where's your costume?"

"Sorry, babe, I'm working security." He planted a kiss on her forehead, despite the bandages. "No costumes for me. Maybe next year."

"Oh, guess what?" Alfie stood too, bouncing up and down on the balls of his feet. "Rumor has it, you guys have a good shot at the Ruffie Award this year."

A small surge of pride shot through Gia.

A local band took to the bandstand, and the sounds of country music filled the air. The scent of funnel cakes from a nearby stand made Gia's stomach growl. Laughter and joy surrounded her.

Harley and Donna Mae took seats at a picnic table across the path from them, plates heaped high with food, and waved.

Gia waved back, thrilled Harley was coming out of his shell and involving himself in community events. He might not be fully ready to immerse himself back in the world, but he was, at least, taking steps in the right direction.

Debby hurried toward them, out of breath by the time she stopped. The furry werewolf costume she wore had to be making her sweat. "Good news, Gia. The kittens Thor found are healthy as can be and ready to go to their forever homes."

"That's awesome, Debby, thank you. I'll be by tomorrow to pick up my little girl."

As it turned out, Thor hadn't taken off for no reason. He'd found a litter of three tiny kittens, apparently abandoned by their mother and just about starving. One of them had a bite taken of its ear and blood matting its fur. Before he would go with Savannah for help, he'd led her to the kittens. She'd had to tuck them into her shirt and take them with her to get him to move.

Gia had fallen in love with the tiniest of the three, black and white with black booties and a piece of her ear missing. Thor was so attached to the little one, he wouldn't leave her side, even after Debby had taken them from Savannah. Though she couldn't be certain, Debby believed Thor heard something attacking them, probably a coyote, and had saved them.

Gia would have taken all three, but Savannah wouldn't part with a little gray and black tabby, and Alfie had called dibs on the all-white one with blue eyes.

Savannah stood and straightened her costume. She'd dressed as a zombie doctor, a clipboard bearing a patient's chart clutched against her chest. "All right, let's do this."

Since Gia was now sporting not only a small bandage on her head from the bump she took falling out of the truck, but one on her shoulder as well, where they'd had to stitch up the bullet wound, she got to be Savannah's patient. "I'm ready."

Savannah turned the clipboard around and held it out to Gia. On a piece of paper stained to look old, its corners burned off, she'd printed in red letters that appeared to be dripping;

Bed 1A
Gia Morelli
—took a bullet for a friend but, thankfully, she's on the mend.

Recipes from the All-Day Breakfast Café!

Gia's Pumpkin Spice Waffles

Ingredients:

1 1/2 cups all-purpose flour
1/4 cup brown sugar
1 tbsp baking powder
1 1/2 tsp baking soda
1/2 tsp salt
1 tbsp pumpkin spice (store bought, or try making your own:
Mix 3 tbsp ground cinnamon, 2 tsp ground ginger, 2 tsp ground
nutmeg, 1 tsp ground cloves. Blend well, and keep the leftover
in an airtight container for next time.)
1 cup pumpkin puree
1 cup almond milk
2 eggs
3 tbsp melted butter

Instructions:

Pre-heat waffle iron, and coat top and bottom with non-stick
spray.

In a large bowl, mix flour, brown sugar, baking powder,
baking soda, pumpkin pie spice and salt.

In another bowl, whisk pumpkin, eggs, butter, and almond
milk until well combined.

Pour wet mixture over the dry ingredients. Mix together until
just combined.

Pour batter into waffle iron, and cook according to waffle
iron directions.

Remove from waffle iron.

Serve with butter and maple syrup. For an extra treat,
sprinkle a bit of cinnamon over the top.

Enjoy!

Gia's Homemade Vanilla Cinnamon Creamer

Ingredients:

- 1 1/2 cups sweetened condensed milk
- 1 1/2 cups milk
- 1 tablespoon vanilla extract
- 2 teaspoons ground cinnamon

Instructions:

Pour condensed milk and milk into a bowl and mix.

Add vanilla extract and mix.

Add cinnamon and whisk until blended.

For a special treat, pour mixture into an ice cube tray and freeze, then add to coffee any time you want and enjoy!

Breakfast Pie

One of the dishes All-Day Breakfast Café owner, Gia Morelli, loves most is Breakfast Pie. In her case, it makes life easier, since the pies are made ahead of time and are easy enough to just slice and serve. They are also delicious re-heated, so they make for a great time saver when you're in a hurry and want to grab something quick. Simply make them up on the weekends, slice them, and all you have to do is heat one slice up whenever you're hungry.

Gia makes several different kinds; western (ham, peppers, onions, and cheese), meat lovers (bacon, sausage, ham, and cheese), veggie (spinach, squash, zucchini, broccoli, mushrooms, and tomatoes), and my personal favorite, my dad's original Breakfast Pie, which he makes every Christmas morning!

Original Breakfast Pie Recipe

Ingredients:

1 lb. bacon
1 package breakfast sausage
1/2 lb. ham
1 large green pepper
2 medium onions
5 medium potatoes or 1 bag shredded potatoes
1 dozen eggs
1 bag shredded cheddar cheese
salt & pepper (to taste)

Instructions:

Cut up and shred 5 medium potatoes (or use 1 bag of pre-shredded potatoes)
Chop onions (keep separate)
Chop ham
Chop sausage
Chop green pepper

Crust:

Fry bacon in a large skillet (an electric frying pan works perfectly), then keep the fat in the pan, and chop the bacon. Keep 1/3 for the crust and set 2/3 aside.

Fry potatoes and one chopped onion in the bacon fat (add salt and pepper to taste). When cooked add 1/3 of the chopped bacon and stir.

Press into a pie dish to form the crust.

Pre-heat oven to 350 degrees.

Filling:

Using the same pan (you can use nonstick spray on the bottom if needed) combine and cook breakfast sausage, ham, remaining bacon, green pepper, and remaining onion.

While cooking, scramble 1 dozen eggs.

Once mixture is cooked, add eggs and mix while cooking. Add salt and pepper (to taste)

When done, stir in about 6 oz. of shredded cheddar, then add filling to pie crust. Put in oven.

Bake for 45 minutes.

When just about done, sprinkle shredded cheddar (to taste) over the top and return to oven until cheese melts.

Serve and enjoy!

Keep reading for a special excerpt of *A Cold Brew Killing*. By Lena Gregory!

A COLD BREW KILLING
An All-Day Breakfast Café Mystery

Lena Gregory

When an ice cream vendor discovers a frozen stiff, Florida diner owner Gia Morelli has to serve up some just desserts…

Gia has become good friends with Trevor, a fun, flirtatious bachelor who owns the ice cream parlor down the street from her popular All-Day Breakfast Café. Trevor has the scoop on all sorts of local attractions and activities. But when he bursts into her diner, trembling and paler than a pint of French Vanilla, she can tell something's very wrong. Trevor points her toward his shop then passes out cold. When Gia runs down to his shop, she discovers a chilling sight—a dead body in the open freezer. But the ice cream man's troubles are just beginning. The police suspect him of this murder a la mode, especially when details of his questionable past surface. Gia believes in her friend and is determined to clear his name and find the real cold-blooded killer before someone else gets put on ice…

Look for A COLD BREW KILLING on sale now!

Chapter 1

"Oh, please, gag me." Savannah Mills slid the tip of one long, lime-green nail beneath the tab of a diet soda can and popped it open. With one eye on the TV, she poured it into a glass over ice. "That man has no more business being mayor than I do."

Gia Morelli finished wiping down the counter from the breakfast rush, tossed the rag into a bin beneath the counter, and turned toward the muted TV. "What did Ron Parker ever do to you, and why do you insist on drinking soda from a can when there's a perfectly good fountain right behind you?"

Savannah kept her gaze on the TV and waved Gia off. "I like it better from the can, more bubbly. And Ron never did anything to me. It's the way he presents himself, all squeaky clean and snooty. In the meantime, that man is as phony as a three-dollar bill."

Earl Dennison, the elderly gentleman who'd been the All-Day Breakfast Café's first customer and still hung around regularly, reached over the counter, grabbed the TV remote, and turned up the volume. Then he sat back down on his usual stool and dug into his massive breakfast. "What makes you say that?"

"Just look at him, that slick grin plastered on his face everywhere he goes." She lifted a brow toward Earl and wagged a finger at the TV. "I don't care what anyone says; no one is that happy all the time."

Though Gia could see Savannah's point—Ron Parker stood behind a podium, his smile so big he had to speak through clenched teeth—she didn't need the two of them arguing over politics. The few customers who still lingered over breakfast or coffee didn't seem to be bothered by the conversation, but still... "Knock it off, you two, or I'll ban all talk of politics in the café until after the election is over."

Earl held up his hands, still clutching his fork. "Hey, not our fault there's nothing else on the TV but election coverage."

"Yeah, well, I don't want anyone getting riled up in here." Gia fiddled with the valve on the new Cold Brew Coffeemaker sitting on the counter behind the register.

"True enough. People do tend to get worked up over politics," Earl agreed.

Gia accidentally nudged the valve handle, just a little, and coffee poured out onto the floor. She flipped it back into place and grabbed a handful of paper towels. "Shoot!"

Earl cleared his throat—to cover his laughter, no doubt. "Granted, I don't know much about making cold coffee, but isn't that thing a little big?"

"Ya think?" Savannah snickered. "How much does it hold, anyway?"

Gia's cheeks heated. She mopped up the spill and tossed the paper towels into the garbage pail, then mumbled, "Fifty gallons."

Earl laughed out loud. "What on earth are you going to do with fifty gallons of cold coffee?"

"Hey, in my defense, I got a good deal on the machine. Besides, Trevor split the cost with me, and every day when it's ready, I'm going to send half down to the ice cream parlor for him." Gia wet a wad of paper towels and bent to clean the stickiness off the floor.

The front door opened.

"Well, I'll be doggoned," Savannah said, amusement clear in her voice. "Speak of the devil."

Gia looked up at the back of Savannah's head. "Who is it? Trevor?"

Savannah shot a grin over her shoulder at Gia. "Nope."

With most of the stickiness cleaned up enough for the moment—she'd give it a good mopping later—Gia stood and stared straight into Ron Parker's trademark smile.

"Good morning, good morning." He approached the counter, his hand held out. "Ron Parker. Nice to meet you."

Gia shook his hand. "Gia Morelli. It's a pleasure to meet you."

The leggy blonde standing next to him, wearing a mini skirt and a halter top, held out a pamphlet, a hundred-watt smile deepening her dimples.

Ron took the pamphlet and handed it to Gia. "I'm just making the rounds, visiting all of the establishments along Main Street, hoping to share my message."

Gia took the proffered pamphlet and glanced at Ron's smiling face on the front cover before dropping it onto the counter. Savannah was right; he'd do better to drop the fake grin. "Thank you. I'll be sure to read through it later."

"Of course." Ron looked around the café. "I have to admit, I expected you'd be busier."

Gia bristled. Business had improved quite a bit in the past few months. Unfortunately, not as much as she'd hoped. "You probably should have come earlier, when the breakfast crowd was still here. You could hang around for a little while if you want, maybe have something to eat and catch the lunch rush. Can I offer you a cold brew coffee?"

His smile diminished, just a little, but Gia still caught the change.

"No, thanks. Can't stand the stuff. I wouldn't mind a black coffee and a blueberry muffin, though. To go." He gestured toward his assistant, and for a minute Gia thought he was going to ask her what she wanted. "Get that for me, will ya, hon?"

Savannah swiveled on the stool, until her back faced Ron, then pursed her lips and stared pointedly at Gia.

Gia had known Savannah long enough to spot an *I told you so* look, even in her peripheral vision. She ignored her and turned to pour his coffee.

By the time she got his order ready and rang it up, Ron had already swept through the room, shaking hands and making promises, and was ready to leave. He held both hands out in front of him, his forefingers and thumbs extended like pistols. "It was a pleasure to meet y'all. I sure hope I can count on your votes."

Thankfully, Savannah waited for him to leave before she started in. "I hate to say I told you so—"

"You don't have to. It was written all over your face," Gia said.

"The way he treats his poor assistant is awful. And what's with that outfit she had on? You'd think she'd dress more professionally if she's going to campaign with him. He'd do better to leave her back at the office. People might take him more seriously."

"Not to disagree," Earl piped in, "but some people just talk that way, especially those used to flipping orders and having them obeyed. He might not have meant any offense. And she sure is a mite easier on the eyes than the candidate."

"Hey…" Savannah pointed her almost dagger-length nail toward him. "You watch it now, buddy. You don't see Mitchell Anderson parading a woman around like some sort of prized trophy, treating her like his servant. Of course, he doesn't have to play games like that. Mitch Anderson is no slouch. If you ask me, he's sort of a hottie. And talk about squeaky clean…"

"I'm not sure he's as clean as everyone says," Earl argued. "There ain't no one don't have a skeleton or two buried somewhere."

"Yeah, well, that may be true, but that woman ain't got nothin' buried." Savannah lifted a brow toward the door, where Ron and his assistant had stopped on the sidewalk to speak to a woman pushing a baby stroller. "Look at that skirt; if it were any shorter, you'd be able to see clear to the top of the Christmas tree."

Earl winked at Savannah, then laughed and shoved a forkful of sausage into his mouth.

Savannah shot him a scowl.

Gia left them to their bickering. She'd just opened the register and started to count out the money from the breakfast crowd when the front door opened. She went to drop the bills back into their slots as she looked up, then kept them in her hand. "Oh, hey, Skyla."

"Hi, Gia, Savannah, Earl. Is Willow around? We're supposed to meet for lunch." Skyla Broussard dropped her big canvas bag onto an empty stool and slid onto the one next to it at the counter.

"Yup, she'll be right in. She just brought the garbage out." Gia squashed down the pang of guilt she felt. She'd pretty much managed to go everywhere in the café, and even out back to leave Harley's dinner, but she still parked out front on the street and had someone else take out the garbage whenever possible. And she still hated looking in the direction of the dumpster, ever since she'd found Bradley's body. "Would you like a cup of coffee while you wait? I have cold brew now."

"Just a regular coffee would be great, thanks." Skyla glanced over at Earl. "You're in late today."

"Yup." He puffed up his chest and sat a bit straighter. "Spent all night at the hospital."

"Oh, no." Skyla's hand fluttered to her chest. "Are you all right?"

"Oh, yeah, I mean no, I mean…" Earl's cheeks flushed a deep crimson. "My whole clan spent the night at the hospital awaiting the arrival of Becky Lynn, grandchild number sixteen."

"Oh, Earl, that's awesome. Congratulations."

He nodded. "Thank you. Sure did take her sweet time comin', that one did."

Skyla laughed. "That's okay. The things you appreciate most in life are those you have to wait for."

"Ain't that the truth." Earl soaked a biscuit in gravy and took a bite.

Gia finished counting the twenties and dropped them into the deposit bag, then turned to get the coffee.

Savannah beat her to it. By the time Gia turned, she already had a mug in front of Skyla and the pot held over it.

A couple approached the counter, and the man handed Gia his check and a twenty-dollar bill.

"How was your breakfast?" Gia asked as she took the check from him.

"Very good, thank you."

She held his change out to him and smiled. "I hope you'll come again."

"Thank you. I'm sure we will," the man said as he pocketed his change, then turned to go.

"Bobby, wait." The woman he was with caught his arm, staring past him at Skyla. "Skyla? Skyla Broussard, is that you?"

Skyla turned toward her with a smile, but the instant their eyes met, Skyla's face paled and the smile disappeared. "Gabriella Antonini?"

"In the flesh." Gabriella smiled at the man she was with and rubbed a hand up and down his arm, seemingly unaware of Skyla's obvious discomfort. "Well, Fischetti, now. Bobby and I have been married…well… pretty much forever."

"What are you doing here?" Skyla demanded.

"Um…" Gabriella faltered. "We just got back into town last night. We were going to look you up, but we hadn't gotten around to it yet."

"Actually, we were going to look up all of the old gang." Bobby Fischetti held Skyla's stare. "We were feeling a bit nostalgic, figured a reunion of sorts was in order."

Skyla swallowed hard and nodded. "It was good seeing you."

"Sure thing." Gabriella resumed her perky attitude as if nothing awkward had happened. "We'll let you know when we can all get together."

Skyla just nodded again and watched them go, then shifted her gaze to the TV.

Gia glanced at Savannah and drew her eyebrows together.

Savannah shrugged and shook her head.

After a moment, Skyla took a deep shuddering breath, then said, "So, what do you guys think of Ron Parker?"

"Oh, please, don't get them started." Accepting Skyla's change of subject, though curiosity was dang near driving her crazy, Gia started straightening the condiments on the counter.

With one last glance at Gia from the corner of her eye, Savannah chimed in. "Earl and I were just discussing that. Personally, I prefer Mitchell Anderson. He just seems more honest."

Skyla's eyes darkened, just for a second. If Gia hadn't been looking right at her, she'd have missed it.

Hmm…something there. Skyla was definitely not her usual self this morning, but Gia wouldn't press. There were still customers in the café, and Savannah and Earl were still at the counter with Skyla. Maybe later, if she could get her alone, she'd ask if she was okay. For now, she'd just leave her be.

Gia hadn't yet made up her mind whom to vote for, and she was actively searching for a reason to choose one candidate over the other. Each had strong points, and she hadn't yet come across any major weaknesses for either candidate, but there was still time. Ron's visit definitely hadn't helped his cause. If anything, he'd pushed her more toward Anderson. "You don't like Anderson?"

Skyla tilted her head as if contemplating the question. "I don't think he should be mayor."

Savannah finished pouring Skyla's coffee, then topped off everyone else's and put the pot back on the burner. "You prefer Ron Parker?"

Skyla shrugged. "He's not my favorite, and I don't think he's the best role model for young men and women, but he's better than Mitch."

"Oh, please, Mom, are you bashing Mitch Anderson again?" Willow let the door from the back room swing shut behind her and crossed the café. She laid a hand on her mother's shoulder and kissed her cheek. "Sorry I'm running a few minutes late."

Skyla patted her daughter's hand. "No worries, hon. I'm in no rush."

Gia always enjoyed the interaction between Willow and her mother. She'd never had a relationship with her own mother, but if she had, she liked to imagine it would have been like Skyla and Willow, and if she ever had a daughter of her own, she'd do anything to attain that close of a bond.

It struck Gia, as it often did when seeing Willow and Skyla side by side, how much alike they looked. They shared the same long, dark hair, the same exotic green eyes, and the same petite build, but Willow carried herself with a confidence Skyla hadn't quite mastered.

"So, what's the deal with Anderson?" Willow sat down next to her mother and took a blueberry muffin from a cake dish on the counter. "Why do you dislike him so much?"

"I don't know." Skyla stared down into her coffee cup, stirring the milk around, seemingly mesmerized by the tiny whirlpool. "I just don't care for him."

She was lying. The realization hit Gia like a ton of bricks. She'd never have expected Skyla to lie to Willow.

"Yeah, well, Ron Parker is everything you've taught me not to be." Willow broke her muffin in half. "He's phony and arrogant, and he treats everyone around him like they're his minions."

"Mmm-hmm…" Skyla dug through her bag and pulled out a few singles and held them out to Gia.

"Don't worry about it." Ignoring the money, as she always did with Skyla, Gia glanced up at the TV. A clip of Ron Parker working the crowd at last week's campaign event played in the background while a news anchor rambled on about the election.

"You didn't answer, Mom. Why do you dislike Mitch Anderson so much?"

Skyla dropped the money on the counter, as she always did after Gia refused to take it, then turned to Willow. "Do you want to sit here all day arguing politics, or do you want to eat lunch and go shopping?"

Nice dodge. Maybe Skyla should have been the politician.

"Definitely shopping." Willow took the last bite of her muffin, hopped off the stool, and rounded the counter to grab her purse. "I'll come in a little early tomorrow to help prep since it's Saturday. Thanks for giving me the afternoon off, Gia."

"No problem."

"And thanks for covering for me, Savannah."

"Anytime, kiddo. Have fun."

"Thanks." Willow smiled, waved, and held the door for her mother before bouncing through after her.

Savannah looked after them for a moment, then turned to Gia. The corners of her mouth turned up slightly, but there was no mistaking the sadness in her eyes.

Gia had no doubt Savannah's thoughts were running along the same line hers had earlier. Both of them had lost their mothers when they were young. Only difference was, Savannah grew up surrounded by family who adored her. Gia grew up alone, unless you counted the father who threw her out the day she graduated high school.

Gia waited until they were gone, then leaned close to Savannah. "Skyla seemed a little off today, don't you think?"

"Definitely, but I didn't want to push it in the middle of the café," Savannah said.

"No, me neither, but if I get a chance, I'll try to talk to her." And if the opportunity didn't present itself, Gia would make time to talk to her. Whatever may be wrong, she certainly wasn't acting like herself.

About the Author

Lena Gregory lives in a small town on the south shore of eastern Long Island with her husband and three children. When she was growing up, she spent many lazy afternoons on the beach, in the yard, anywhere she could find to curl up with a good book. She loves reading as much now as she did then, but she now enjoys the added pleasure of creating her own stories. She is also the author of the Bay Island Psychic Mystery series, published by Berkley. Please visit her website at www.lenagregory.com.

*When an ice cream vendor discovers a frozen stiff, Florida diner owner
Gia Morelli has to serve up some just desserts…*

Gia has become good friends with Trevor, a fun, flirtatious bachelor who
owns the ice cream parlor down the street from her popular All-Day
Breakfast Café. Trevor has the scoop on all sorts of local attractions and
activities. But when he bursts into her diner, trembling and paler than a
pint of French Vanilla, she can tell something's very wrong. Trevor points
her toward his shop then passes out cold. When Gia runs down to his
shop, she discovers a chilling sight—a dead body in the open freezer. But
the ice cream man's troubles are just beginning. The police suspect him
of this murder a la mode, especially when details of his questionable past
surface. Gia believes in her friend and is determined to clear his name and
find the real cold-blooded killer before someone else gets put on ice…

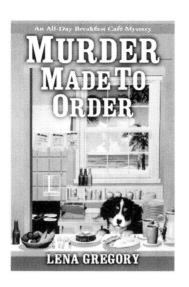

An All-Day Breakfast Café Mystery

MURDER MADE TO ORDER

LENA GREGORY

To save her cozy Florida diner, Gia Morelli must choke down a heaping helping of murder…

New York native Gia Morelli is just getting used to life in Florida when she gets word that the town government wants to shut down her pride and joy: the charming little diner known as the All-Day Breakfast Café. A forgotten zoning regulation means that the café was opened illegally, and hardboiled council president Marcia Steers refuses to budge. Gia is considering hanging up her apron and going back to New York, but before she gives up on her dream, she discovers something shocking in the local swamp: Marcia Steers, dead in the water. There's a secret buried in the books at town hall, and someone killed to keep it hidden. To save her café and bring a killer to justice, Gia and her friends will have to figure out a killer's recipe for murder…

For Florida diner owner Gia Morelli, there's no such thing as too much breakfast—unless it kills you...

When Gia Morelli's marriage falls apart, she knows it's time to get out of New York. Her husband was a scam artist who swindled half the millionaires in town, and she doesn't want to be there when they decide to take revenge. On the spur of the moment, she follows her best friend to a small town in Central Florida, where she braves snakes, bears, and giant spiders to open a cheery little diner called the All-Day Breakfast Café. Owning a restaurant has been her lifelong dream, but it turns into a nightmare the morning she opens her dumpster and finds her ex-husband crammed inside. As the suspect du jour, Gia will have to scramble fast to prove her innocence before a killer orders another cup of murder...

"Hold on to your plates for this fast-paced mystery that will leave you hungering for more!" —J.C. Eaton, author of the Sophie Kimball Mysteries

Printed in the United States
by Baker & Taylor Publisher Services